Praise for
Forever in Blue:
The Fourth Summer of the Sisterhood

"*Pants* fans who privately wondered whether the magical jeans—or the series—would hold up through another summer of hard wear can rest assured they do."　　　　　—*The Bulletin*, Recommended

"A strong, satisfying conclusion that won't disappoint fans."
　　　　　　　　　　　　　　　　　　　　　　　—*Booklist*

"Lively prose, snappy dialogue and a complex intertwining of four stories mark this outstanding series . . . an ode to love and friendship to delight Brashares's legions of fans."　　　—*Kirkus Reviews*

"The series' legion followers will eagerly follow each gal through her summer of ups and downs and will again be heartened by the teens' rock-solid friendship."　　　　　　　　—*Publishers Weekly*

"Fans will . . . delight in the story."　　　—*School Library Journal*

"Talk about good jeans: Expect lotsa laughter and tears for the Sisterhood of the Traveling Pants in the fourth and final volume of this well-worn series."　　　—*Entertainment Weekly*, "The Must List"

"[Brashares] takes good care of her characters as well as her readers."　　　　　　　　　　　　　—*The Columbus Dispatch*

"It's no wonder these stories are so popular."　—*Detroit Free Press*

"The treat of the season."　　　　　　　　—*The Sunday Republican*

"Brashares delivers the goods, with a meaty, satisfying final hurrah."　　　　　　　　　—*The Mercury News* (San Jose)

"A great read."　　　　　　　　　　　　—*Daily News* (New York)

"This is a book that avid readers of the series are likely to run out for, grab and devour in one sitting." —*Pittsburgh Post-Gazette*

"Fans of the series will certainly want to follow the lives of the four friends in this fourth book." —*KLIATT*

"A great ending to the series. *Sisterhood* followers who are eagerly awaiting this final book will not be disappointed." —*Voice of Youth Advocates*

"Ann Brashares has created a wonderful, heartfelt series for teens (and adults) around a pair of pants." —Amazon.com

Other books by Ann Brashares

The Sisterhood of the Traveling Pants
The Second Summer of the Sisterhood
Girls in Pants: The Third Summer of the Sisterhood

Forever in Blue

The Fourth Summer of the Sisterhood

Ann Brashares

Delacorte Press

Published by Delacorte Press
an imprint of Random House Children's Books
a division of Random House, Inc.
New York

This is a work of fiction. Names, characters, places, and incidents either are the
product of the author's imagination or are used fictitiously. Any resemblance to actual
persons, living or dead, events, or locales is entirely coincidental.

ALLOYENTERTAINMENT   Produced by Alloy Entertainment
151 West 26th Street
New York, NY 10001

Visit us on the Web! www.randomhouse.com/teens
www.sisterhoodcentral.com

Educators and librarians, for a variety of teaching tools, visit us at
www.randomhouse.com/teachers

The Library of Congress has cataloged the hardcover edition of this work as follows:
Brashares, Ann.
  Forever in blue : the fourth summer of the Sisterhood / Ann Brashares.
    p. cm.
Summary: As their lives take them in different directions, Lena, Tibby, Carmen, and
Bridget discover many more things about themselves and the importance of their
relationship with each other.
  ISBN: 978-0-385-72936-9 (hardcover)
  ISBN: 978-0-385-90413-1 (Gibraltar lib. ed.) [1. Best friends—Fiction.
2. Friendship—Fiction. 3. Jeans (Clothing)—Fiction. 4. Conduct of life—Fiction.]
I. Title.
  PZ7.B73759For 2007
  [Fic]—dc22

                                                    2006018782

ISBN: 978-0-385-73401-1 (tr. pbk.)

Printed in the United States of America

10 9 8 7 6 5 4 3 2 1

First Trade Paperback Edition

For my sweet Susannah
... when she's ready

Acknowledgments

With admiration I thank Jodi Anderson, first and always.

After four books and six years together, I thank my cohorts at Random House with ever-deepening warmth and appreciation: Wendy Loggia, Beverly Horowitz, Chip Gibson, Judith Haut, Kathy Dunn, Marci Senders, Daisy Kline, Joan DeMayo, and many others who have invested themselves wholeheartedly in this project. I thank Leslie Morgenstein and my friend and agent, Jennifer Rudolph Walsh. What a lovely time we've all had.

I thank my parents, Jane Easton Brashares and William Brashares, and my brothers, Beau, Justin, and Ben Brashares. You can't pick your family, they say, but I would pick them.

I lovingly acknowledge my husband, Jacob Collins, and our three children, Sam, Nate, and Susannah.

Forever in Blue

And see she flies

And she is everywhere

—Nick Drake

PROLOGUE

Once upon a time there were four girls. Young women, you might even say. And though their lives traveled in different directions, they loved each other very much.

Once upon a time before that, these same girls found a pair of pants, wise and magical, and named them the Traveling Pants.

The Pants had the magic of teaching these girls how to be apart. They taught them how to be four people instead of one person. How to be together no matter where they were. How to love themselves as much as they loved each other. And on a practical level, the Pants had the magic of fitting all four of them, which is hard to believe but true, especially considering only one of them (the blonde) was built like a supermodel.

Okay. Full disclosure. I am one of these girls. I wear these Pants. I have these friends. I know this magic.

I am in fact the blonde, though I was kidding about the supermodel part.

But anyway, as it happens with most kinds of magic, these Pants did their job a little too well. And the girls, being extraordinary girls (if you don't mind my saying so), learned their lesson a little too well.

And so when the girls' lives changed that final summer, the Pants, being wise, had to change too.

And that is how this tale of sisterhood began, but did not end.

The only true paradise is

paradise lost.

—Marcel Proust

Gilda's was the same. It always was. And what a relief too, Lena found herself thinking. Good thing you could count on human vanity and the onward march of fitness crazes requiring mats and mirrors.

Not much else was the same. Things were different, things were missing.

Carmen, for instance, was missing.

"I can't really see how we can do this without Carmen," Tibby said. As was the custom, she'd brought her video camera for posterity, but she hadn't turned it on. Nobody was quite sure about when posterity started, or if maybe it already had.

"So maybe we shouldn't try," Bee said. "Maybe we should wait until we can do it together."

Lena had brought the candles, but she hadn't lit them. Tibby had brought the ceremonial bad eighties aerobics music, but she hadn't put it on. Bee had gamely set out the bowls of Gummi Worms and Cheetos, but nobody was eating them.

"When's that going to be?" Tibby asked. "Seriously, I think we've been trying to get together since last September and I don't think it has happened once."

"What about Thanksgiving?" Lena asked.

"Remember I had to go to Cincinnati for Great-grandma Felicia's hundredth birthday?" Tibby said.

"Oh, yeah. And she had a stroke," Bee said.

"That was after the party."

"And Carmen went to Florida over Christmas," Lena said. "And you two were in New York over New Year's."

"All right, so how about two weekends from now? Carmen will be back by then, won't she?"

"Yeah, but my classes start on June twentieth." Lena clasped her hands around her knees, her large feet bare on the sticky pine floor. "I can't miss the first day of the pose or I'll end up stuck in a corner or staring at the model's kneecap for a month."

"Okay, so July fourth," Tibby said reasonably. "Nobody has school or anything that Friday. We could meet back here for a long weekend."

Bee untied her shoe. "I fly to Istanbul on June twenty-fourth."

"That soon? Can you go later?" Tibby asked.

Bridget's face dimmed with regret. "The program put us all on this charter flight. Otherwise it's an extra thousand bucks and you have to find your own way to the site."

"How could Carmen miss this?" Tibby asked.

Lena knew what she meant. It wasn't okay for any of them to miss this ritual, but especially not Carmen, to whom it had mattered so much.

Bee looked around. "Miss what, though?" she asked, not so much challenging as conciliating. "This isn't really the launch, right?" She gestured to the Pants, folded obediently in the middle of their triangle. "I mean, not officially. We've been wearing them all school year. It's not like the other summers, when this was the huge kickoff and everything."

Lena wasn't sure whether she felt comforted or antagonized by this statement.

"Maybe that's true," Tibby said. "Maybe we don't need a launch this summer."

"We should at least figure out the rotation tonight," Lena said. "Carmen will just have to live with it."

"Why don't we keep up the same rotation we've had going till now?" Bridget suggested, straightening her legs in front of her. "No reason to change it just because it's summer."

Lena bit the skin around her thumbnail and considered the practical truth of this.

Summer used to be different. It was the time they left home, split up, lived separate lives for ten long weeks, and counted on the Pants to hold them together until they were reunited. Now summer was more of the same. Being apart wasn't the exception, Lena recognized, it was the rule.

When will we all be home again? That was what she wanted to know.

But when she thought about it logically, she knew: It wasn't just the answer that had changed, it was the question. What was home anymore? What counted as the status quo? Home was a time and it had passed.

Nobody was eating the Gummi Worms. Lena felt like she should eat one or cry. "So we'll just keep up the rotation," she echoed wanly. "I think I get them next."

"I have it written down," Tibby said.

"Okay."

"Well."

Lena looked at her watch. "Should we just go?"

"I guess," Tibby said.

"Do you want to stop at the Tastee Diner on the way home?" Bridget asked.

"Yeah," Tibby said, gathering the effects of a ritual that hadn't happened. "Maybe we can see a late movie after. I can't handle my parents tonight."

"What time are you guys taking off tomorrow?" Bee asked.

"I think our train's at ten," Tibby said. Lena and Tibby were taking the train together: Tibby was getting off in New York to start film classes and her Movieworld job, and Lena was heading up to Providence to change dorm rooms for the summer. Bee was spending time at home before she left for Turkey.

Lena realized she didn't want to go home just yet either.

She picked up the Pants and cradled them briefly. She had a feeling she could not name exactly, but one she knew she had not had in relation to the Pants before. She had felt gratitude, admiration, trust. What she felt now still contained all that, but tonight it was mixed in with a faint taste of desperation.

If we didn't have them, I don't know what we would do, she found herself thinking as Bee pulled the door of Gilda's shut behind them and they walked slowly down the dark stairs.

One's real life is so often
the life that one does
not lead.

—Oscar Wilde

"Carmen, it is beautiful. I can't wait for you to see it."

Carmen nodded into the receiver. Her mother sounded so happy that Carmen had to be happy. How could she not be happy?

"When do you think you'll move in?" she asked, trying to keep her voice light.

"Well, we will need to do some work. Some plastering, painting, refinishing the floors. There's some plumbing and electrical to do. We want to get most of it out of the way before we move in. I hope it will be by the end of August."

"Wow. That soon."

"*Nena*, it has five bedrooms. Is that unbelievable? It has a beautiful backyard for Ryan to run around in."

Carmen thought of her tiny brother. He could barely

walk yet, let alone run. He was going to grow up with such a different life than the one Carmen had.

"So no more apartment, huh?"

"No. It was a good place for the two of us, but didn't we always want a house? Isn't that what you always said you wanted?"

She'd also wanted a sibling and for her mother not to be alone. It wasn't always easy getting what you wanted.

"I'll have to pack up my room," Carmen said.

"You'll have a bigger room in the new house," her mother rushed to say.

Yes, she would. But wasn't it a bit late for that? For having a house with a yard and a bigger room? It was too late to redo her childhood. She had the one she had, and it had taken place in her small room in their apartment. It was sad and strange to lose it and too late to replace it.

Where did that leave her? Without her old life and not quite coming up with a new one. In between, floating, nowhere. That seemed all too fitting, in a way.

"Lena dropped by yesterday to say hi and see Ryan. She brought him a Frisbee," her mother mentioned a little wistfully. "I wish you were home."

"Yeah. But I've got all this stuff going on here."

"I know, *nena*."

After she hung up with her mother, the phone rang again.

"Carmen, where are you?"

Julia Wyman sounded annoyed. Carmen glanced behind her at her clock.

"We're supposed to be doing a run-through on set in . . . now!"

"I'm coming," Carmen said, pulling on her socks as she held the phone with her shoulder. "I'll be right there."

She hustled out of her dorm and to the theater. She remembered along the way that her hair was dirty and she'd meant to change her pants, because the ones she was wearing made her feel particularly fat. But did it matter? Nobody was looking at her.

Julia was waiting for her backstage. "Can you help me with this?" For her role in the production, Julia wore a long tweed skirt, and the waist was too big for her.

Carmen bent down to work on the safety pin. "How's that?" she asked, pinning the waistband in the back.

"Better. Thanks. How does it look?"

Julia looked good in it. Julia looked good in most things, and she didn't need Carmen to tell her so. But Carmen did anyway. In a strange way, it was Julia's job to look good for both of them. It was Carmen's job to appreciate her for it.

"I think Roland is waiting for you onstage."

Carmen stepped onto the stage, but Roland didn't appear to be waiting for her. He didn't react in any way when he saw her. These days she felt her presence had the same effect as a ghost—nobody noticed her, but the air suddenly got cold. Carmen squinted and tried to make herself small. She did not like being onstage when the lights were on. "Did you need something?" she asked Roland.

"Oh, yeah." He was trying to remember. "Can you fix the curtain in the parlor? It's falling off."

"Sure," she said quickly, wondering if she should feel guilty. Was she the one who put it up last?

She positioned the ladder, climbed up three rungs, and aimed a staple gun at the plywood wall. Set building was strange in that it was always about the impression, made to be seen from particular angles and not made to last. It existed in space and time not as a thing, but as a trick.

She liked the *chunk* sound of the staple clawing into the wall. It was one of the things she'd learned at college: how to operate a staple gun. Her dad was paying a lot of money for that.

She'd learned other stuff too. How to gain seventeen pounds eating cafeteria food and chocolate at night when you felt lonely. How to be invisible to guys. How to not wake up for your nine o'clock psychology class. How to wear sweatshirts almost every day because you felt self-conscious about your body. How to elude the people you loved most in the world. How to be invisible to pretty much everyone, including yourself.

It was lucky she'd gotten to know Julia. Carmen was very fortunate, she knew. Because Julia was one of the most visible people on campus. They balanced each other out. Without Julia on the campus of Williams College, Carmen privately suspected she might disappear altogether.

It was different being a girl with a boyfriend.

Bridget meditated upon this as she walked along Edgemere Street on the way from Lena's house to her own. Her meditation had begun moments before, when a guy she knew vaguely from high school leaned out of his car and yelled "Hey, gorgeous!" and blew her a kiss.

In the past she might have shouted something at him. She might have blown him back a kiss. She might have given him the finger, depending on her mood. But somehow, it all seemed different now that she was a girl with a boyfriend.

She had spent almost a year getting used to it. It was particularly complex when you only saw that boyfriend for a day or two every month—when he went to school in New York City and you went to school in Providence, Rhode Island. Your status was more theoretical. For every guy who shouted from his car window, for every guy you passed on the way to Freshman Psychology who sort of checked you out, you thought, *What he doesn't realize is that I have a boyfriend.*

Each time she saw Eric's remarkable face, each time he appeared at the door of her dorm room or came to meet her at Port Authority in New York, it all came back. The way he kissed her. The way he wore his pants, the way he stayed up all night with her getting her ready for her Spanish midterm.

But it became theoretical again after Eric told her about Mexico. He'd gotten a job as assistant director at their old camp in Baja.

"I'm leaving the day after classes end," he'd told her on the phone in April.

There was no uncertainty in it, no question or lingering pause. There was nothing for her.

She clamped her hand harder around the phone, but she didn't want to betray the chaotic feelings. She wasn't good at being left. "When do you get back?" she asked.

"End of September. I'm going to stay for a month with my grandparents in Mulegé. My grandmother already started cooking." His laugh was light and sweet. He acted as though she would be as pleased for him as he was for himself. He didn't fathom her darkness.

Sometimes you hung up the phone and felt the bruising of your heart. It hurt now and it would hurt more later. The conversation was too unsatisfying to continue and yet you couldn't stand for it to end. Bridget wanted to throw the phone and also herself against the wall.

She had presumed her and Eric's summer plans would

unfold together in some way. She thought having a boy-friend meant you planned your future in harmony. Was it his certainty about her that made it so easy for him to leave, or was it indifference?

She went for a long run and talked herself down. It wasn't like they were married or anything. She shouldn't feel hurt by it. She knew it wasn't personal. The assistant director job was a windfall—it paid well and put him close to his faraway family.

She didn't feel hurt, exactly, but in the days after he told her, she got that fitful forward-moving energy. She didn't feel like hanging around missing him. If she hadn't been caught by surprise, caught in a painful presumption, she probably wouldn't have signed up for the dig in Turkey quite so fast.

Eric couldn't expect her to sit around waiting for him. That was not something she could do. How long could she coast on having a boyfriend when that boyfriend planned to be away from May to late September? How long could they coast as a couple? She wasn't a theoretical kind of person.

It was after the conversation about Mexico that she really started to wonder about these things. After that it seemed like for every guy she saw on her way to class, she had the feeling that her status as a girl with a boyfriend was something demanded of her rather than something she had very eagerly given.

❊   ❊   ❊

18

Tibby glanced at the time on her register. There were four minutes left in her shift and at least twelve people in line.

She scanned in a pile of six movies for a prepubescent girl wearing sparkly silver eye shadow and a too-tight-looking choker. Were the girl's eyes bulging or was Tibby imagining it?

"You're gonna watch all these?" Tibby asked absently. It was Friday. Late fees kicked in on Monday. The girl's gum smelled strongly and fakely of watermelon. As the girl swallowed, Tibby thought of fishermen's pelicans, with the rings around their necks so they couldn't gulp down their catch.

" 'Cause I'm having a sleepover. There'll be, like, seven of us. I mean, if Callie can come. And if she can't, I shouldn't be getting that one, because everybody else hates it."

Were we like that? Tibby wondered while the girl went on to describe each of her friends' specific movie requirements.

Now her shift was over by two minutes. Tibby cursed herself for having begun the conversation in the first place. She always forgot that annoying fact of question-asking: People tended to answer.

She had eleven customers still to serve before she could reasonably close down her register, and she was no longer getting paid. "This one's closing," she called to incipient number twelve before he could invest any time in her line.

The next person up was a goateed young man with a Windbreaker over his doorman coat. When it flapped open, Tibby could see that his name was Carl. She wanted to tell him that his movie was all right, but the ending stank and the sequel was an insult to your brain, but she made herself think the comment and not say it. That would be her rule going forward. She might as well admit to herself that she liked talking more than listening.

She closed out her register, said her good-byes, and walked along Broadway before turning onto Bleecker Street and then into the entrance to her dorm. The bad thing about her job was that it paid barely over minimum wage. The good thing about her job was that it was three blocks away.

The lobby of her dorm was cool and empty but for the security guard at his desk. It was all different now that it was summer. No students jabbering, no cell-phonic symphony of ring tones. A month ago, the big bulletin board had been laden with notices twenty thick. Now it was clear right down to the cork.

During the school year, the elevator ride was socially taxing. Too much time to stare and appraise and judge. In the normally crowded space she'd felt a need to be something for each of her fellow passengers, even the ones whose names she didn't know. Now, with it empty, she felt herself merging into the fake wood-grain wall.

Tonight the halls would be empty. The summer programs didn't start until after July fourth. And even then there would just be new, temporary people, not her friends, and not the kind you worried about in the elevator. They'd be gone by the middle of August.

It was a strange thing about college. You felt like you were supposed to be finding your life there. Each person you saw, you thought, *Will you mean something to me? Will we figure into each other's lives?* She'd made a few actual friends on her floor and in her film classes, but most people she saw she kind of knew off the bat wouldn't mean anything. Like the swim team girls who decorated their faces with purple paint to demonstrate school spirit, or the guy with the fuzzy facial hair who wore the Warhammer T-shirt.

But then again, chimed in the voice she'd recently come to think of as Meta-Tibby (her do-right self, never hurried or snappish), who would have guessed that first day in the 7-Eleven that Brian would become important?

In the four years since she'd first met Brian, many things had changed. Though Brian insisted he'd loved her from the first time he met her, she'd thought he was a doofus for the ages. She'd been wrong. She was often wrong. Now she got a deep abdominal tingle whenever she thought of being near him. It had been nine months since they'd . . . what? She hated the term *hooked up*. Nine months since they'd swum in their underwear after hours in the public pool and kissed fiercely and pressed themselves together until their hands and toes turned pruney and their lips blue.

They hadn't had sex yet. Not officially, in spite of Brian's pleas. But since that night in August, she felt as though her body belonged to Brian, and his body to her. Ever since that night in the pool, the way they loved each other had changed. Before it they each took up their own space. After it they took up space together. Before that night if he touched his ankle to hers under the dinner table, she blushed and obsessed and sweated through her shirt. After that night they always had some part touching. They read together on a twin bed with every part of their bodies overlapping, still concentrating on their books. Well, concentrating a little on their books.

Tonight this place would be quiet. On some level she missed Bernie, who practiced her opera singing from nine to ten, and Deirdre, who cooked actual food in the communal floor kitchen. But it was restful being alone. She would write e-mails to her friends and shave her armpits and legs before Brian came tomorrow. Maybe she would order pad thai from the place around the corner. She would pick it up so she wouldn't have to pay the tip for delivery. She hated to be cheap, but she couldn't afford to lay out another five dollars.

She fit her key into the loose lock. So imprecise was the lock she suspected it would turn for virtually any key in the dorm. Maybe any key in the world. It was a tarty little lock.

She swung open the door and felt once again the familiar appreciation for her single. Who cared if it was seven by nine feet? Who cared if it fit more like a suit of clothes than an actual room? It was hers. Unlike at home, her stuff stayed the way she left it.

Her gaze went first to the light pulsing under the power button on her computer. It went second to the steady green light of her camera's battery, fully charged. It went third to the glimmer of shine in the eyeball of a large, brown-haired nineteen-year-old boy sitting on her bed.

There was the lurch. Stomach, legs, ribs, brain. There was the pounding of the heart.

"Brian!"

"Hey," he said mutedly. She could tell he was trying not to scare her.

She dropped her bag and went to him, instantly folding up in his eager limbs.

"I thought you were coming tomorrow."

"I can't last five days," he said, his face pressed into her ear.

It was so good to feel him all around her. She loved this feeling. She would never get used to it. It was too good. Unfairly good. She couldn't dislodge her worldview that things balanced out. You paid for what you got. In happiness terms, this always felt like a spending spree.

Most guys said they'd call you tomorrow and they called you the next Saturday or not at all. Most guys said they'd be there at eight and showed up at nine-fifteen. They kept you comfortless, wanting and wishing, and annoyed at yourself for every moment you spent that way. That was not Brian. Brian promised to come on Saturday and he came on Friday instead.

"Now I'm happy," he said from her neck.

She looked down at the side of his face, at his manly forearm. He was so handsome, and yet he wore it lightly. The way he looked was not what made her love him, but was it wrong to notice?

He rolled her over onto the bed. She pried off her running shoes with her toes. He pulled up her shirt and laid his head on her bare stomach, his arms around her hips, his knees bent at the wall. If this room was small for her, it barely contained Brian when he stretched out. He couldn't help kicking the wall now and then. Tonight she was glad not to have to feel guilt toward the guy in 11-C.

It was something like a miracle, this was. Their own room. No hiding, no fibbing, no getting away with it. No parent to whom you must account for your time. No curfew to bump up against.

Time stretched on. They would eat what they felt like for dinner — or at least, what they could afford. She remembered the night they'd had two Snickers bars apiece for dinner and ice cream for dessert. They would fall asleep together, his hand on her breast or the valley of her waist, and wake up together in the sunshine from her east-facing window. It was so good. Too good. How could she ever afford this?

"I love you," he murmured, his hands reaching up under her shirt. He didn't hang around for that beat, that momentary vacuum where she was meant to respond in kind. His hands were already up under her shoulders, unbending himself over her for a real kiss. He didn't need her to say it back.

She used to have the idea — an untested belief, really — that you loved someone in a kind of mirror dance. You loved in exact response to how much they were willing to love you.

Brian wasn't like that. He did his loving openly and without call for reciprocation. It was something that awed her, but that set him apart, as though he spoke Mandarin or could dunk a basketball.

She plunged her hand under his T-shirt, feeling his warm back, his angel bones. "I love you," she said. He didn't ask for the words, but she gave them.

. . . and down they forgot

as up they grew

—e. e. cummings

There were so many things you took for granted. So many things you hardly noticed until they were gone. In Carmen's case, one of those things was her identity.

She did have one once, she thought as she put the last of the props away in the darkened and empty theater.

She had once been the only child of a single mother. She had been one quarter of a famously inseparable foursome. She had been a standout math student, a fashionista, a good dancer, a control freak, a slob. A resident of apartment 4F. Now these things were gone, or—for the moment, at least—undetectable. She had come up with nothing to replace them. Except for maybe Julia. She was lucky to have Julia.

Ideally, you grew up in a house with a family and then you went to college. You left your home and family there, kind of waiting for you. You left a hole roughly the size and shape of you. You got to come home and fill it every once in a while.

Maybe this was only an illusion. Nothing stayed the same. You couldn't expect your family to sit there in suspended animation until you came back. That required a babyish narcissism that not even Carmen could muster. (Well, maybe she could muster it a little.) But so what if it was an illusion? Illusions could be really helpful sometimes.

The important thing was that home stayed where it was and you got to move. You could always plot your location in the world by your relationship to it. *I'm so far from home*, you could think, when in, say, China. *I'm so close to it*, you could think, when you turned the last corner and saw it again.

As Carmen's mother liked to point out, teenagers and toddlers were very much the same. They both liked to leave their mother, so long as their mother did not move.

Well, Carmen's mother did move. She was a moving target. Home was a time and no longer a place. Carmen couldn't return to it.

As far as Carmen was concerned, that made the leaving a lot harder. It also made the plotting of your location very tricky indeed.

For the first seven months of the school year, nothing felt familiar and nothing felt real. Except for maybe food. She felt as though she'd stepped out of the flow of time. She watched it go past, but she didn't take part. She just waited there, wondering when her life would start again.

She had lived big before. She really had. She was ambitious, she was pretty. She was a young woman of color.

Now she felt like a ghost. The pale, starchy cafeteria food made her pale and starchy. It blurred her lines.

She depended too much on her context to know herself. The faces of her friends and her mother were mirrors to her. Without them she couldn't see herself; she was lost. She'd first realized it that strange and lonely summer in South Carolina when she'd met her stepfamily.

She and Win Sawyer, the guy she'd met last summer, had gotten together a couple of times in the fall, but she had purposely let it trail off. She didn't know or like herself enough to be knowable or likable when she was with him. She had nothing to offer.

It turned out that she wasn't very good at making friends. That was one of the problems that came of having three pals, ready-made, practically waiting for you to be born so they could befriend you. She hadn't had to work that muscle you use to make friends. She doubted she even had that muscle.

Her first mistake was believing that she and her roommate, Lissa Greco, would be instant friends, and that their relationship would be a stepping-stone to social consequence. Lissa set her straight pretty quickly. She'd arrived at Williams with her two best friends from boarding school. She was petulant and undermining to Carmen. She wasn't looking for another friend. She accused Carmen of stealing her clothes.

In the beginning Carmen was disoriented by her loneliness and wanted desperately to see Tibby, Bee, and Lena. But as time passed, she started to avoid them in subtle ways. She didn't want to admit to them or herself that she wasn't quite making the go of college that she'd hoped.

Once, she went to Providence and saw Bee in her glory: her soccer friends, her glorious roommate, her eating friends, her partying friends, her library friends. She saw Lena in her different kind of glory, quiet in the studio, surrounded by her beautiful sketches. The weekend she spent in New York with Tibby, it was three of them to the room, including Brian, and Tibby won a departmental prize for her first short film.

Carmen didn't want them coming to see her here, where she had no glory at all. She didn't want them to see her like this.

She first met Julia in the late winter in the theater department, where Carmen was signing up for a playwriting class. Julia mistook her for a theater type. "Have you worked on sets?" she'd asked Carmen.

Carmen couldn't figure out whom she was talking to. "Me?" she'd finally asked. She wasn't sure which was more surprising: that Julia took her for a set builder or that Julia was talking to her at all.

How low I have fallen, Carmen thought miserably. Nobody in high school would have mistaken her for a set builder. She'd been one of the cute girls, particularly by the end of high school. She showed off her belly button in tiny shirts. She flirted outrageously. She wore red lipstick to take her SATs.

Carmen tried to scrape together a little bit of dignity. "No, I'm not really a set person," she said.

"Oh, come on. Everybody's a set person. Jeremy Rhodes is directing a production of *The Miracle Worker* for senior week, and we're getting desperate," Julia explained.

Carmen recognized Julia from the cafeteria. She was one of the few freshmen that people knew about. She was beautiful and somewhat dramatic-looking, with her pale white skin and her long black hair. She wore vintage jackets and long bohemian skirts and made a certain amount of noise with her various pins and beads and bangles. She was small and thin but used the oversized gestures of a person who knew she was being looked at.

"Well, sorry," Carmen said.

"Let me know if you change your mind, okay?" Julia said. "It's a really cool group of people. Really tight."

Carmen nodded and fled, but she did think about it. She thought wistfully of having things to do and "really cool" people to do them with.

Julia approached her again in the cafeteria a few weeks later. "Hey, how's it going?"

Carmen felt self-conscious because she was eating alone. She was torn between being unhappy that Julia was seeing her this way and being happy that all the rest of the people there were seeing her with Julia. "All right," Carmen said.

"Did you get into the writing class?"

"Nope," said Carmen. "How's the play going?"

"Really good." Julia smiled a winning smile. "Still looking for people to join up."

"Oh, yeah?"

"Yeah. You should really think about it. Jeremy's very

31

cool. There are only three performances and they don't start until after exams. Why don't you come tonight? We have a rehearsal at seven. Just see what you think."

"Thanks," Carmen said, feeling almost absurdly grateful. Grateful that Julia had noticed her, remembered her, talked to her, invited her to something. Did Julia know how alone she was here? "Maybe I will," she said.

So grateful was she, she probably would have agreed if Julia had invited her to drink poisoned Kool-Aid.

And that was how, one week later, Carmen found herself standing on a ladder wearing a tool belt. If her friends saw her, they would not recognize her. No one in her high-school graduating class would recognize her. Or at least, she hoped they wouldn't. She didn't recognize herself. But really, who was herself? Who?

If she knew that, she probably wouldn't be standing on the ladder wearing the tool belt.

And now, six weeks after that, Carmen was doing the same thing, only it had lost its feeling of absurdity. She belonged there more than anywhere else. You could get used to almost anything.

And she did appreciate having something to do, someplace to go after dinner besides her dorm room. She appreciated that Julia was nice to her. Julia introduced her around. She made sure that if the cast and crew were going to get cappuccinos after rehearsal, Carmen came too. Carmen appreciated the hilariously mean impression of Lissa that Julia did to cheer her up when her roommate did something nasty.

In the theater group, which included many upperclassmen, Carmen felt like she was an add-on to Julia, a low-budget hanger-on friend. She had to remind people of her name too often. But still. It was better being out and about as a friend of Julia than eating candy in her room as a nobody.

Once in a while she felt sorry for herself. She felt like the prince in "The Prince and the Pauper," being mistaken for someone unimportant. *Do you even know who I am?* she thought. *Do you even know who my friends are?*

But really, if someone called her bluff, what would she say? Maybe she could answer the second question, but not even she knew the answer to the first.

What are you getting out of this? she silently asked Julia, these weeks later, as she pinned Julia's skirt for the third time and Julia gave her a squeeze of thanks. That was the part she couldn't figure out.

When Julia came to her in April with brochures from the Village Summer Theater Festival in Vermont, Carmen was startled and, of course, grateful.

"These are full-scale productions with a lot of really well-known actors," Julia said. "Do you want to do it? It's mid-June through the second week in August. It's hard to get in for acting, but they're always looking for crew. It could be a great experience."

Carmen was so pleased to be invited, she would have agreed for the sole reason that she'd been asked. Later she had to get her parents to agree to pay.

"Carmen, since when are you interested in theater?" her father had wanted to know when she called him to ask for the check. She'd reached him on his car phone on his way home from the office.

"Since, I don't know . . . Since now."

"Well, I guess you've always been dramatic," he mused aloud.

"Thanks a lot, Dad." This was the kind of stuff you had to put up with when you asked for money.

"I mean that in the best sense, Bun. I really do."

"Right," she said tightly.

"And I remember you as the fierce carrot in the salad in your first-grade play."

"Tomato. Anyway, I'm not doing acting."

"Then what are you doing?"

"Behind-the-scenes stuff."

"*Behind-the-scenes* stuff?" He acted like she'd said she was going to eat her own ears.

"Yeah." She was starting to feel defensive.

"Carmen, sweetie, you've never done anything behind the scenes in your life."

He was in quite the chatty humor, wasn't he? she thought darkly.

"So maybe it's about time," she said.

She heard him turn off the car's ignition. It was quiet. "Bun, if this is really what you want, then I am willing to pay for it," he said.

It was easier when he was being annoying. When he was nice, she found she actually had to think.

Was it what she wanted? She thought of Julia. Or was Carmen just wanting to feel wanted?

She took stock of her options. Bee was going to Turkey, Tibby was taking classes in New York, and Lena would be in Providence. Her mother and David were ditching her apartment—her home—and fixing up a large suburban house on a street she had never even heard of.

"It's really what I want," she said.

Bridget stood in the bathroom looking for a toothbrush in the disorderly medicine cabinet, realizing just how long it had been since she'd spent a night at home.

It wasn't the product of any design. It was just one thing and then another. Over Thanksgiving, she'd stayed up so late talking at Lena's she'd just crashed on the couch. She'd been in New York over Christmas break, first with Eric uptown, then with Tibby downtown. She'd gone down to Alabama to visit Greta for spring break. She'd taken all-night buses the time she came home in February.

And now, on the eve of her trip to an excavation in a remote place halfway across the world, she was touching down at home.

She kept her eyes straight ahead in the hallway. She didn't want to see how badly the carpet needed to be vacuumed. She wasn't going to spend her short time here cleaning the stupid house.

In her room she sifted impatiently through her duffel bag again. She didn't feel like putting any of her stuff on the shelves. She had piles of laundry, but she wouldn't do it here. She kept her contact points minimal: her feet and whatever bit of floor space was required by the bottom of her bag. To sit or lie down extended that contact uncomfortably.

She remembered her seventh-grade camping trip, the ranger teaching them the principle of low-impact camping. "When you leave the wilderness, make it like you were never there." That was how she lived in her own house. Low-impact living. She ate more, drank more, laughed more, breathed more, slept more at any of her friends' houses than at her own.

She knocked on Perry's door. She knocked again. She knew he was in there. Finally she pushed the door open. He was staring at his computer screen. He had big earphones on, that was why he hadn't heard her.

What was it with her dad and her brother and their damned earphones? The house was as quiet as a crypt.

"Hey!" she said, about a foot from his ear. He looked up, disoriented. He took off his earphones. He wasn't used to being disturbed.

He was deep into one of those online war games he'd been playing since the beginning of high school. He did not want to chat. He wanted to get back to his game.

"Do you have a spare toothbrush somewhere? I thought I packed mine, but I can't find it." She always felt bullish and noisy in this house.

"Sorry?"

"An extra toothbrush. Do you have one?"

He shook his head without thinking about it. "Uh-uh. Sorry." He turned his eyes back to the screen.

Bridget stared at her brother. For some reason she

thought of Eric, and with that thought came the dawning of a certain set of objective facts. Yes, her family was alienated. On their best days they were eccentric. They were not happy; they were not close. But still. Here she was standing in front of Perry, her own brother — her twin, for God's sake — whom she had hardly seen this year.

She pushed a pile of techie magazines out of the way and hoisted herself onto his desk. She was going to talk with her brother. They hadn't had a single real conversation since Christmas. Out of guilt alone, she would torture him.

"How's school?"

He fumbled with something on the back of his monitor.

"What have you been taking this semester? Did you do the wildlife class?"

He continued to fumble. He looked at her once, wishfully.

"Hey, Perry?"

"Yeah. Oh, sorry," he said. He left the computer alone. "I've actually been taking time off this semester." He spoke to the arm of his chair.

"What?"

"Yeah. I haven't been taking classes this semester."

"Why not?"

His look was blank. He wasn't used to having to answer questions. He wasn't used to having to present his life or explain his decisions.

"What did Dad say?" she asked.

"Dad?"

"Yeah."

"We didn't really discuss it."

"You didn't really discuss it." She was talking a little too quickly, a little too loudly. Perry made a face like his ears hurt.

"Does he know?"

Perry's eyes would not engage. She felt as if she were speaking over a PA system rather than specifically to him.

She didn't care if he wouldn't look at her. She made herself look at him. She wanted to see him through objective eyes.

His hair had always been darker than hers, and now it had turned completely brown, probably accelerated by his staying inside all the time. He had untended fuzz on his upper lip, but otherwise he looked as though he had barely entered puberty. She glanced away, a churning feeling in her chest.

He was so slight and she so tall it was a wonder they were related, let alone twins. But then, maybe it wasn't a wonder at all. Maybe it was part of the harsh duality of being born together. What one got, the other didn't. And Bridget had always been strong. She couldn't help picturing them stowed together in her mother's stomach, taking what resources they could.

It was the zero-sum problem with twins. If one was smart, the other felt dumb. If one was bossy, the other was meek. The equation was too easy.

Bridget knew she'd always taken more than her fair share. But was it her job to stay small to encourage him to be big? If she withdrew, would he come forward? Was it her fault he had come out this way?

"I guess Dad knows," Perry finally answered.

She stood up. She felt frustrated. What was Perry doing if not going to school? He didn't have a job. Did he have any friends? Did he ever leave his room?

"I'll see you later," she said tightly.

"You could ask him," he said.

She turned around. "Ask who?"

"Dad."

"About what?"

"About the toothbrush."

Fill what is empty,

empty what is full, and

scratch where it itches.

—Tallulah Bankhead

Lena didn't feel lonely easily. Somehow, knowing she had friends was enough to keep her happy. She didn't actually have to talk with them or see them all the time. It was like other things: So long as she had an aspirin in the cabinet, she didn't really need to take one. So long as the toilet was readily available, she could wait until the last second to use it. As long as the basic resources existed for her, her needs were small.

She thought of this on the first day of her summer painting class. The instructor was new to her, the monitor was new. The students were unfamiliar. She was using a new kind of brush. She would probably like these things once she got used to them.

And in the meantime, Tibby and Carmen were on the other end of her cell phone. The Traveling Pants would come her way soon. Annik, her former teacher, was available for art-related crises, even the little ones. Her old kind of brush was sitting there at the ready, just in case. These were the things that made her bold.

But did it count as boldness when she kept herself so covered?

"Up there. There's a space," she heard the instructor, Robert, saying to a late arrival. Lena's main hope for the other students was not that they provide friendship or commiseration. It was that they not set up too close to her and obstruct her sight lines. She tensed up as the new person came closer and relaxed again when he/she passed behind her and kept on going to the far side of the studio. Potential threat averted. She didn't need to take her eyes from the model.

When the timer dinged and the model broke her pose, Lena finally looked up. She saw dark brown hair poking above the newly set-up canvas, curly and not very well trained. A tall person, most likely male. She quickly looked down. It was familiar dark brown hair. She tried to think. She kept her eyes down as she went into the hall.

Lena had developed the habit years before of avoiding eye contact. It was a sad capitulation, in a way, because she loved to look at people's faces. She wanted to be an artist, after all. She had good, informative eyes, and she liked to use them. The trouble was, whoever she looked at was usually looking back. And though she liked looking, she did not like being looked at. Brain-wise, she was perfectly designed for invisibility. Face-wise, she knew she was not. She'd always been striking. She'd always gotten attention for it.

That was one of the things she loved about drawing and painting models. It was the only time in her life she got to look and look and look and nobody looked at her.

She walked back to her easel after the five-minute break, gearing up for the next twenty-five minutes of concentrated work. The late person with the hair was still at work. It made her sort of curious. She saw a hand and a palette. It was a man's hand.

For the first minutes of the pose, she thought about the hair and the hand across the way and not about her drawing. That was strange of her. Well, maybe she did avoid eye contact, but she apparently fell for a mystery as hard as the next person.

At the break, she waited for the face to emerge from behind the canvas. She waited for him to find her face and look at her. Then the world would be normal. He would look at her for a few seconds too long and then she could not care about him anymore.

Did she know him? She felt like maybe she did.

Another break passed and he did not so much as peer around his canvas. How frustrating. She actually positioned herself to get a look at him. She had to laugh at herself in the process, craning her neck. The laugh brought in the smell of linseed oil and oil paint and she felt happy in a visceral, smell-induced way.

Desire was just the dumbest thing. You wanted what you wanted until it was yours. Then you didn't want it anymore. You took what you had for granted until it was no longer yours. This, it seemed to her, was one of the crueler paradoxes of human nature.

She remembered a pair of brown wedge boots. She'd seen them at Bloomingdale's and passed them up because they cost over two hundred dollars. They probably had lots of pairs in the back, she'd thought. Certainly they would have her gargantuan size in stock. She could always come back.

And yet when she did go back two days later, they were all gone. She asked the saleslady, who said, "Oh, those wedge boots sold out instantly. Very popular. No, we're not getting any more."

At which point, Lena became obsessed. It wasn't that other people wanted them. It was that she couldn't have them. No, that wasn't completely it either. Partly, at least, it was the fact that they were genuinely lovely boots. She scoured the Internet. She researched the manufacturer, she searched eBay. She would have bid three hundred dollars for those two-hundred-dollar boots, and yet she never found them. "The boots that got away," Carmen said jokingly once, when Lena rhapsodized about them.

So how did desire, hopelessly tricky as it was, relate to love? It wasn't the same. (She hoped it wasn't the same.) It wasn't entirely different. They were certainly related. By blood, though, or more like in-laws? she wondered.

What about Kostos? There was desire, no question. What else? Would she have continued to love him if he had continued to be available to her? Yes. The answer came before she finished thinking the question. Yes. There was a time when he loved her and she loved him and they both believed they could be together. Indeed, such a time it was, it had effectively wrecked all the rest of her times.

But could she have gotten over Kostos if he hadn't been taken from her so forcibly? If she'd just been allowed, over the course of months or years, to discover that he snored or that he was prone to zits on his back or that his toenails grew inward and made his feet stink?

She stopped. Wait a minute. Objection. She demanded that her mind rephrase its question. Would she have gotten over him *more easily* had he not been forced away? She was over him now. Yes, she still thought about him, but not nearly as much. No, she hadn't yet been with anyone else, but . . .

For the rest of class, Lena found herself looking again and again at the hand to the right of the canvas across the way and the shock of hair above it. He was a lefty, she realized. Kostos was a lefty.

He worked through the breaks. She couldn't get so much as a peek at him.

The last pose ended and Lena packed her things away slowly. She hung around, pretending to be thinking (well, she was actually thinking, wasn't she). At last she drifted into the hallway.

And because the truth must be told, Lena (who didn't care) loitered for fourteen minutes in the hallway until he finally came out of the classroom and she got her look at him.

She did know him. Okay, no, she didn't know him. But she knew of him. He wasn't her year. Maybe one or two years older. She had certainly seen him.

He wasn't the sort of person you would forget, appearance-wise. He was tall, with raucous hair, dark gold skin, and some very good-humored freckles.

His name was Leo, and she knew that because he had a reputation. Not for being a player, so far as she knew, but for being able to draw. And that, of all things, was a turn-on to one Lena Kaligaris, Greek virgin.

Her small circle of friends and acquaintances at RISD, art geeks that they were, whispered most fervently about the people who could or couldn't, did or didn't. Draw, that was. And this young man of the hair and hand stood among the few, almost legendary people who could.

She watched him with a surprising little thrill in her stomach and waited for him to notice her. How often did she want that? Not often. What she really wanted, she informed herself, was for him to look at her in a particular way. It wouldn't matter if he had a serious girlfriend or wasn't even into girls at all. She wanted him to give her the look, the slightly extended appraisal that would drain him of his mystery and transform him into a regular person. (She did want that, didn't she?) It was this familiar look that confirmed her peculiar power, easily possessed and rarely wanted.

These were the things that freed her. These were the things that made her bold.

But he didn't look at her like that. He didn't look at her

at all. He fixed his eyes ahead and he kept on walking, bringing to mind for the second time that afternoon the memory of the brown wedge boots.

"I got in."

Brian slipped the news in between the mu shu pork and the fortune cookies.

"You what?" Tibby demanded, unsure she had heard him properly.

"I got in."

"You did?"

He looked slightly sheepish. He cracked his fortune cookie in quarters and then eighths, and then it was a crumble.

"That's so great! I knew you would. How could you not?"

Ever since Brian had hatched the idea of transferring to NYU from the University of Maryland, his grades had been faultless.

"I just want to sleep beside you every night," he had told her back in December. "That's all I want."

She knew he would get in. She knew he would make it work. That was how he was.

"What does it say?" he asked, pointing to the fortune in her hand.

" 'Beware the prevalence of ideas,' " she read. She crunched on her cookie. "My lucky numbers are 4 and 237. How about yours?"

" 'You are sexy,' " he read.

"No way! It doesn't say that. Let me see it!"

He smiled suggestively and handed it over.

It actually did say that. How unfair. "So what about the money?" she asked, tossing her fortune into the remains of the plum sauce.

"Well."

"Not good?" She felt the sesame noodles climbing back up her esophagus.

"I got six thousand."

"Oh." She swallowed. "Dollars?"

"Dollars."

She tried to think. The waiter slapped the bill down on their table without stopping.

"Out of twenty-two thousand."

"Oh."

"Not including room and board."

"Oh." She flicked her chopsticks around. "How come not more?"

"My stepfather has more money than you'd think."

"But he doesn't give you any of it," Tibby burst out. In her world, parents paid for college, and if they couldn't cover it, they helped you get the loans to pay the difference.

Brian didn't look bitter in the least. He didn't even look irritated. What Tibby thought of as a right, Brian didn't hope for. "I know. Yeah. But that's how it works."

"It's not fair that they count his money against you. Can you explain that he's not going to pay *anything*?"

Brian shrugged. "I'm saving."

"How much have you got?"

"One hundred and seventy-nine." He picked up the bill.

She grabbed it from him. "I've got this."

"No. I want to."

"You're saving."

"I know. But I can save and also buy you dinner."

"And take the bus up here almost every weekend and buy me CDs?" She didn't mean to sound mad at him.

He took out his wallet. She saw a corner of the condom he'd stashed there three or four months ago. "So we're ready, when we're ready," he'd told her when she'd first noticed it. He fished out a bill—a twenty, crumpled and weary, as though it were the last of its kind.

"Come on. Please let me." She got her wallet out too.

"Next time," he said, getting up, leaving her clutching her extraneous wallet.

He always said that. His arms were around her as soon as they made it to the sidewalk. It surprised her that they could walk in that degree of embrace.

On the way up in the elevator they took advantage of being alone. As soon as they were inside her room, Brian went to his duffel bag and unzipped it. "To celebrate," he said, pulling out a bottle of wine.

"Where did you get that?" she asked. Brian was not your fake-ID type.

He tried to look mysterious. "I found it someplace."

"Like in your house?"

He laughed. "It was sitting around. It's old."

She picked it up and looked at it. It was red wine from 1997. "Very funny."

"Hang on." He disappeared down the hall and came back with a corkscrew and two plastic cups from the communal

49

kitchen. He didn't really know how to use the corkscrew and neither did she. At last, laughing, they poked the cork into the wine bottle. First he poured two cups and then he put on a Beethoven CD, the fifth concerto for piano, which he knew she loved.

"It's loud," she said.

"Nobody's here," he said.

"Oh, yeah."

They sat cross-legged, facing each other on the floor. When they touched cups, the soft plastic gave, making no sound.

"To us together," she said, knowing how happy it made him by the flush of his skin. She felt shy all of a sudden. She wanted to say something ironic, but nothing came. She took a long drink of wine.

"Is it good?" he asked, pulling her feet to get her to come closer.

"I don't know. Is it?"

He drank some more. "Tastes kind of old."

"I think I like it," she said. She liked all the things about that moment, and the wine went along with them.

"Here's more."

"You have some too."

She turned and lay back against him, wine in her blood and music in her ears. She guessed there were people who lived their whole lives without getting to be this happy. That thought was the single note of unhappiness in her happiness.

He whistled along with the violins for a few bars. "I

think this is the best night ever," he said in a quiet voice, thinking her thoughts, as he often did.

"Except maybe the night of the pool."

"Right." He considered. "But I didn't know you as much then. I thought I did, but now I know I didn't. And imagine how it will feel next year or the one after?"

Brian was unafraid to think of the future, believing she was in it. He talked about them when they were thirty as easily as when they were twenty. He talked about babies and who would get Tibby's extra-long second toe. He wanted all of it. He wasn't afraid of saying so.

He liked to tell her his dreams, and he always dreamed in *we*. "Who's *we*?" she asked the first time he recounted to her a long, complicated scenario.

He looked at her, perplexed, as though she was kidding around with him for no good reason. "You and me."

It couldn't keep getting better, Tibby decided. It just couldn't. There was a law of physics that prohibited it. Seriously, there was some kind of law. Conservation of joy. No joy could be added to the sum in the universe without some being taken away. They were taking more than their share as it was.

He poured more wine. She realized in an indistinct way that she was getting drunk. She realized it on one level and felt it on another.

The bottle and the plastic cups were somehow shoved out of the way and now they were kissing on the linoleum floor.

The second movement of the concerto began, too beautiful for anything. "How about the bed?" she suggested faintly.

Usually she was the one who kept guard in these situations. She'd made the decision that they weren't supposed to make love yet. They were both virgins. He was more than ready, but she still wasn't sure. And as much as he pleaded, he didn't push; he was a gentleman.

Now she pressed against him, her hips seeming to know what to do without even bothering with her brain. Her shirt was off, without her quite noticing. Some time ago, Brian had gotten the knack of her front-fastening bra.

She managed to free him of his shirt. There was nothing better than feeling his bare skin against hers, and those few fine hairs in the middle of his chest.

If he was doing this, she wondered vaguely, and she was doing that, then who exactly was minding the store?

They were hurtling forward now, doing the things they often did, but faster and more. Her body wasn't consulting her at all anymore. She wanted to be closer to him; she wanted him inside her.

She meant to stop. To say hang on, wait up. Just to think, at least. To get her whole self on board. But she couldn't say stop. She didn't want to. She wanted to feel him inside. He was so close now.

"Do we have . . . ?" she began faintly.

"Yes," he said almost before a word was out of her mouth. He fumbled for less than a second before locating the familiar condom and tearing it open.

"Do you want to . . . ?"

"I don't know. . . ."

She loved him. She knew she did.

And then in a moment, simple and pure, they were together in a way they hadn't been before.

Oh, life is a glorious cycle

of song, / A medley of

extemporanea; / And love is

a thing that can never

go wrong; / And I am

Marie of Roumania.

—Dorothy Parker

Opening night came and went. Carmen wore dark clothes and knocked herself out changing sets and managing props. She kept her focus tight; there was no room for error. Although she did good work, it was the kind of job where people only noticed you if you screwed up.

Of all the people Carmen clapped for, she clapped the loudest for Julia as Annie Sullivan. She made sure there was a bouquet of roses to be presented to her onstage. She was proud of her friend. With Julia, even pride took on the tint of gratitude.

Carmen had worked hard. She'd learned things. She'd answered her own questions without needing help. She was largely invisible, granted, but there was something to be said for plain competence.

Afterward she gave Julia a silver bracelet. Julia countered with a plate of brownies for Carmen, which she brought to her room late that evening.

"Hey, did you get your room assignment at Village Theater yet?" Julia asked. She had her paper in her hand.

"I think so," Carmen said, finding the letter on her desk that had arrived that morning from Vermont.

"Forte House, room 3H," Julia read. "Did they put us together?"

"3H. Yep."

"Oh, good."

Once again, Carmen felt fortunate and also relieved. How lucky she was that Julia wanted to room with her. She'd been half afraid when she got the assignment that Julia would prefer a stranger.

"My brother said he'd drive me up. He's visiting some girl at Dartmouth and it's not too far out of the way. Do you want to come? Do you have a ride yet?"

Julia's brother, Thomas, was a conspicuously handsome senior at Williams. Carmen was too overwhelmed in his presence to chirp out a single word. She was not only invisible but mute. "That'd be great. I hadn't planned a ride yet."

"Oh, good," Julia said again, looking genuinely pleased. "Do you want to go get coffee?" she asked.

"Sure," said Carmen, and as she wandered along next to an exuberant Julia, she felt herself in awe of Julia's Mexican skirt, of the particular dark red color of her tank top, of her thinness and her confidence to wear a tweed cap that would have fallen pretty flat on almost anyone else. Again Carmen felt the gladness to have someone to do things with. Not just any someone, but one of the most striking people in the school.

Carmen stood in line at the student union to get them both lattes and arrived back at the table to see Julia holding court among a bunch of sophomore boys. Carmen slipped in silently beside her. She laughed at Julia's witticisms and admired her ease.

For the hundredth time she wondered what Julia saw in her. This friendship was an incredible boon to Carmen, but what was Julia getting out of it? There were other girls around campus as glamorous as she was. As friends they would have suited Julia a lot better, and yet she hung around with dull, mute, invisible Carmen.

Carmen stared into her coffee cup while Julia told a funny story about the sound system going haywire in the second act of the play. Carmen felt bad for not being a worthier friend. She should think of things to say too, not sit there like a moron. She should have *something* to offer.

Julia did not belong with a loser in an oversized sweatshirt. If for no other reason, Carmen determined she would pull herself together for Julia's sake.

Lying against Brian, her face sticking to his sticky chest, Tibby felt warm, thin tears dripping from the corners of her eyes, running over the bridge of her nose, tap-tapping onto his rib cage. They were some of the truest and most mysterious tears she had ever cried. When she put her hands up to his face, she realized his eyelashes were also wet.

She wanted to stay like this forever. She wanted to sink into his body and live there. She also realized she really had to pee.

Sometime or other she rolled onto her back and he sat up. She touched her flushed cheeks.

"What—" An odd sound occurred in his throat.

She sat up too, caught by it.

"What?" she said, dazed.

"I—there was—I'm not sure—"

"Brian?"

"The condom—I think it was— It's not—"

"Not what?" She didn't even want to look.

"Not . . . on."

"What do you mean?" Her voice was flat, but her muscles were coiling.

"God, Tib. I'm not sure. Maybe it broke. I think it broke."

"You do?"

He was investigating, his hair falling forward over his face. He reached a hand toward her, but she had already stood up, dragging the covers with her.

"Are you sure?" Her voice was rising. Worries were seeding and spreading, pushing up stems like in a time-lapsed movie.

"It'll be okay. We'll— I'll—"

"Are you sure it broke?" She was clutching the covers around her with two hands. She thought with hatred of the incompetent condom that had lived in his wallet all these months.

He sat like Rodin's *Thinker* on the bare bed. "Yes, I'm pretty sure. I don't know when it happened."

She could get pregnant. She could be getting pregnant

right now. What about STDs? Herpes? What about, God, AIDS?

No, he was a virgin. He said he was a virgin. He had to be. He was, wasn't he? "It happened when we were having sex," she said sharply.

He looked up at her, trying to understand the strange tone of her voice.

She could get pregnant! Easily! This was exactly how it happened! She needed to think. When was her period? These were the things that happened to tragic girls who weren't nearly as cautious or practical as Tibby.

What should she do? What did this mean? For all this time, being in all these strange places in her life, she had taken a certain refuge in the fact that at least she was still a virgin. At least that category of fears was not hers to fear. It was the single transom she had not crossed.

She wasn't a virgin anymore! Why had she let herself forget that it mattered?

She looked at Brian, almost as far away as he could be in a room so small. She should be having these worries aloud, with him, not just alone. But she couldn't help it.

She wished she could dress without his seeing. She turned away.

"Tibby, I am sorry. I'm so sorry this happened. I didn't even know—"

"It's not like you did anything. . . ." Her words were backed by minimal breath and floated to the wall.

"I just wish . . . ," he said.

✽   ✽   ✽

59

Bridget's stomach had been groaning since she'd woken up that morning, but when her father put a plate of eggs on the table for her, she fitfully roved around the kitchen instead of sitting down with them.

"Dad, why did you let Perry quit school?" she asked.

Her father was dressed in shapeless twill trousers and a tweed jacket, the same outfit he'd worn to work as long as she could remember. He was a history teacher and associate dean at a private high school, and he was clueless in the way she imagined only a longtime high school administrator could be. He'd made a career of tuning out teenagers. He was in good practice when it came to his own.

"He didn't quit. He took some time off."

"Is that what he said?"

Her father adopted his look of silent retreat. He didn't like to be demanded of. He resisted her in his passive way. "You should eat if you want me to drop you on my way to school," he said quietly. He was always eager to drop her places.

"Why is he taking time off? Did you ask him that? Three courses at Montgomery Community College is not exactly overwhelming."

He poured his coffee. "Not everyone belongs in the Ivy League, Bridget."

She glared at him. He was trying to force her to back off. He knew she was neither a scholar nor a snob, that she felt defensive about going to Brown. He probably calculated that this would shut her up, but it wasn't going to work. "So he's going back to school in the fall?" she said volubly.

Her dad put forks on the table. He sat down to eat. "That's what I expect."

She tried to grab hold of his gaze. "Is that really what you expect?"

He salted his eggs. He paused, waiting for her to sit down. She didn't want to sit down. When it came to him, she was a passive resister, too. It was one of the few things they had in common.

He'd made these eggs as a gesture. He'd done it for her. And yet the sight of them turned her stomach. Why couldn't she receive what few overtures he made?

He refused to give her what she wanted. She refused to take what he gave.

She sat down. She picked up her fork. He ate.

"I'm worried about him," she said.

He nodded vaguely. His eyes wandered to the newspaper on the table beside him. On most mornings the *Washington Post* was his breakfast companion, and she sensed he wasn't enjoying the break in routine.

"It seems like he's just . . . rotting away in his room."

Her father looked at her finally. "His interests are different than yours, but he does have them. Why don't you eat?"

She didn't want to eat. She didn't want to do what he said. She felt that if she ate, she'd be acceding to him, to this life in the underworld, and she wasn't willing to do it.

"Does he see anyone? Does he leave the house? Do his interests include anything other than staring at a computer day and night?"

"Don't be so dramatic, Bridget. He'll be fine."

All at once she was furious. She was standing and her fork was clattering around on the floor. "He'll be fine?" she shouted. "Just like Mom was fine?"

He stopped chewing. He put his fork down. He looked not at her but through her, past her. "Bridget," he said in a low rumble.

"Why don't you look around! He is not fine! Why won't you see it?"

"Bridget," he intoned again. The more times he said her name, the less she felt she was even in the room with him.

"This is no way to live! Can't you see that?" She felt the tears in her throat and behind her eyes, but she wouldn't cry. He wasn't safe enough for crying, and hadn't been in a long time. *It's too lonely this way.*

He shook his head. Of course he couldn't see it. Because it was how he lived too.

"Bridget. You live the way you choose. You let Perry do the same."

And me. You let me be, he might as well have added.

She wouldn't sit down. She wouldn't eat his eggs. But she would live the way she chose. She would do that for him.

She grabbed her duffel bag and her backpack and walked out of the kitchen and out of the house. That was what she chose.

* * *

"So when he called, I told him I couldn't talk," Julia explained, sitting cross-legged on Carmen's twin bed in their small dormitory room in Vermont. "I felt bad and everything. I don't know how to tell him that I'm not going to be into it this summer."

It was funny. The setting was new—the campus of a performing arts center that housed the theater festival—but the situation was the same—Julia sitting on a dorm-room bed at night telling Carmen the latest episode in her off-again relationship with Noah Markham, scholar and stud.

Carmen nodded. She had finished putting all her stuff away, so she started refolding things.

"I mean, what if I meet someone here, you know? Have you looked around? There are a lot of good-looking guys. Probably half of them are gay, but still."

Carmen nodded. She hadn't really looked around yet.

"A place like this, anything can happen. You know how costars are always falling in love on movie sets and ruining their relationships?"

Carmen read *Us Weekly* often enough to know the truth of this. She put a bottle of the shampoo they both liked on Julia's dresser. She saw the familiar black-and-white picture of Julia's mother in the silver frame. Julia kept it in her dorm room at school. It was a glamorous picture taken by some famous photographer whose name Carmen only pretended to know. Julia's mother had been

63

a model, Julia told her. She was beautiful, certainly, but Carmen also registered that Julia's mother almost never called.

Carmen didn't put out any pictures of her family, but taped inside the cover of her binder she kept a small picture of Ryan on the remarkable day that he was born. She'd also taped a picture of the Septembers at Rehoboth Beach, the last time they'd all been together. Sometime during the winter she'd moved it from inside the front cover to inside the back cover, because though the sight of it made her happy, it made her happy in the saddest possible way.

Julia watched Carmen arranging the room. "Hey, did you pick up the Teramax conditioner?"

Carmen raised her eyebrows. "I don't think so. Was it on the list?"

Julia nodded. "I'm pretty sure I wrote it on there."

Carmen scoured the pharmacy bags but couldn't find conditioner of any sort. "I must have missed that somehow." She felt guilty, though she didn't even use it.

"Don't worry about it," Julia said.

"I'll pick some up when we go into town," Carmen said apologetically.

"Seriously, it's fine," Julia assured her.

Julia fell asleep at some point, but Carmen lay in her bed. She had to remind herself where she was.

After a while she got up and checked the list that she and Julia had made for her to take to the pharmacy. Teramax conditioner was not on it.

She went out to the hall to call Lena. Lena didn't answer, so she left a message. Tibby didn't answer either, and Bridget had already left for Turkey.

Even though it was late, she called her mom.

"*Nena*, hi. Is everything okay?" her mom asked in a groggy voice.

"Fine. We're just settling in here."

"How does it seem?"

"Good," Carmen said without really thinking about it. "How's Ryan?"

Her mom laughed. "He threw his shoes out the window."

"Oh, no. His new walking ones?"

"Yes."

Carmen pictured Ryan and his tiny sneakers and she pictured her mom racing around trying to locate them.

"Street or courtyard?"

"Street, of course."

Carmen laughed. "So what else is going on?" she asked, somewhat wistfully.

"We met with the painters today." Her mother said it as though she'd met with the president.

"Oh, yeah?"

"We're having them skim coat every wall. We're starting to choose colors."

Carmen yawned. She didn't have much to say about skim coating.

"Okay, Mama, well, sleep tight."

"You too, *nena*. I love you."

Carmen tiptoed back into the room and crawled into bed, careful not to wake Julia, who was a light sleeper.

Carmen knew her mother loved her. That used to provide a certain sufficiency. That alone had been enough to make her feel like somebody.

It used to feel like she and her mother were almost one person, living one life. Now their lives were separate. Her mother's identity wasn't one she could tag along with anymore.

It didn't mean her mother didn't love her. She'd given Carmen life, but she couldn't be expected to keep giving it. And yet Carmen wasn't sure how to live by herself.

She tucked her hands under her pillow, and even though she could hear Julia's breathing a few feet away, she felt terribly lonely.

When Lena got to her room that night, she called Carmen back, hoping it wasn't too late. "I have to ask you something and don't jump all over me," she said, after giving Carmen a chance to relocate to the hallway.

"As if I would," Carmen said, too curious to pretend to be hurt for long.

"Am I over Kostos, do you think?"

"Did you meet someone else?" Carmen asked.

Lena gazed at the ceiling. "No."

"Did you *look at* someone else?"

Lena felt herself blushing and was glad Carmen couldn't see. Carmen had always combined an extravagant capacity for near psychic brilliance and total obtuseness, but she rarely used them both at the same time. "Why do you ask?"

"Because I think you will be officially over Kostos when you talk about—even really look at—somebody else."

"Isn't that a little simplistic?"

"No," said Carmen.

Lena laughed.

"One of these days you are going to fall in love and forget about him. Sooner or later it has to happen. I'd hoped it would be sooner."

Lena crossed her feet under her on the bed. Could she forget Kostos? Was that what she was supposed to be striving for? She'd so far aimed at "getting over" him, whatever that meant, and she often prided herself on making strides toward that goal. But it was hard to imagine forgetting. She wasn't really the forgetting type.

"I don't know if that's possible."

"I think it is. I think it will happen. And you know what else I think about Kostos?"

Lena sighed. She had reached her limit of saying the name Kostos out loud and far exceeded her limit of hearing it said by others. "No, smarty. What?"

"I have this weird premonition that as soon as you forget about Kostos, you are going to see him again."

Lena felt activity in her stomach. It had both the heavy quality of sickness and the fizz of excitement. She was glad the bathroom was right there.

"Oh, you do, do you." Lena tried to calibrate her voice for lighthearted sarcasm, but it sounded dark as mud.

"I really do," Carmen answered solemnly.

Lena hung up the phone with the suspicion, perhaps even the hope, that Carmen had veered into the obtuse.

Pain is inevitable;

Suffering is optional.

—Greta Randolph

She'd had her period on the drive from school home to Bethesda, hadn't she? Tibby tried to remember the usual accompaniments—the stained underwear, the forgetting to buy tampons or pack them, the needing to stop at a gas station to take care of urgent matters.

"Tibby Rollins?"

She and Bee had driven down together. Bee had borrowed her roommate's car in Providence and picked her up in New York on the way. Tibby remembered at least two gas station stops. One was for actual gas, the other for more of a personal emergency. But was the emergency bleeding through her pants or was it needing a box of Krispy Kremes? She couldn't remember. She was a virgin then, and virgins were entitled to blessed ignorance about when their periods came and went.

"Tibby Rollins?"

She turned with irritation toward the sound of her manager's voice. Charlie always called her by first and last names, as though there were three other Tibbys on the premises.

"Charlie Spondini?" she said back.

He frowned at her. "The return box is so jammed up nothing will fit in the slot. Do you mind?"

"I do mind. That is inconsiderate of our customers and our financial dependence on late fees." Sometimes she could make him laugh, but today she knew she was just being rude. She almost wished he would fire her.

"Tibby Rollins . . ." He looked more tired than angry.

"Okay, fine," she said. She moved to the giant cardboard return box under the counter and began unloading.

She and Bee had driven down on June fourth. If she did have her period then, that meant . . . What did it mean? Was she supposed to know when she ovulated? She hated that stuff. She'd been through her mom's fertility treatments, the thermometers and kits. She didn't want to live in the same world as that.

"Excuse me?"

Tibby looked up. It was a customer. He had tinted glasses and a gray comb-over. "Do you know if you have *Striptease*?"

"What?" She glared at him with distaste.

"*Striptease*?"

Ick. "It's in Drama if we have it."

"Thanks," he said, and turned to the aisles.

"It's a total piece of crap," she informed his back.

At home her message light was blinking. Usually she found sustenance in Brian's sweetly romantic messages. Tonight she had to force herself to listen.

"Tib, I found out about the pills you can take." His voice sounded strained and worried. "I don't think it's too late. I'll come up tonight if you want me to go with you. I have the address of the Planned Parenthood. It's not far—just on Bleecker Street. I can—"

She jabbed the Erase button and her room was quiet. She didn't want to know the address of Planned Parenthood. She didn't want to have that kind of life. She didn't want to get examined by a gynecologist and fill a prescription. She wanted her sexual experience to be strictly over the counter.

Why had she done it? Why had she let Brian talk her into it? *He didn't really talk you into it,* said the voice of Meta-Tibby. There hadn't been much talking going on at all.

But he was the one who wanted to so badly. He was the one who'd wanted it and pleaded all these months. He was the one who'd carried the shoddy condom around in his wallet. He was the one who'd been so sure that doing it would bring them closer.

Every black thought she had stuck itself to that stupid condom and to Brian for carrying it so eagerly and so long.

Tibby flipped on her tiny TV. The local news was on channel seven. Tibby kept it on this station, because there was an anchorwoman she liked. She was older, probably almost sixty, and her name was Maria Blanquette. She had brown skin and intelligent and imperfect features, and unlike most news talkers, who wore thick masks of makeup, Maria looked like an actual person. She did this "Manhattan Moments" segment where she was supposed to showcase all the celebrity doings in New York City. But instead of adulating the celebrities, as most entertainment spots did, Maria laughed, and she had a laugh unlike anything else on TV. It was loose and raucous and totally unpolished. Tibby sat through hours of news for those moments.

Tibby watched hopefully, but Maria didn't laugh today. Tibby suspected her producers had probably warned her to can it.

Usually Bridget liked airplane food. She was one of the very few people who did.

If you scarfed it all down while it was steaming hot, it tasted pretty good. If you thought about it too much and let it get cold, she now realized, it wasn't so appealing. That was true of many things in life.

Tonight it sat on her tray table. Eric was in Baja. She imagined he was diving into the Sea of Cortez. It was almost dinnertime there, and he always used to swim before dinner. And here she was, thirty-five thousand feet over the Atlantic. Both of them suspended over water, neither of them with their feet on the ground.

"Eric acts like I don't need anything," she'd said to Tibby on the phone a few days before.

"Maybe you act like you don't need anything," Tibby had said. She'd said it gently, but still it cut its way into the center of Bee's brain.

She felt a tingle of anxiety, being so far from the ground and hurtling so quickly in the opposite direction of Eric and home and the things she needed.

It was dark in the cabin, dark outside her window. She wasn't completely alone. Interspersed throughout the cabin were lots of people from her program. She'd be spending her summer with them. They were strangers now, but friends theoretically. It was too bad Bridget wasn't a more theoretical person.

She liked short flights better, where you stayed in the same day. She felt faint discomfort at flying directly away from the sun.

She put her cold hands on the Pants, feeling the comfort of uneven stitches of yarn and the puffiness of the fabric paint Carmen used.

What did she need, really? She needed her friends, but she had the Traveling Pants. It was like having her friends with her. The Pants allowed her to hold on to her friends no matter what.

Greta was in her house in Burgess, where she always was. If Bridget calculated the time there, she could figure out exactly what Greta was doing. Tuesday at seven was bingo. Wednesday morning was shopping. No matter how fast or far Bridget went, Greta stayed still.

And there was Eric. One time in her life she had needed

Eric and he had been there. He had known exactly what to do. She never forgot that.

And home. Technically speaking, that meant a dingy clapboard house containing her brother and her father. She swallowed hard. She gave her uneaten tray of food to a passing flight attendant. Did they need her? Did she need them?

These weren't the right questions. They were N/A. She remembered getting three N/As on her first-grade report card and worrying that she'd failed those subjects. When she told her father, he'd laughed and fiddled with her hair. "That means Not Applicable, Beezy. It doesn't mean you failed anything." He'd been able to comfort her back then. Back then she'd tried harder, too.

Now it wasn't a home where needs were had or met. If Perry or her dad needed her, it didn't matter, because they wouldn't accept her help anyway. If she needed them . . . well, she didn't. They had nothing to give that she wanted.

She couldn't help them. She didn't need them. That was the truth. Not everybody got a close family. Not everybody needed one.

She was flying away from the sun, but it would be there to meet her when she landed. They were just taking different routes to the same place.

She felt herself relaxing into her seat, unsticking her mind from the continent behind, looking to the one ahead. She couldn't help her dad or Perry. She couldn't. Her job was to look forward, to make as good a life as she could. She didn't need to look back anymore.

She pulled off her sneakers and tucked her feet under her. She crossed her arms and held her hands in her armpits to keep them warm. When she woke up, she'd be in Turkey. On another continent, in another hemisphere, on another sea.

She felt the tingle starting. But this was the tingle of excitement instead of fear. The one that made you hungry rather than sick. The one that came from looking ahead and not behind.

In a way it was the same tingle. It just felt a lot better.

Carmen doodled on the handouts while aspiring theater types—known here as apprentices—from all over the country sat listening to the presentations in the main theater building. Julia painted her toenails, which seemed like kind of a ditzy thing to do. But she painted them black, which seemed to Carmen like an actressy thing to do.

Carmen looked around at the number of decked-out kids. Julia wasn't the only one in layers of vintage clothes and inky black eyeliner. It almost made Carmen laugh to think that though Julia stood apart from all the schlumpy kids at school, Carmen stood apart from the glamour queens here.

The director of the big and coveted Main Stage production, Andrew Kerr, made his presentation first.

"This year we're putting on *The Winter's Tale*. As I'm sure you know, for every decade anniversary of the theater we do an all-Shakespeare summer, and this year is number thirty. We've got some wonderful professional actors involved.

Here's the thing." He cleared his throat to get attention. "This Main Stage mounts a professional, Equity production. But by tradition we open only one role to an apprentice. One role, and it's typically not a lead. That's the way it is every year. You are welcome to try out, but callbacks will be minimal. Don't waste too much energy on it. There are many great roles for you in the Second Stage and community productions. All of you will have some part in one of them."

Most of the kids knew this already. But it was hard not to be hopeful. Carmen suspected a lot of them were going to waste a lot of energy on it, regardless of what Andrew Kerr said. She was beginning to realize that actors, as a general category, were hopeful, and they also had strong self-esteem.

"All the auditions begin together. Then we'll follow up with separate callback lists for each of the three productions."

Was anyone else here going straight to crew? Carmen wondered. Was she the only predefeated theater apprentice in America?

"Auditions begin not tomorrow, but the day after. Sign-up sheets are in the lobby. Good luck to all of you."

Carmen wondered whether she'd get the chance to work on sets for the big production. She guessed not. There were actual known set designers and builders arriving here. Well, she'd be happy working on one of the other shows.

After the meeting, Julia was inspired. "Let's go back to the room and get to work."

"I don't think I have anything to work on yet," Carmen said, falling a little bit behind Julia's energized stride.

"I was hoping you would run lines with me," Julia said.

* * *

Some bodies like change better than others. The rest
of Bee's group was sacked out over the three rows of the
old Suburban, one of several large and battered vehicles
owned by the Consortium for Classical Archaeology. Bee
sat straight as a palm, studying the countryside between
Izmir and Priene. Now they were close enough to the coast
that you could see the Aegean out the right-hand windows.

"Ephesus is a few kilometers to the left," said Bob
Something, a graduate student, who was driving the car.
"We'll spend at least a day there this summer."

Bridget squinted eastward, remembering the pictures of
Ephesus from her archaeology class. The sun had indeed
arrived along with her.

"Also Aphrodisias, Miletus, and Halicarnassus. These
are some of the best ruins you'll ever see."

She was glad she was awake, because otherwise Bob
would have had no one to tell this to and she wouldn't have
heard it.

"What about Troy?" she asked, beginning to feel a little
breathless. Here she was in this incredible place, farther
from home than she'd ever been. There was as much history here in this soil as anywhere on earth.

"Troy is north, up near the Dardanelles. It's fascinating
to read about, but there isn't as much to look at. Nobody
from our group is making that trip, as far as I know." He
had a faded orange alligator shirt and a round face. She
thought he must have recently shaved a beard, because his

chin and lower cheeks were pale and the rest of his face was pink.

"I read the *Iliad* in school last semester," Bridget said. "Most of it." In addition to her ancient archaeology class, she'd taken Greek literature in translation. She hadn't realized it at the time, but looking back, she considered it by far her most engrossing academic experience. You couldn't always know what would matter to you.

When they pulled into the site, Bridget was surprised at how small and basic it was. Two very large tents, several smaller ones, and beyond them, the dusty, roped-off shapes of the excavation. It sat on a high hill overlooking a river plain and, just beyond that, the Aegean.

She left her bags in one of the tents, which had canvas walls over a wooden platform. It held only four cots and some open shelving, but it seemed quite romantic to her. She was nothing if not a veteran of rustic summer venues.

The new arrivals groggily gathered for a welcome meeting, and Bridget exercised the bad habit of looking around and deciding who was the best-looking guy in the room. It was a habit that predated her being a girl with a boyfriend, and she hadn't entirely managed to eradicate it.

In this case, the room was actually a large, open-sided tent, which would serve as their meeting room, lecture room, and cafeteria. The best view was of the Aegean, but there were a few good faces, too.

"This is a comparatively remote site, folks. The plumbing is rudimentary. We have four latrines and two showers.

That's all. Make friends with your sweat this summer," said Alison Somebody, associate director, in her not very welcoming welcome. She had a kind of boot-camp mentality, Bridget decided. She was excited about privation.

Well, Bridget could get excited about privation too.

"We've got a generator to serve the field laboratory, but the sleeping areas are not wired. I hope nobody brought a hair dryer."

Bridget laughed, but a couple of women looked uneasy.

It was a small and fairly new dig, Bridget gathered. About thirty people altogether, a mix of university and scientist types and a few civilian volunteers. It was hard to tell, amid all the T-shirts and cargo pants and work shirts and Birkenstocks, the professors from the graduate students, from the college students, from the regular citizens. Most of them were American or Canadian; a few were Turkish.

"There are three parts to this site, and all of us spend some time in each of them. If you are a student and you want credit, you must attend lectures Tuesdays from three to five. We'll take a total of four trips to other sites. The schedule's on the board. All trips are mandatory for credit. That's the school part. That's it. Otherwise, this is a job and we work as a team. Questions so far?"

Why were organizational types so joyless? Bridget wondered. Who wouldn't want to see the Temple of Artemis at Ephesus?

It was lucky, in a way, that Brown University was situated in a relatively urban setting and not in a tent, because it was difficult to concentrate with the sea winking at you like that. She began to tune Alison out in favor of her habit. There was one good-looking guy who she guessed was also a college student. He had black curly hair and very dark eyes. He was Middle Eastern, she thought. Maybe Turkish, but she heard him speaking English.

Another one was sort of good-looking. He looked old enough to be a graduate student. He had reddish hair and so much sunscreen on his face it cast a blue tint. That was maybe not so sexy.

"You're Bridget, right?" Alison asked, startling her from her habit.

"Yes."

"You're in mortuary."

"Okay."

"What does mortuary mean?" Bridget asked a tall girl named Karina Itabashi on their way to the field lab.

"It means dead people."

"Oh."

After lunch Bridget settled in for her first lecture and discovered an interesting thing: The best-looking guy was neither the possible Turk nor the sunscreen-slathered redhead. The best-looking guy was the one standing in front of her, lecturing about artifacts.

"Okay, folks." The best-looking guy had been holding an object behind his back, and now he presented it to them. "Is this object in my hand a technofact, a sociofact, or an ideofact?" The best-looking guy was looking directly at her, wanting her to answer his question.

"It's a tomato," she said.

To his credit he laughed rather than throwing the tomato at her. "You have a point, uh . . . ?"

"Bridget."

"Bridget. Any other ideas?" Various hands went up.

She'd thought he was a graduate student when she'd first seen him eating a sandwich under an olive tree earlier that day. He didn't look like he could be thirty. But he'd introduced himself as Professor Peter Haven, so unless he lied, he was one. He taught at Indiana University. She tried to picture Indiana on the map.

At sunset that night after dinner in the big tent, a bunch of people gathered on an embankment on the hilltop to watch the sun go down. Several six-packs of beer were on the ground. Bridget sat next to Karina, who had a beer in her hand.

"Do you want one?" she asked Bridget, gesturing to the supply.

Bridget hesitated, and Karina seemed to read her expression. "There's no drinking age here, as far as I know."

Bridget leaned over and took one. She'd been to enough parties over the last year that she'd formed a solid acquaintanceship with beer, if not an actual friendship.

On Karina's other side, Bridget recognized one of the directors, and she was struck here, as she had been at dinner, by the mixing of the team. The group wasn't hierarchical, the way school was. Age-wise, it wasn't nearly as homogeneous. If anything, people assembled more according to the area of the site where they worked than according to age or professional status. She realized how accustomed she was to looking out for authority figures, but here she wasn't finding any.

"Where are you digging?" she asked a woman who sat down next to her. She recognized her as Maxine from her cabin.

"I'm not. I'm a conservator. I'm working on pottery in the lab. What about you?"

"Mortuary. For starters, at least."

"Ooh. How's your stomach?"

"Good, I think."

She saw Peter Haven at the other end of the group. He was also drinking and laughing over something. He had a nice way about him.

The sun was down. The moon was up. Maxine lifted her beer bottle and Bridget tapped it with hers. "To mortuary," Maxine said.

"To pottery," Bridget added, never having drunk beer with a conservator before. It was good to be an adult. Even the beer tasted better here.

It's innocence when it

charms us, ignorance

when it doesn't.

—Mignon McLaughlin

If Leo had looked at her as planned, Lena wouldn't have had to think about him several times that night, or tried to figure out his last name so she could Google him.

She certainly wouldn't have felt the need to go to the empty studio on a Saturday morning when all self-respecting art students were still in bed. She went there to sneak a look at his painting, secretly hoping that maybe his artistic skills were not all that his reputation promised.

She checked first on her own painting. It was a standing figure of a thick-thighed woman named Nora. Lena could convince herself of Nora's beauty only as long as Nora was standing still. As soon as she changed her expression or opened her mouth, the concept crashed to the floor and Lena had to build it again at the start of each pose.

But those thighs of Nora's did have their strange grace and, more importantly, presented Lena with an unsubtle view of mass, so hard to re-create in two dimensions. Lena liked how that part of her painting was coming.

Now, embarrassed even though she was alone, she edged across the scuffed linoleum. She considered the empty model stand, the unmanned easels, the high, creaky casement windows, the fern that nobody watered, the leftover smells. An empty studio reminded Lena of the world at night. It was hard to reconcile that the night world was the same place as the day.

Lena remembered a summer lightning storm when she was in middle school. She was wide awake at midnight and bravely made her way down the stairs in her nightgown to sit on the front porch and watch. A burst of lightning flashed, midnight became noon, and Lena was jarred to see that all the things in the mysterious night world were exactly the same as they were in the cheery, prosaic day.

After that she spent a lot of time convincing herself that what you saw, even what you felt, had an unreliable relationship to what was actually there. What was actually there was reality, regardless of whether you saw it or how you felt about it.

But after that she'd started drawing and painting and had to unravel all the convincing she'd done. There was no way to access a visual reality beyond what you saw. Reality was what you saw. "We are trapped in our senses," her old teacher, Annik, told her once. "They are all we have of the world."

And so they are the world, Lena remembered thinking then, and many times since.

You couldn't paint a thigh based on how you knew it was, in darkness or in light. You had to paint a thigh based exactly on how the light particles entered your eyes and how you perceived it from that angle, in that room, at that moment.

Why did she spend so much of her life unlearning? It was so much harder than learning, she mused as she timidly made her way around Leo's canvas.

She was almost scared to look—scared of its being worse than it was supposed to be but more scared of its being better.

She waited until she was fully in front of his painting to take it on.

After three days in the studio, his painting was really only begun. More suggestion than execution. And yet it was so far beyond hers she felt like crying. Not just because hers looked so amateurish in comparison, but also because his had a gesture and a quality, even at this young stage, that was unaccountably sad and lovely.

She was devoting her life to art school, and she knew she could learn a lot of things here, but in a flash of recognition, she also knew that this couldn't be taught. She couldn't say why this painting struck her so, what was the particular insight into the pathos of Nora, but she felt it. And she felt her own set of standards and ambitions swirling down the toilet. She could practically hear the flush.

She put her fingers to her eyes, unnerved to feel actual wetness. She had hoped these would be conceptual tears, not wet ones.

She thought of Leo. His hair and his hand. She tried to reconcile the look of him with this painting.

And in a rush she felt ashamed of her fatuous games as she realized she was going to be thinking about him whether or when or how he ever looked at her.

LennyK162: Hellooooo, Tibby. Are you in there? You are not answering calls and your friends are concerned. Bee is writing up the missing person report and I am designated to call Alice. Please advise.

Tibberon: I am here, O hilarious one.

"Please call me back before five if you can, Tib," Brian said.

Tibby lay on her bed as she listened to the end of his message. She didn't want to call him back. If she actually spoke to him, rather than leaving him messages when she knew he was at work, she probably wouldn't be able to be angry at him.

"It'll be okay, Tib," he said in closing.

Why was he always saying that? What power did he have to make it so? Maybe it wouldn't be okay. Maybe she really was pregnant.

Anyway, okay for whom? Maybe it was her body and not his.

And what if she was pregnant? What would he say then? What if he wanted her to keep the baby? He had talked about babies before. What if he secretly wanted something like this to happen?

Meta-Tibby had something to say about this, but regular Tibby shut her up fast.

Brian probably romanticized the notion of having a baby. He probably thought it would be this beautiful thing between them. Well, Tibby had seen the whole process up close and personal, and it wasn't pretty. She had seen her mother's gigantic belly, pregnant with Nicky, with all the scary red stretch marks across it. She knew how little you slept and how much babies cried. And in one of the most surreal experiences of her life, she had weathered the whole bloody, bloody thing as Christina's unwilling labor partner. She knew the power of birth, both for beauty and terror. She was the last girl in the world who could write it off as cute and sexy.

She couldn't be. What if she was?

If her last period had ended on the fifth, say . . . or maybe it was the sixth? And then you counted twenty-eight days. No, it was twenty-one days, right? From the last day? From the first day?

Tibby had puzzled over this question at least one hundred times, and still she got confused in all the same places.

Brian worked as a busboy at a Mexican restaurant in Rockville on Wednesday evenings. She waited until she knew his shift had started to call him back.

"I don't think you should come this weekend. I think I'm going up to Providence to hang out with Lena. Okay? Sorry about that."

She hung up quickly. She felt her face twisted in an unpleasant shape. She was too preoccupied to feel her own shame at lying or even to do it convincingly.

If it had been the fifth, then her period—if it was going to come—was going to come by the twenty-sixth. But what if it hadn't been the fifth? It could easily have been the sixth or seventh. Then she would have to wait until Sunday. How could she wait that long?

And what if it didn't come on Sunday? What if it didn't come at all?

No. She couldn't think that thought. She couldn't bring herself to think it, and yet she couldn't fully think any other.

She wasn't really going to Providence. She didn't want to see her friends now. Not until she got her period. If she went, she would have to tell them what was going on. They knew her too well to accept her evasions or her lies. She didn't want to say the feared word out loud to her friends, because that would make it feel true.

She hated not telling them that she had finally done it. She needed to tell them such an important piece of information. But the aftermath of having done it was too painful to share, and the two things were inextricable.

She couldn't see Brian right now. She didn't want to talk about what had happened. What if he wanted to have sex again? He would, wouldn't he? What would she do?

Brian shouldn't have been so insistent on it, she found herself thinking. *We should have just stayed how we were.*

She didn't feel like eating, she didn't feel like sleeping. There was nothing to look forward to, nothing to feel happy about, and nothing she could bring herself to do.

And yet she had very specific plans for the weekend. She would wait and hope for the one thing she really wanted. She would wait and hope that it would come.

"Oh, my God. It's a piece of a skull. Somebody get Bridget."

Bridget laughed and turned around.

Darius, the good-looking Middle Easterner, turned out not to be Turkish, but Iranian by way of San Diego. He was also in mortuary, and at this moment he was pointing to a wall of dirt.

She moved in. She put down her usual pointy trowel in favor of finer instruments. In a little over a week she had already earned a reputation for fearlessness. In the face of moldering bones, snakes, worms, rodents, spiders, and bugs, no matter how big, she was unperturbed. Not even the stench of the latrines got to her. Though in truth she almost never peed inside.

At five-thirty in the evening, her dirty, sweaty colleagues were wandering toward camp, but she was still working on the piece of bone. It was actually quite a large piece. It was painstaking work. You couldn't just dig it out. Every bit of soil had to be cleared and screened with care. Every bit of bone, every fragment of clay or stone had to be sent to the lab. Everything had to be recorded in context by means of a large three-dimensional grid. She had to photograph each thing with a digital camera and number it by basket and lot.

"The difference between looting and archaeology is preserving context," Peter had told her. "The object itself, whatever its worth, represents a small fraction of its value to us."

By six-thirty, only Peter was still there with her. "You can go," she said. "I'm almost done."

"I don't feel right, leaving you alone in a grave," he said.

She liked him there, with the sun behind him. She'd let him stay.

"I've named him Hector," she said, coaxing the skull from the dirt.

"Who?"

"Him." She pointed to the hole that would have been his nose.

"That's a heroic name. Why do you think it's a he?"

She wasn't sure if he was asking her or quizzing her. "By the size. We found a part of a female skull yesterday."

He nodded. "And what did you name her?"

"Clytemnestra."

"I like it."

"Thanks. I'm keeping an eye out for the last few bits of her. Her skeleton is almost complete."

"Oh, so that's Clytemnestra. I heard about her in the lab."

Bridget nodded. "The biology guys are excited about her."

Once almost all the dirt was processed, she gingerly lifted Hector's skull. She began to brush out the grooves as she'd been taught.

"It doesn't get to you, does it?"

She shrugged. "Not really."

"Something will eventually. It seems so far back, I know, but something always gets through."

"But there isn't much tragedy in a death that took place three thousand years ago, is there?" Bridget mused aloud. "Old Hector would be long dead no matter what great or awful things happened in his lifetime."

Peter smiled at her. "It puts mortality in perspective, doesn't it?"

"Yeah. Why do we worry so much about everything when we're just going to end up here?" she asked. She felt quite cheery considering she was standing in a burial site holding a large section of a human skull.

He laughed at her, but he seemed appreciative. He sat down at the edge of the trench to consider. She had the odd perception that he had fine ears. He seemed to hear the full extent of what she said and meant, no matter how loudly or quietly she spoke. When you shared a context, it made hearing easier.

"No question a recent death feels more tragic," he reasoned. "I guess because we're still experiencing the world that the dead person is missing. We are still around to miss them."

Did he have such a tragedy in his life? she wondered. Could he tell that she did?

She pushed her hair back. She realized she'd drawn a streak of dirt across her forehead. "Our moral connection to people expires after a certain amount of time. Don't you think? Otherwise how could we dig up their graves?"

"You are exactly right, Bridget. I couldn't agree more. But how long a time? Two hundred years? Two thousand? How do you calculate the moment when a person's death becomes scientific rather than emotional?"

She knew he was asking the question rhetorically, but she actually wanted to answer it. "I'd say you calculate it by the death of the last person whose life overlapped with theirs. The point when they lose the power to help or hurt a living soul."

He smiled at her certainty. "That's your hypothesis?"

"That's my hypothesis."

"But don't you think the power to help or hurt can extend far beyond a person's natural life?" he asked.

"I don't," she proclaimed, almost reflexively. Sometimes she felt the magnet of certainty more than truth.

"Then you, my friend, have a thing or two to learn from the Greeks."

Lenny,
    I enclose the Pants with a little bit of ancient dirt and a picture of me with my new boyfriend, Hector. He's not so lively, you may say. But he's got the wisdom of the ages.
            A whole lot of love from yer pal Bee
        (and a toothy kiss from yer pal-in-law, Hector)

Carmen did run lines with Julia. She ran them for hours on end for two straight days. Julia wanted to try a range of parts before she settled on her audition strategy.

Carmen was relieved when Julia went to the office to photocopy more pages so Carmen could at least have a break and check her e-mail. She had a list of unread messages from Bee and Lena and her mom and her stepbrother, Paul.

When Julia got back, she immediately noticed a picture Carmen had printed out and left on her desk.

"Hey, who's this?" Julia asked. She picked up the paper and studied it.

It was a picture of Bee in Turkey holding a human skull and pretending to kiss it. Bee had sent it over the Internet, and it had made Carmen laugh so much she'd printed it out.

"That's my friend Bridget," Carmen said.

"Really?"

"Yeah."

Carmen knew it was strange of her that she didn't talk about her friends more to Julia. She mentioned them in passing once in a while, but she never expressed what they really meant to her. She wasn't sure why. It was as though she had put them and Julia into two different compartments. They didn't mix. She didn't want them to mix.

"She's your friend?" Julia looked vaguely doubtful, like perhaps Carmen had clipped the picture from a magazine and was just pretending.

Maybe that was why, Carmen thought.

"She's amazing-looking. Check out those legs," Julia said.

"She's a jock."

"She's pretty. Where does she go to school?"

It was funny. Carmen didn't think of Bee as pretty, exactly. Bee didn't have the patience for it. "Brown," she said.

"I thought about going there. Williams is a lot more intellectual, though."

This from a girl who read not only *Us Weekly* each week, but *Star* and *OK!* as well. Carmen shrugged.

"Her hair looks kind of fake. She should use a darker shade."

"What?"

"Does she color it herself?"

"Bridget? She doesn't color her hair at all. That's her hair."

"That's her real hair?"

"Yes."

"Are you sure?"

"Yes."

"That's what she tells you, anyway," Julia said, half jokingly, but Carmen didn't find it funny.

She looked at Julia, wondering what was up. Was she honestly competing with a girl she'd never met?

"Hey, let's go pick up something quick for dinner and bring it back here," Julia suggested later, after another hour of lines. "I want to keep studying."

"You can stay here," Carmen offered. "I'll go get it." She

was frankly glad to get away from lines, glad to be outside. The grounds of the place were beautiful, especially in the evening light. There were miniature weeping trees along the paths and huge annual gardens around the main buildings.

In her appreciation of the flowers, she lost track of the cafeteria, known by the apprentices as the canteen. She walked until she got to a pretty hillside overlooking the valley. It was lush and so sweet in this light.

Carmen stood there looking at it for a long time. She was already lost—she couldn't really get more lost, could she? When you belonged nowhere, you sort of belonged everywhere, she mused.

She wondered how long it had been since she'd used her senses to perceive beauty. It was like she had been frozen for all these months and was only now beginning to thaw.

She realized that another person from the campus was nearby, appreciating the same view. It was a woman she had not yet seen or met.

"It's beautiful, isn't it?" the woman said.

Carmen sighed. "It really is."

They fell into step together along the path. "Are you part of the theater program?" the woman asked. She was wide hipped and somewhat graceless. She wasn't an actress, Carmen decided, and felt a sense of camaraderie.

Carmen nodded.

"What are you trying out for?"

Carmen pushed a stray hair behind her ear. "Nothing. I'm doing sets, hopefully."

"You're not going to try out for anything?"

"No."

"Why not?"

"Because I'm not an actress."

"How do you know? Have you tried?"

"I guess not. No." *Though my father claims I'm dramatic,* she added silently.

"You should try it. It's really the strength of this program."

"You think so?"

"Absolutely."

"Huh." Carmen spent two seconds pretending to consider this so she wouldn't seem rude. "Hey, would you point me in the direction of the canteen? I got off track and I have no idea where I'm going."

"Sure," the woman said. She pointed to the left when the path split.

"Thank you," Carmen said, looking over her shoulder.

"What's your name?" the woman asked.

"Carmen."

"I'm Judy. Good to meet you, Carmen. You try out, okay?"

Carmen couldn't say okay if she didn't mean it. "How 'bout I'll think about it?"

"That's all I can ask," the woman said.

Later, when Carmen was trying to fall asleep and all the lines and lines and lines were scrabbling around in her head, she did think about it. She mainly thought of why she would not do it.

Right now I'm having

amnesia and déjà vu at

the same time.

I think I've forgotten

this before.

—Steven Wright

Lena walked around with that overstimulated feeling. She didn't like it very much. She forgot to eat and she wore eye makeup to painting class. She forced herself to look at Leo only once every pose and to keep to herself during breaks. She hoped, she silently begged for him to notice her. She racked her brain to find ways to hedge these hopes, to keep them safe.

She looked at her painting in a new way. At first she was so disgusted by it, she could barely look at all. But then she settled down. She tried to relax and see better and deeper than she had before. She felt like a track runner who was pushing herself to break a five-minute mile only to have somebody tell her it could be done in four. If it could be done, then she had to reframe her sense of possibilities. She had to at least try.

She thought about Leo. She asked around a little, casually, she hoped, and learned that he was in his third year, that he didn't live on campus and was rarely seen at campus events. His mystique only grew.

The next Saturday the Traveling Pants arrived from Bee. Lena wore them for courage and struck out from the safety of her dorm room. Not for the courage to talk to Leo; the courage to visit his painting again.

She was so intent on her agenda, so eager and yet so furtive, she almost felt like she had gone into the empty studio to steal something. She walked straight past her painting in favor of his. She stood in front of it, as she had been secretly longing to do all week. For every session he worked on it, she found herself wishing she could watch, to see exactly what he did. How could she now retrace a whole week's worth of work?

She needed to think about her own painting with as much vigor, she knew, but for now she was living in the world of possibilities.

If she could have crawled inside the paint, she would have, so desperate was she to understand what he did, how he did it.

"You learn a lot in art school by looking around," Annik had said to her on the phone a few nights ago.

How true this was. She found herself only wanting to hear what Robert the instructor said when he was talking to Leo.

The beauty of Leo's work waned as she took it apart, dissected it. And then she'd lose her focus for one second and it snuck up on her again. Finally she stopped trying so hard and let her eyes fuzz a bit as she just admired it.

It wasn't that she hadn't seen transcendent paintings before; she had. She'd stared at paintings that were far more accomplished than this. She'd been to the National Gallery hundreds of times. She'd been to the Met and other great museums, big and small.

But Leo was painting exactly the same subject she was—in the same studio, at the same angle (though in mirror image), by the same light. He was an art student, not a master. This was apples to apples: They were handling the same forms and dimples and hairs and shadows. It made her able to appreciate what he was doing in a thrilling though humbling way.

She just looked at it. The lines of the shoulders. The elbows. For some reason she thought of her grandfather. Emotions Lena usually stowed down deep came to hover at the surface. She felt a flush in her cheeks and the wateriest of tears flood her eyes. She thought of Kostos next, and she thought of the fact that she hadn't really thought of him in a few days.

Was Carmen right? Was she really capable of forgetting him? Was that what she should be striving for?

She wasn't sure she wanted to be striving for that. How disorienting it felt. She wasn't sure she wanted to be the forgetting type, even if she could be. If she forgot Kostos, she feared she'd forget most of herself along with him. Who was she without him?

"What do you think?"

Lena was so deep down in her brain she felt she had to travel miles to get back to the sound and the light. In quick succession she realized that Leo was standing a few feet away from her, that he was talking to her, that she was standing in front of his painting for no reason she was prepared to explain, and that she had tears running down her face.

Instantly her hands went to her face and she wiped them off. She pressed wet fingers to her thighs and remembered she was wearing the Traveling Pants. Well. These weren't the first tears to dry on the Traveling Pants.

He looked at her and she scrambled to think of what was supposed to happen. He was looking at her Pants. Should she try to explain them? But he had said something, hadn't he? He had asked a question. Did that mean she was supposed to answer it? So manic was the fluttering of her thoughts she feared it was audible.

"It's okay if you don't like it," he said, wanting to help her out.

"No! I do like it!" she nearly shouted at him.

"I'm having problems with the head." He reached out with his thumb, and to Lena's horror, actually smudged a patch of wet paint that composed Nora's jawbone.

"No!" she burst out. Why was she shouting at him? She made herself be quiet. She realized she didn't want him to look at her quite this hard.

"Sorry," she hurried to say. "I just—I like that part. I don't think you should smudge it." She wondered if she was more connected to his painting than he was.

"Oh. Okay." He thought she was crazy. She wished he would go back to not looking at her at all.

She tried to calm down. She wasn't going to be cool, so

she could at least be honest. "I really love your painting. I think it's beautiful," she said at a normal volume.

He looked at her in a different way now, trying to gauge her tone, surprised by her sincerity. "Well, thank you."

"The thing is, though . . . looking at it makes me realize I have no idea what I'm doing." Who could have known that Lena would actually talk to Leo? And that when she did, she would be so disarmed she'd be truthful?

He laughed. "Looking at it makes me realize I have no idea what *I'm* doing."

She laughed too, but miserably. "Shut up," she said.

Had she just told him to shut up?

"It's true, though," he said. "I look at it in a certain way and I only see what's wrong with it. Isn't that what we all do?"

"Yeah, but most of us are right," she said ruefully.

Was she actually having a conversation with Leo right now?

He laughed again. He had a nice laugh.

"I'm Leo," he said. "Where are you set up?"

She pointed to the easel directly across the room from his, trying not to feel too crushed by the fact that he really hadn't noticed her at all. "Lena," she said in a slightly defeated voice.

"Are you a year-rounder or here for the summer?"

"All year," she said crampily. "I only finished my first, though."

He nodded.

The fact of this conversation settled upon her at last.

Here was Leo. In an otherwise empty studio. Did he have a girlfriend? Did he have a boyfriend? Did he make time in his life for such frivolity?

She realized he wanted to work on his painting. She suddenly felt so self-conscious she couldn't carry on. She made an excuse and fled.

When she got home, she twisted and turned in her unmade bed for a while, and then she called Carmen.

"Guess what?"

"What?"

"I think I have a crush."

Carma,

Here are the Pants and a little sketch I made of Leo. From memory, not from life. (And no, I'm _not_ thinking of him day and night. _God_.)

Funny hair, huh?

He did not realize I was in his class. I think I'm making a big impression around here.

Love you,
Len

At seven-thirty the light waned and Peter still sat with Bridget at the edge of the trench. She knew he felt he had to stay because he was supervising, and also to show her he appreciated her work ethic. She only hoped he was enjoying it as much as she was.

"Hey, Bridget?" he said at last.

"Yeah?"

"Can we go get some dinner?"

"Oh, fine, fine." She pretended impatience. "Let me finish recording."

"We'll drop the stuff by the lab on the way."

They fell into step companionably. She tried wiping her face and made it even dirtier.

"Would you call me Bee?"

"Bee?"

"Yeah, as in bumble."

"Okay."

"That's what my friends call me. You can call me Bridget if you want, but I may think you are slightly mad at me."

He smiled at her. "Bee, then."

They washed up hurriedly by the outdoor pump, but dinner had been cleared from the big tent by the time they got there.

"It's my fault," she said.

"It is," he agreed in his agreeable way.

The Turkish ladies who provided most of the food service kindly found some leftover bread and hummus and salad for them. One of the ladies brought over an unlabeled bottle full of strong red wine. It was a tricky business drinking wine after working in the sun all day. Bee mixed hers with water.

Was this awkward? she wondered.

It wasn't awkward exactly. It was good, slanty fun. He was handsome and he was nice and she was drawn to him for these and probably other reasons.

Would it be less awkward if he weren't so handsome and nice? Would it be less fun?

What about the fact that she was a girl with a boyfriend? That he was . . . who knew what?

Was having a boyfriend honestly supposed to make you not feel attracted to people? Was it supposed to make you not attractive?

And now she wondered, how did he see her? Was it all in her mind, this tension she felt in the way they reached for things and shared the space?

Oh. She felt like smacking herself. She was incorrigible. Why was she feeling this way?

Hmm. Was she feeling this way?

What way was it, exactly?

The sun was long past set, but they walked along the hillside toward the embankment. She felt the dizziness, the giddiness of the wine. Was his tread a little happier, a little less directed too? They intended to join what was left of the party like they did most nights, but it had mostly scattered. There was some awkwardness about whether to sit down. At least in her mind. He did sit down and she joined him. Was it strange that they should be spending time together like this?

No. If she weren't incorrigible, it wouldn't be.

Incorrigibly, she pulled the elastic out of her hair. It was coming out anyway, she told herself, though she didn't quite buy it. Her hair was unusually long from not having Carmen around to trim it since they'd gone to college. It was down to her elbows, almost, halfway down her back. It had the particular feature of absorbing moonlight. She knew he had to notice it. He was probably wishing he hadn't sat down with her.

Why was she behaving this way? She was older now. She'd learned her lessons. What was she trying to prove?

Her limbs had that forward tingle. She couldn't help herself.

Was it all in her mind?

It was, wasn't it? Maybe that was for the best.

She looked at his eyes to try to gauge the mood of the moment faithfully, but he unexpectedly met her gaze. They stayed there for a moment too long before they both looked away.

Shit.

He fidgeted. He clapped his hands together as if he were summarizing an argument. "So, Bridget," he said. "Tell me about your family."

She felt her body bending away from him without actually moving. She had nothing to say about her family at present. "So, Peter," she said, a little too fierce. "Tell me about yours."

How much the air had cooled. In a dry place like this the sun left and took all the heat. There was nothing in the air to hold it. "Let's see. My kids are four and two. Sophie and Miles."

His kids were four and two. Sophie and Miles. It had seemed to her that this might come at the end of the questioning rather than first thing out. She had somehow thought he'd tell her about his parents or his siblings. Her brain fitfully worked backward. He was a father, which presumably meant he was a husband.

"And your wife?"

"Amanda. She's thirty-four."

"Are you thirty-four too?"

"Almost thirty."

"Older woman."

"Right."

She had misread him. She had let her thoughts get away from her. It was time to get them all back.

Do not spoil what you

have by desiring what

you have not.

—Epicurus

The Traveling Pants called to Carmen from under her bed. The other times Carmen had gotten them in the last several months, she had carried them from place to place, but she had not actually worn them.

The Pants were outstanding, and Carmen hadn't been in the mood to stand out very much. She hadn't been in the mood to answer questions Julia would certainly ask about them. It was again the issue of the compartments. She couldn't figure a way to introduce that Carmen to this one. Also, she was scared she was too fat.

She pulled her suitcase from under her bed and felt for where she'd stashed them earlier that morning when they'd arrived by FedEx from Lena. There they were, carefully folded into her suitcase like a false bottom.

For some reason, on this day, she had the urge to put them on. Maybe because it was beautiful outside or because she'd had a lot of coffee. Maybe it was because Lena had a crush on a guy named Leo, and that made Carmen happy and also made her think that the world was opening up.

It was a slightly scary urge, because she was worried about what she would discover. Though she had opted not to try on the Pants, they had never opted not to fit her. She didn't want to force them.

But she also knew that since she'd started working on *The Miracle Worker* in the spring, she'd almost completely stopped her late-night affair with candy. During the past two months she'd been careful about what she ate, mostly in her efforts to be a more worthy friend for Julia.

Holding her breath, sucking in her stomach, wishing she could suck in her backside, she pulled them up, up, up, and over. They went. Who could doubt their magic now? God, they fit. How good they felt. How happy they made her.

She went to the mirror and really looked at her reflection for the first time in months. She pulled on a pink T-shirt and struck out for the wide world. For the first time in ages she didn't feel ashamed of herself.

It was certainly because of the Traveling Pants that she wandered into the lobby of the theater where the auditions were taking place.

"You're in the next group," a woman with a clipboard told her. "Go ahead in."

The woman was mistaken, Carmen knew, but she went in anyway because she was curious. Had Julia gone yet?

A guy was up there reading from *Richard III*. Carmen sat in a seat toward the back and listened. She grew sleepy, enjoying the language if not necessarily absorbing the meaning.

"Carmen?"

She heard her name and she looked around. Had she actually fallen asleep?

She squinted.

"Carmen, is that you?"

She leaned forward. A woman was standing up in the second row. She realized it was Judy, who had pointed her on the path to the canteen the night before.

Carmen waved, feeling self-conscious.

"We're going to break for the afternoon in a few minutes," she said, "but we'll take you now if you're ready."

Meaning they would take her now to audition? Judy must have thought she'd come to try out. It certainly looked that way. Otherwise, why was she here?

Carmen meandered toward the stage. She paused at Judy's aisle, where Judy was sitting with Andrew Kerr and a couple of other people Carmen didn't know.

"I didn't really . . . I didn't really prepare anything," Carmen whispered, hoping her voice would reach Judy but not the others. "Do you want me to come back another time?" *Like never*, she thought.

"Just go ahead," Judy said. She must have been one of the assistant directors, Carmen thought.

Carmen walked up onto the stage, wondering what in the world she was doing. She did not feel comfortable standing under these lights. She had nothing to say, nothing to read. "I'm more interested in sets," she said lamely to the assembled group. She thought she heard someone laugh in the back.

The other people in Judy's row looked annoyed, but Judy was patient. She came up to the stage and handed Carmen some pages. "Just read Perdita. It's fine. I'll read Florizel's lines."

"Are you sure?" Carmen asked. She felt stupid. Everyone else had memorized parts and prepared them and performed them with a clear sense of intent. Here she was reading from pages she had not even provided.

She did know some of these lines, though. They were from *The Winter's Tale*. She'd practiced them with Julia. That spurred her on, because the words, though strange, were familiar and pleasing to her.

Judy started the scene as Florizel, and then gave way to Carmen with an obvious lead-in.

Carmen cleared her throat.

> "Sir, my gracious lord,
> To chide at your extremes, it not becomes me—
> O, pardon, that I name them!—your high self,
> The gracious mark o' the land, you have obscur'd
> With a swain's wearing; and me, poor lowly maid,
> Most goddess-like prank'd up."

She stopped and looked up.

"Keep going," Judy said.

So Carmen kept going. She was getting to the part she most liked, and she read it with a certain joy. At the end of the last page she stopped. She looked around. She felt stupid again.

"Okay. Thanks," she called to them generally, squinting to see Judy in spite of the lights blasting her retinas. "Sorry about that."

She trundled offstage and let herself out the back door into the sunshine.

She actually laughed aloud when she got outside, because the whole thing was so bad and ridiculous.

Oh, well. Another adventure for the Pants, she thought affectionately.

There were so many odd reversals on the way to growing up.

Tibby was fourteen before she got her period for the first time. She was the last of her friends. She wished for it. She imagined how it would be. She bought a box of maxi pads and kept them under her bathroom sink just in case. It stayed there unopened for months. She worried she would never get it. She worried there was something wrong with her. She wished and wished for that first spot of blood to bring her into union with her friends.

And then it came. The happiness at getting what you want is not usually commensurate with the worry leading up to it. Relief is a short-lived emotion, passive and thin. The agony of doubt disappears, leaving little memory of how it really felt. Life aligns behind the new truth. Her period was always going to come.

Three months later she had fallen into the convention of

hating her period and dreading it just the way everybody else did. She suffered the cramps badly. She lay curled up in her bed for hours. She took Midol. The pads, once prized, became a nuisance. Why had she ever wanted them? She stained all her clothes and washed them herself, because she was embarrassed to have Loretta see.

And now, almost five years later, she was back to pining for her period. She kept a constant monitor on her abdomen, at work, at home. She watched TV with part of her brain and thought about her uterus with the other. Was that a cramp she felt, that little twinge? Was it? Oh, please?

She thought about her uterus straight through work Friday and Saturday morning. She thought about it as she walked to Fourteenth Street to buy food and a magazine. She thought about it as she walked past the places that had become meaningful to her over the last year—the place where she'd gotten a terrible haircut with her friend Angela; the Mexican place favored by film students where they served cheap margaritas and almost never carded. She thought about her uterus through the long afternoon and night while she ignored her ringing phone and listened to messages left by people who loved her.

I'll just get through this, she thought. *Then I'll call everybody back.*

She worked Sunday. She wore a pad, just in case. She thought she felt a cramp.

"Tibby Rollins, where are you going?"

Tibby froze on her way through the Comedy aisle. She cleared her throat. "Uh. Nowhere?"

She couldn't say she was going to the bathroom again. She'd already been six times and it wasn't even noon. Every time, she checked her underwear hopefully. Every time, she returned to the floor in an agony of worry.

"Do you mind taking register three?"

"Okay. Fine."

If it didn't come today, was it officially late? Did that mean . . . ? A wave of panic mounted and broke. But maybe her last period hadn't really ended on the sixth. Maybe it had been the seventh.

This was her pattern. She talked herself up. She panicked. She talked herself down.

A customer was waving his hand in her face.

"Sorry?" she said, blinking.

"Have you seen this?" he asked. He was in his twenties, she guessed. Yeesh. So strong was his cologne she could practically taste it.

"Yes," she said, trying not to breathe in.

"Is it a good date movie?"

Tibby didn't mean to roll her eyes. It just happened.

He murmured something unfriendly and walked away.

She watched him go, considering her uterus. Was that a cramp she felt? Or was she just hungry? She made sure Charlie wasn't looking when she snuck off to the bathroom again.

❋ ❋ ❋

Julia was a nervous wreck for callbacks the next day.

"It'll be good," Carmen assured her. "I'm sure you were great."

"Let's hope Judy thought so," Julia said nervously, chomping on her pinky nail.

"Judy?"

"She's the casting director."

"Really?"

"Yeah. Why? Do you know her or something?"

"Not exactly, no."

Most of the kids were eating lunch when word went out that the lists were posted. Carmen was waiting in line to get coffee for her and Julia, and she feared she might get trampled like a hapless British soccer fan.

She watched the stampede. She drank her coffee by herself, enjoying the relative quiet.

Later, after the hoopla had died down, Carmen did wander by the lobby to check the lists. Why not? She checked the community theater list first, thinking it the least absurd possibility, and then the Second Stage. Her heart did pick up a little speed as her eyes passed from *I to J* to *K to L*. To *M*. Her name was not there.

Not exactly a surprise, she said to herself as she walked outside, taking the long way back to her room. She was mildly embarrassed that she'd even looked.

Was she disappointed? She wanted to read her heart honestly.

No. She felt pretty happy. She was wearing the Traveling

Pants and they still fit her, and even on an empty path she felt herself among friends.

O Tibbeth,
    Wherefore art thou ignoring thy friends?
    I sendeth thou a phone card. Please calleth me backeth.
    And I encloseth the Pants.

Loveth,
Thy loving and
most theatrical wench,
Carmen. Eth.

When Bridget reported for duty the next workday, Peter was not in the grave. She casually waited until around noon to casually ask cabinmate Carolyn why not. "I think he moved over to the house excavation."

"Oh," she said casually.

He was not the Tuesday lecturer, and she didn't see him at dinner the following night.

"A bunch of people went into town for dinner," Maxine mentioned.

Town was about thirty-five minutes away and Bridget had not yet been there, but suddenly she felt herself growing curious about it.

The next day, Alison announced to the team in mortuary that they'd made a big advance in the house dig, and asked for a couple of volunteers to shift. Bridget's hand shot up.

"We found a new part of the foundation and a new floor," Peter explained animatedly to the newly expanded group after lunch.

Was he surprised to see her there? Did it matter?

"We've cleared the floor in one small area, and we want to keep going. It's a tamped-earth floor, made of . . . well, earth. It can be hard to distinguish from the rest of the earth, if you know what I mean."

Bridget found herself on her hands and knees with her trowel. They were deep in, the shadows were long. Other members of the crew were carefully lifting off layers of the ground in front of her. Where she knelt there was less than a foot of loose dirt where they'd left off with the coarser tools.

She felt around with her hands, cupping mounds of it into the nearest bin. Peter had told her what to look for, but she sensed she would do better with her hands. She most urgently did not want to dig through and wreck the integrity of the floor.

She kept two palms on the edge of the flat and moved them along, feeling with her hands. It was all earth, yes, but some of it had been constructed and maintained purposefully and the rest had poured haphazardly into the negative space. Even after two and a half millennia, she could begin to feel the difference.

That was the thing with digging, she was starting to understand. You went into it with the instincts of a looter: Dig around, find something valuable and cool, and bring it to a museum. She'd fancied herself a wannabe Indiana

Jones. But the real thing was finding the effects of the human will. The planning, the wanting, the attempting of these ancient people was what connected you to them. Their effort was the difference between the random, all-over, everywhere-including-your-scalp dirt and this precious floor.

That was what they could learn from the gravesite, Peter had explained to her. You could learn a lot more about a people from how they buried, cared for, and commemorated their dead than from an ancient body randomly struck down by the side of a road.

"We do not like random," she'd teased Peter after one of his pep talks.

"No, we don't, do we?" he said, laughing, as he was quick to do.

This floor was not random. She closed her eyes and concentrated all of her self into her palms, almost in a trance as she felt along. She knew she probably looked ridiculous, but she didn't care. She remembered her grandfather describing how Michelangelo sculpted bodies out of blocks of marble. Her grandpa had been reading a book about the artist during a long-ago summer she'd spent in Alabama with him and Greta. She remembered him saying how Michelangelo looked for the body inside the block. He saw it and sensed it in there, and with his chisel he freed it.

Well, Bridget thought, a floor was a more prosaic thing, granted, but she was going to free it.

Her fingers were so sensitized she almost shouted when they ran into something hard and quite purposeful, but not the floor. Carefully she shook it off and held it in the patch of sunlight.

"Look at this," she called.

Peter hopped down into the room, followed by Carolyn and another guy. "Wow. That's great. That's most of a lamp. Look, you can see some of the painting on it."

She felt the moist terra-cotta against her fingers and followed the smooth, molded shape.

"That's where they would pour the oil. Probably olive oil." Peter pointed to a little well at the top. "They'd float the wick right there." He nodded at her approvingly. "I bet you can't find the missing piece."

She was such a sucker for a dare. He could obviously tell that.

"I found it," she said less than a minute later.

He hopped back down again, mirth spread over his features. She was glad to provide so much entertainment.

"Well done, Bee." He raised a hand to whack her on the shoulder, but put it down again without making contact. "Do your recording and bring it to Maxine. She'll be happy to have a whole one."

Always carry a flagon of

whiskey in case of

snakebite, and

furthermore, always carry

a small snake.

—W. C. Fields

"Love's *Labour's Lost* is such a great play," Carmen declared. "You were awesome reading the speech of Lady What's-Her-Name."

"Rosaline," Julia said flatly.

Carmen was trying to cheer Julia up about the fact that she'd gotten called back for the community production, the least desirable in her mind, and not the other two. But Julia wasn't having it.

"Rosaline. Right. You have to admit the play's a whole lot funnier than *Richard the Third*."

Richard III was the production on the Second Stage. Carmen could already perceive a hierarchy developing between the kids who'd gotten called back for Second Stage and the larger number who'd gotten called back for the Community Stage.

"Yeah. But they don't even sell tickets. It's, like, free. It's outdoors. It's not even real."

"How can you say that? Of course it's real. Andrew said it's the best attended of all of them, by far."

"That's because it's free," Julia said. "Anyone can go."

"That's a *good* thing. Anyway, at least you got called back," Carmen said. She wasn't even sure why she said this. She had made up her mind not to tell Julia about her ludicrous tryout, but here she was eager to debase herself to make Julia feel better.

"Everyone got called back," Julia said.

"That's not true."

"What are you talking about? Melanie Peer said that everyone who tried out got called back for something."

"No, they didn't."

"How do you know?" Julia was sitting up straighter now.

"I didn't get called back," Carmen said, with a perverse note of triumph.

Julia looked at her in outright astonishment. "You tried out?"

"Yeah."

"You're kidding."

"It *was* kind of a joke, but no. I really tried out."

"Really? Why?"

"I have no idea. It was kind of a mistake, actually."

"Who did you read?"

"Perdita."

"No."

"Yeah."

Julia looked like she might laugh, but she made a wince of sympathy. "You didn't get called back."

"No way."

"Oh, well. It was brave of you to try."

"That and stupid."

Julia patted Carmen on the arm and laughed. It looked like this method of cheering her up really was working.

Lena wasn't sure how much of it was attributable to Leo, but she knew that every hour she wasn't in her painting class she wished she were.

"Hi, Lena," he said to her on Thursday as she was leaving painting class, girding herself for three long, bleak days of not painting and not getting to see Leo.

"Hi," she said, taking almost absurd pride in the fact that he still knew her name.

"How's it going?" he said.

"Pretty good," she said blandly. She smiled blandly. "How are you?" she asked blandly.

"Just fine."

Please be interesting, she begged of herself.

She was wearing her hair down and had put on mascara for the fourth day in a row. She was boring as crap, but at least she looked good.

"I don't know if I can make it to Monday," Leo said. He distractedly pushed his hand around in his hair and made it stand up more.

"What do you mean?"

"I mean no painting. I'm right in the middle of this thing I'm trying to figure out. It'll be gone by Monday. It's too long to go, you know?"

She nodded. Oh, how she knew. She wasn't sure her reasons were quite as pure as his, but she was taken aback to think they felt exactly the same way.

"I'm thinking of seeing if Nora would work extra hours over the weekend. I'd have to ask Robert, I guess." He pushed his hair around again despondently. "Would you want to go in on it with me?"

She was nearly frozen by the thought. She cherished his phrasing. "Uh."

She tried to figure. She'd have to come up with around eight or nine dollars an hour. How could she do that? She had no money. She ate Cup O' Noodles almost every night from the twenty-four pack she'd bought at Costco with her parents' membership. That was as close as her father got to financial aid. Her mother had slipped her eighty dollars at the beginning of the summer, and she'd made it last for almost three weeks.

But how could she say no? She couldn't. She'd pawn her watch. She'd steal her mother's diamonds. She'd borrow money from Effie, for God's sake.

She swallowed. "I'd love to go in with you," she chirruped.

"Are you Carmen Lowell?"

Carmen looked up from the table at the canteen to see a guy she didn't know staring at her with odd intensity.

She was so surprised she didn't answer. A year ago she might have imagined he was staring at her like that because he thought she was cute, but now she was so conditioned to invisibility she found his gaze disturbing. Suddenly she worried she'd set off all the sprinklers in her dorm or something.

"Yes, she's Carmen Lowell," Julia said, looking mildly impatient with both of them.

"Well, dude. Congratulations. Sophia over there thought it was you, but I said I didn't think you were trying out."

Carmen could not have been more mystified. She would have liked to say something, but she just gaped like a hooked fish.

"Congratulations for what?" Julia asked.

"The callback," he said.

Julia put her fork down. She cast a protective look at Carmen. "She didn't get called back."

Carmen nodded.

"I'm pretty sure you did." Why did this guy proceed to talk as if to Carmen and not to Julia, who was the one conversing with him? This added another unsettling layer. "Didn't you check the list?"

"She did check it," Julia said, almost combatively.

"Then maybe you should check it again," the guy said to Carmen.

"He has no idea what he's talking about," Julia muttered once he'd left, resuming her dinner of salad and Diet Coke.

Carmen stood up. She had an odd idea blossoming in her mind and she needed to choke it off before it really started to get to her.

"You said you checked, right?" Julia asked.

"Yeah. I might go check again, though." Carmen picked up her tray with the remnants of her dinner on it.

Julia stood too. "I'll come with you. I'm done."

As they walked toward the Main Stage, Julia talked and Carmen fretted.

"That guy probably looked at one of the tech lists and got confused," Julia said.

"Yeah, probably."

But the thing Carmen was thinking when she pushed open the doors to the lobby was that she had checked the lists, but only two of them. She hadn't thought to check the third, because it was somewhere else, she didn't know where, and it just seemed too preposterous to go around looking for it.

Wordlessly, both she and Julia walked to the lists and ran their eyes along the columns. Indeed, Carmen's name was not there.

"One thing," Carmen murmured on the way out. She bent her steps to the other side of the entrance, where she now saw a much smaller list posted.

"That's the Main Stage list," Julia said.

Even so, Carmen walked up to it and looked. There were seven names on the list, and hers was one of them.

To: Carmabelle@hsp.xx.com
From: Beezy3@gomail.net
Subject: dirt + me = love

Carma,

I have a new love. Don't tell Hector.

I have fallen in love with a dirt floor. I am obsessed. I am devoted.

I am its humble servant.

I am going to marry it. I am going to have dirty, flat children with it.

But fear not, Carma. I'll still love you guys even though you're rounded and clean. Just, you know, not in that way.

Love,

Mrs. Bee Vreeland Dirtfloor

After the initial shock wore off, Julia wanted to talk about it.

"It's unbelievable, Carmen, it really is," she said.

She wanted to know every detail of Carmen's happening into the theater, her discussion with Judy. She wanted Carmen to reenact every word of her muddled tryout.

And then, all of a sudden, Julia didn't want to talk about it anymore. She said she was tired and fell asleep in under five seconds.

So Carmen lay there twisting in her sheets, wondering if Judy was playing some subtle trick on her. What could it mean?

And now she was supposed to prepare for a real audition for the following evening? How was she supposed to do that? She had no idea how you did that.

Anyway, what was the point? She was not an actress. She did not like the lights. She would not get the part.

Her audition had proven to her that she had no business on the stage, even if it had failed to prove so to Judy.

The next morning she got up early. She walked around until nine o'clock, when she could find out the location of Judy's office and, subsequently, Judy.

"I think you might have made a mistake," she said, hovering nervously in front of Judy's desk.

Judy took off her reading glasses. "What mistake?"

"You put me on the callback list for *The Winter's Tale*."

Judy looked at her a little strangely. "That wasn't a mistake."

"I think it might have been."

"Carmen, are you the casting director or am I?" Judy didn't look mean, exactly, but her straight-across eyebrows were intimidating.

"I know. I know. It's just that I don't think I'd be right for it."

"You don't even know which part we're going to cast!"

"Well, that's true, but I don't think I'd be right for any of them."

"Can you please leave that to me?" Judy was getting annoyed now.

"Judy. Seriously. I don't know how to prepare for an audition. I'm bad at memorizing. I would not do a good job. I think there are so many people who would do a good job. My friend Julia Wyman, for instance, would do a great job. I heard her read Perdita, and she did it so much better. She memorized the whole thing." Carmen realized how juvenile she probably sounded.

"Carmen, no offense to your friend Julia, but I see that girl twenty times a day."

Carmen was puzzling over how this could be, until she realized Judy was speaking figuratively.

"She's polished, she's poised and ambitious, but that's not what I'm looking for right now. When she reads Perdita I hear a shepherdess who thinks she's a princess. I want a shepherdess who thinks she's a shepherdess."

Carmen did not completely follow, but she didn't want to argue.

"I'm looking for somebody who is a little more porous, you know? Someone who is fragile, who is less sure of everything."

Carmen nodded, imagining for the first time that Judy wasn't completely out of her mind.

When she got home, she called her mother.

"Carmen, congratulations! That's exciting!"

"Mama, it's not exciting. It's scary. I don't think I want to do it. I don't know how." Her voice never sounded whinier than when she spoke to her mother. "You know I'm not an actress!"

Her mother was silent while she mulled this over. "Well, *nena*, you have always been dramatic."

"Mama!"

Why did everyone keep saying that?

Never had a weekend passed more slowly. Lena remembered the old adage about knowing whether you'd chosen the right career by how you felt on Sunday night. Well, what light did it shed on your personal life when you abhorred Friday night?

She lived for Monday painting class. She lived twice when Leo came up to her easel at the first break.

"Robert says we can't do it," he said unhappily.

"Why not?" she asked.

"We can't use the studio. Some bullshit about insurance and you need a security person in the building. I don't know. He says we can't hire Nora off the books either."

"Really?"

He shook his head.

"That sucks," she said, though a little too happily. She was elated that he was seeming so much like her friend.

"Yeah."

Well. It was good not to have to steal her mother's diamonds. But how could she get through another weekend?

The timer dinged and they both went back to painting. At the end of class she took a long time putting away her stuff and was thrilled when he wandered back over to her easel.

"It's not that I have to paint Nora," he said as they walked together down the hall and out into the sunshine. "I mean, that would be great. But I just want to keep painting. We should be working every day. I feel like I start over every Monday."

"I know what you mean," she said boringly.

He walked pretty fast, she realized. She practically jogged to keep up with him.

"I could work on a still life or something," he said. "But I'm doing the figure this summer. That's what I want to think about. It's not the same to stare at a couple of pears."

"Yeah."

He stopped. "Do you want to get a cup of coffee?"

"Sure," she said.

He led her around the corner. "This place has good iced coffee," he said.

"Great," said she. His freckles were nice.

He ordered two. "Do you have time to sit down for a minute?"

How 'bout an hour? she felt like saying. *How about seven?* She couldn't help laughing at herself a little.

"I do" was what she said.

They sat.

"I have a lot of minutes," she added overhonestly.

"Yeah?"

"Yeah. I guess I am kind of underscheduled this summer." Why was it that when her mouth obeyed her she was chokingly boring, and when it didn't she was mortifying? Where was the in-between?

He looked at her. Did he feel sorry for her? It wasn't exactly sexy to admit you had nothing to do.

"I mean, I have painting," she hurried to say. "I have work-study in the library eight hours a week. But none of my friends stuck around this summer, so . . ."

"Right."

"Yeah."

He shook the ice around in his iced coffee. He looked regretful. "I have to be at work soon. But what are you doing tomorrow night?"

She turned pink. She felt stupid. Charity and romance did not go together. "Well. That's really nice of you, but—"

"But what? Come over for dinner. You can't go acting like you have other plans."

She laughed. "I can't, can I?"

"Anyway, it will be good. Here." He fished around in his bag for a piece of paper and a pen. He wrote down his address. "About seven?"

"Okay," she said weakly.

When he left the coffee shop, the air slowly leaked out of her. Leo had asked her to dinner. She had a date with Leo.

Some part of her was pleased. Other parts knew there was nothing like the artifice of a date to ruin a relationship. Especially a date born out of pity.

It is a characteristic

of wisdom not to do

desperate things.

—Henry David Thoreau

The Traveling Pants came on Monday. Tibby's period did not. A watched period, she worried, does not come.

She decided to change her strategy. She would tempt fate. She wore a pair of slight, lacy underpants and pulled the Traveling Pants on over them. She went to register for her summer classes.

With a small part of her brain, she filled out forms in the lobby of the main film building and consulted the catalog. With the remainder of her brain, she thought about not thinking about her uterus anymore.

Since the first time she'd ever worn the Traveling Pants, she'd had this secret worry that she would get her period while wearing the Pants. You couldn't wash the Pants, of course. It was the first and most infamous rule. Tibby had often imagined the shame of bleeding on the Traveling Pants and then needing to send them on. She imagined secretly washing them and hoping no one would ever find out.

It was this fear that led her, from the first summer onward, to wear her hardiest underwear whenever she wore the Pants, and also to wear a liner of some kind. She happened to know she was not the only member of the Sisterhood to do so. It was kind of a basic courtesy at this point.

But not today. Today she took the ultimate risk. Whatever it took she would do, she both thought and did not think as she strode into her dorm room late that afternoon.

"Tibby?"

She reared back against the door. Her blood whisked around her veins in a hectic way. In all the times Brian had appeared in her room, he had never truly startled her before.

"Sorry," he said, recognizing her distress. Usually he sat on her bed, but today he was standing. When he tried to put his arms around her, she shrugged away.

"Today isn't a good day," she said.

"You didn't answer the phone. I wanted to make sure you were okay."

"Okay."

"Are you?" He wanted so much to talk to her. She could see that. But she was holding herself too carefully. She couldn't open up a little or at all.

"Don't you work tonight?" she asked.

"I traded shifts."

"What about tomorrow morning?"

"I'll be back for that," he said.

"You're going back tonight?"

He nodded. "I just wanted to see you."

This was her first moment of relief. He wasn't staying.

"Okay. Well."

His hair was lank. When did he last take a shower?

"I know you're worried. I'm worried. I just wish I could—"

"You can't," she said quickly. She looked at the ground. "This is where you are happy that you're the boy and I'm the girl."

He wore his hurt openly. "I'm not happy."

She saw how miserable he was, how miserable she was making him. She thought of the Pants and her single-minded wish. What wouldn't she ruin? What wouldn't she sacrifice for a dot of blood?

"I know you're not happy," she said regretfully.

"I wish I could do something."

She wanted him to leave. That was what he could do. She wanted to be alone with her uterus. "If I think of something, I'll tell you," she said, opening the door and stepping aside for him to go through it.

"Will you?"

"Yeah."

"You promise?"

"Yeah."

"Tibby?"

"Yeah?"

He looked like he might cry. He wanted to be able to talk.

We shouldn't have done it, she wanted to say. *We opened ourselves up to all this. Why did you want to so much? Why did you make me believe it would be all right?*

She knew she should be having this talk with Brian. Instead, she had it, once again, with herself.

"What?" she pressed, knowing full well what he wanted.

He looked at her for another moment and turned to go.

She felt mean. She was mean. She hated herself more than she hated him.

He walked to the elevator. He had come all this way, and now he was going all the way back. Only Brian would do a thing like that.

Usually these gestures moved her. She appreciated the way he was, the way he trusted himself and her, regardless of how the rest of the world worked. Usually she understood the particular ways he felt and the things he did.

Tonight she felt differently. After she closed the door she wondered what half-sane person would travel twelve hours to see a girl for ten minutes.

Julia worked on the Princess of France while Carmen, self-consciously, worked on Perdita.

"Perdita means lost child, did you know that?" Carmen asked, looking up from her book the night before the callback. The room had been silent for so long, she wanted the comfort of a little conversation.

"Yes. I know that," Julia said flatly.

Carmen tried not to feel hurt. "Do you want me to read Berowne or the king for you?" she asked.

"No, thanks."

Later, it seemed to her that Julia felt bad. "Do you want me to read with you?" Julia offered.

"Um, sure. That's really nice. Do you want to be Polixenes?"

"Fine."

"Okay, so I'll start where she goes." Carmen squinted at the page, knowing she should try it from memory. "Uh, 'Sir, welcome . . .' "

"Go ahead."

" 'Sir, welcome! / It is my father's will I should take on me / The hostess of—' "

"No," Julia interrupted. "It's 'hostess-ship,' not 'hostess.' And you don't say 'of.' It's a contraction. You say 'o.' You say 'hostess-ship o' the day.' "

"Right," Carmen said. She tried it again.

Julia stopped her after another three lines. "Carmen, have you read Shakespeare before?"

"Not that much. Not out loud. Why?"

"Because your meter is all wrong. Rhythmically it just sounds wrong."

"Oh." They were close enough friends that Carmen had trouble believing Julia meant to sound as mean as she sounded.

"And it's not like I have time to teach it all to you either," Julia said. "I have a lot of work to do for my own callback."

"Fine," Carmen said. She felt like she was going to cry.

Julia shut her book, seemingly blind to what Carmen was feeling.

Carmen kept her eyes on her script.

"Listen, Carmen, no offense, but are you sure you should bother with this? It doesn't seem like your kind of thing, you know? It's going to take a lot of work, and the chances of it working out are pretty small. Maybe you should just blow it off. That's probably what I would do if I were you."

Carmen did not want to cry. "I already tried to get out of it," she said almost inaudibly. "I told Judy she'd made a mistake."

"You did?" Julia's voice was loud and quick. "And what did she say?"

"She said she didn't."

Julia's normally pretty face did not look pretty at this moment. It looked pinched and suspicious. Carmen tried to use her imagination to restore its prettiness, to remember why they were friends.

"Didn't what?"

"Think she'd made a mistake."

"Well, yeah. But you know yourself better than she does."

Carmen nodded wordlessly. She lay on her bed and turned her face to the wall. What was wrong with her? Julia was being a witch to her and all she felt like doing was crying. Where was the famous Carmen temper? She was a master at standing up for herself.

But that Carmen felt like someone she only knew about from a long time ago. That Carmen wasn't this Carmen.

This was a faded Carmen. She'd lost her mojo for that kind of thing.

Maybe you needed to feel strong to stand up for yourself. You needed to feel loved. She'd always been better at acting up with people she trusted to love her.

She wished she could just fall asleep and sleep straight through her callback audition and forget about the whole thing. Maybe Julia wasn't simply being mean. Maybe she was being honest and it was the honesty that was tough to swallow. Carmen didn't know how to read Shakespeare. Her meter was undoubtedly wrong.

She wished she could sleep, but she couldn't. Even long after Julia turned off the light, Carmen lay there feeling wretched about herself. She felt despair, and apart from the Pants, she couldn't think of a way to feel better.

And then she thought of one small way. Quietly she picked up her script from the bottom of her bed. Quietly she walked out of the room and into the hallway.

She sat down outside her door in a spot where the light was good. Feeling an odd sense of rebellion, she stayed in that spot and studied the lines.

She read them all. Not just Perdita's, but the whole play. She read it again, and then, through the remaining hours before morning, she read Perdita's part, each time with more care. She didn't try to memorize it or figure out what Julia meant by the meter. She just tried to understand the play.

Carmen didn't know how to act like an actress. But it

dawned on her that she wasn't supposed to. She was supposed to act like Perdita. She was supposed to act like the lost daughter of estranged parents—a flawed but repentant father, a beleaguered but upright mother who gets carried off to sea. Maybe that was something she could try to do.

A single day is enough to

make us a little larger.

—Paul Klee

As Lena dressed for her alleged date, she realized she hadn't thought of Kostos in two days. Compared with how she used to be, two days was forever. Was she forgetting yet? Did that constitute forgetting? Maybe the fact that she was still asking meant no, not yet.

Lena wanted to look pretty, but not date pretty. She didn't want to try too hard, but she did want him to notice that she was attractive. Or was thought to be so. That struck her as funny. *You may not have noticed it, Leo, but I am thought to be attractive.*

She liked and admired Leo for not seeming to notice, but she did also want him to. Here she had this supposedly striking quality, and it mostly caused her strain and annoyance — vapid attention and endless comments and people assuming she was a princess or a snob. She might as well take advantage of it once in a while.

Without meaning to, she was suffused with the memory

of the last time she'd wanted to take advantage of it. It was at her bapi's funeral, when she knew she'd see Kostos.

Lena lost track of her preparations. She dropped the eye pencil on her dresser. She sat on her bed, her hands tucked under her. That was the hardest day to remember.

She stared at her feet for a while and then out the window at the building across the way. This did not count toward forgetting, she realized.

When she finally got up, she dispensed with the makeup and the hair fiddling. She changed back into her comfortable shoes that made her feet look like the boats they were. She hedged; she left herself how she was.

She walked along with the address flapping in her hand. Where did he live? Did he have a roommate? Was this going to go along a standard date format? Or was this simply the gesture of a charitable friend? She wasn't sure which she wanted less.

She turned onto his street. She knew the street, but not this part of it. It was deserted and a little bit dodgy, she recognized, and yet the old industrial loft buildings were staunchly romantic.

She stopped in front of 2020. She buzzed 7B. 7B buzzed back. She pushed into the building and made sure the door was shut behind her.

Of all the hundreds of possibilities she had considered, one of the few she hadn't met her at the door.

"Hi, I'm Jaclyn. You're Lena?"

Lena gaped for a moment too long and then stuck out her hand. "I am. Hi."

Jaclyn was a tall African American woman who appeared to be in her early forties. She was wearing a paint-spattered denim work shirt over olive green cargo pants and elegant brown slides. She had three sparkly clips in her long braided hair. She was beautiful.

Lena's brain was rushing around as she looked past the woman into the apartment. It was a gigantic loft. The ceiling must have been twenty feet high in the main room, and around it was a balcony suggesting a second floor. The railings were hung with huge tapestries and a few ancient-looking carpets.

The effect of the woman and the place were quite dazzling to all of Lena's senses, but her brain was wondering how she, Lena, could possibly fit into it. Leo was less conventional than she'd even guessed. And apparently he liked older women.

Leo appeared behind Jaclyn. "Hey. Welcome. Come in."

She followed them through the big room to an open kitchen under the balcony. The table was set, and pots were steaming on the stove. The air was spicy and garlicky.

"I hope you like, uh, flavorful food," Jaclyn said. "Leo uses a head of garlic every time he makes dinner."

Another sense dazzled. Another surprise about Leo. Lena nodded. "I'm Greek," she said.

Jaclyn smiled. "Excellent," she said.

Leo was manning all four gas burners with an admirably cool head. Lena had grown up in a family of cooks, but she couldn't manage even one burner.

"Mom, could you get me the butter?" Leo called.

All the bits and pieces swirling in Lena's head came apart and recombined. Jaclyn was his mom?

Jaclyn got the butter. More evidence that she was indeed his mother. There wasn't anyone else around who could be his mother.

Lena looked from Jaclyn to Leo and back. Huh. She considered Leo's dark gold skin. It made sense now. Lena saw, now that she really looked, how much of his mother's beauty Leo had.

Lena realized that as a dinner guest it was not desirable to be completely mute. "Can I help with anything?" she asked politely.

"I think we're set," Jaclyn said, looking for something in the cupboard. "Leo, how's it going?"

"A couple minutes," he said. "Hey, Lena, will you bring me the plates and I'll fill them up here?"

She was glad to have a job. She gathered and carefully stacked the yellow plates. "These are beautiful," she murmured.

"They're my mom's," Leo said.

It took her a second to realize that he didn't just mean that his mom owned them.

"You mean like . . ."

"She made them. She's a ceramicist. Mostly."

"You made these?" she said stupidly to Jaclyn, who was setting glasses on the table.

"Yep. Water with dinner? Juice? Wine?"

"Water, please," Lena said. She couldn't help looking at Jaclyn with bald admiration. She was beautiful. She was young. She made exquisite yellow dinner plates. Lena suddenly wondered about Leo's dad. Was there a dad? There were only three plates.

Lena thought of her own mother with her tailored beige clothes and her shiny briefcase.

Lena's taste buds were her only sense yet undazzled, and a few bites of dinner did the trick. It was a spicy curry with lamb and vegetables over some eventful and delicious kind of rice. "This is so good," she said to Leo, her awe undisguised. "I can't believe you made this."

He laughed and she realized it hadn't come out all compliment, as she had intended. "I mean, not because you don't seem like you could cook," she added lamely. "Because I'm so bad at it."

Why was she always putting herself down in front of him? What charm, exactly, did that hold?

"You probably haven't practiced that much," Leo said.

"That's true. Everybody else cooks in my family, so I haven't needed to yet." She thought of all her ramen noodles with silent shame. "My grandparents owned a restaurant in Greece."

The conversation rolled on from there. Jaclyn wanted to hear all about her family and how her parents ended up in America. Lena talked for a while, and when she remembered she was shy and lost, Jaclyn rescued her with a funny story about the time she went to Greece with an old boyfriend, lost him in a market near the Acropolis, and never saw him again.

After that Lena discovered that Leo's dad was a

businessman from Ohio who was no longer in the picture and that Jaclyn had brought up Leo mostly on her own.

"She supported us selling her ceramics and her tapestries," Leo explained with obvious pride.

Lena admired the tapestries and then all the other lovely things lining the walls and shelves. The whole place was filled with things the two of them had made. Drawings, pots, sculptures, paintings. It was almost overwhelming to Lena.

She thought of the empty beige walls of her house and of the hard, minimal surfaces of metal and polished stone. Her parents, hailing from a romantic, disheveled homeland, had grown up in ancient, disheveled houses. Now they wanted only American sleekness.

You grow up, Lena thought, about herself and them. *You leave home. You see other ways of living.*

Lena looked around, intoxicated by her sense of longing. She wanted this.

It was late and Bee still had two hands and two knees against the floor. She had cleared several more feet and could not leave it. She'd work through dinner. She'd do it by moonlight if she had to. She could do it in the dark. She'd dreamed about it the past three nights. She simply loved the feeling of finding the floor, inch by inch, under her hands. By now she really trusted herself to know where it was.

The difference tonight was that Peter was kneeling two feet away, clearing next to her. He had not yet learned the floor as she had, but she was slightly proud to note that he had put aside his trowel and adopted her technique. She was faster, smoother, and surer every hour she worked.

"You can go," she said. "Seriously. I'm fine. I'm a crazy nutjob, I know. I can't help it. But I swear I won't ruin anything."

"I know you won't," he said almost defensively. "I'm not staying for you."

She laughed. "Good to know."

He had the slightly abstracted look she also wore when she had her hands on the floor. "I mean." He raised his dirty hands. "It's addictive."

"Don't I know."

"Worse than pistachios."

"So much."

He disappeared briefly to find a spotlight and hook it up to the generator. He hopped back down.

"Hey, look," she said. She held up a large piece of pottery. "Another one." They had piles of them. They had left off with the proper labeling as it got later and later in the night.

"From the kalyx krater," he said.

"I think."

"Dude. We might find the whole thing." He was excited. He did what he did for good reasons. She could understand wanting to spend your life like this.

"Dude, we might," she teased him back.

He left again later to find a few pieces of pita bread and

a large chocolate bar and a half-empty bottle of red wine. He gallantly shared them with her.

After the eating were long periods of silent work. Occasionally she heard laughter from over the hill, where the nightly party was rolling on.

"Another sherd," he said. "It's from a lamp."

"Arrrrg!" she erupted. "Say *shard*! Don't say *sherd*." The word *potsherd* was the single thing about archaeology she really did not like.

He passed her a challenging look. "Sherd."

"Stop it!"

"Sherd."

"I hate that."

"Sherd."

"Peter! Shut up!"

"Sherd."

She reached over and shoved him hard. He was not only startled, he was poorly balanced. He fell over into the dirt.

Even though she felt bad, she was laughing too hard to stop. She walked over to him on her knees. She wanted to say sorry, but she couldn't get it out.

He reached up and shoved her in retaliation. She fell onto her back, laughing so hard she was practically suffocating. They both lay in the dirt, punch-drunk and wine-drunk.

Once he'd gotten his breath and sat up, he reached out his hand. "Truce?" he said, hauling her up.

She was back on her knees. He was still holding her dirty hand in his. He pulled it toward his chest.

"Truce," she meant to say, but she started laughing again midway through.

"Sherd," he said.

"How'd it go?" Julia asked when Carmen joined her for a late dinner after her audition. By Julia's expression, it looked to Carmen as though she had a specific idea in mind about how Carmen should answer.

It was a disaster, Carmen was supposed to say. *I made a total fool of myself.*

She could tell that that was what Julia wanted to hear, and that if she said it they could both laugh over it and be close again.

Carmen put her tray down and sat. But if Julia was actually her friend, why did she want to hear that? And if Carmen was so good at standing up for herself, why did she feel the need to say it? Why did Julia require that she be a failure, and why did Carmen go along with it?

"I'm not sure," Carmen said slowly, honestly. "I couldn't really tell."

"Did Judy say anything?" Julia looked impatient, unsatisfied.

"She said 'Thanks, Carmen.' "

"That was it?"

"That was it."

So cool was the air between them, Carmen figured they'd spend the rest of the meal in punishing silence. But a few minutes later two girls from their hall came up. "Hey,

Carmen, I heard you had a great audition," Alexandra said.

Carmen didn't try to hide her surprise. "Really?"

"That's what Benjamin Bolter said. He said that your energy was very fresh."

Carmen wasn't sure exactly what that meant. "Thanks. I was nervous."

"Nervous can be good," the other girl, Rachel, said.

"Anyway, I really hope you get it. How cool would that be?"

Carmen watched them go, suddenly wishing she were eating dinner with Alexandra and Rachel and not with Julia.

When they were leaving the canteen, Carmen realized that a bunch of kids at the front table were watching her. One of the ones she'd met, Jack something or other, waved at her. "All right, Carmen!" he called out.

She felt herself blushing as she went out the door. She wished she were wearing earrings and some makeup. She felt the drumming of excitement in her chest. It was kind of a responsibility, being visible.

To: Tibberon@sbgnetworks.com
From: Carmabelle@hsp.xx.com
Subject: call me call me call me

Hey, you girl of urban mystery. Will you call me? I have something cool to tell you and I'm not writing it here. You have to call me. Ha.
And don't do that thing you do of leaving a message when you know I won't be there.

* * *

By eleven o'clock that night, Lena was relaxed and happy. Her stomach was full. She knew she was in love. If not with Leo, then certainly with his mother.

"So I asked Nora about posing, even though we're not supposed to hire her," Leo said as they picked at the last of the raspberries and the shortbread cookies.

"What did she say?" Lena asked, her elbows on the table.

"She said she'd think about it. I'm not too optimistic."

"The truth," Lena said, "is I really want to do it, but I probably can't afford to. Unless I steal my mom's jewelry. Which I have considered."

Leo laughed. "It's only eight bucks an hour if we split it."

Lena put her hand to her temple. "I know. But I have *no* money. I'm kind of on my own with school, and it's . . ."

"Ludicrously expensive," Jaclyn filled in. "Did you try for financial aid?"

"I didn't qualify," Lena explained. "My parents have the money, but my dad doesn't really . . . support the idea of my being an artist." Lena usually kept this to herself, feeling ashamed of them. But tonight she said it with a note of pride.

"You should apply for a scholarship," Leo said. "That's what I did."

"Did you get full tuition?" she asked.

"Tuition, stipends, everything. It helps being black," he said. "I qualify for almost every scholarship they've got."

It helps being the best painter in the school, she thought. "I have a partial one," she explained. "I'm applying for the big one for next year. I'll find out in August."

"I'm sure you'll get it," Leo said. "But I'll help you with your portfolio if you want."

Lena flushed with pleasure. "Thanks," she said. She wasn't sure she could let him see all those drawings she used to think were good. "I just need a few finished paintings, you know?"

Jaclyn got up to clear the teacups. "You should do what we used to do when I was in art school."

"What's that?" Leo asked, his feet, in faded blue socks, propped on the corner of the table.

"We used to trade poses with each other. We'd do portraits, figures, whatever. It's free, it's fair. Most of my drawings and paintings from my art school years are of my friends."

"I don't really know that many people in the summer program," Lena admitted.

Jaclyn gestured to Leo. "You know each other. You two can do it."

While Leo was getting on board, Lena was realizing what this meant. She stopped being quite as relaxed. "You mean, like, I pose for Leo and he poses for me?" The way they looked at her, she felt both childish and dumb.

Leo was starting to look eager. "We could split it up however we want. Maybe I could pose for you on Saturday and you could pose for me on Sunday. We could work like that for the next bunch of weekends."

Lena knew she was gaping. She tried to cover a little more of her wide eyes with her eyelids.

"It's good for an artist to pose, too. I've heard that," Leo was saying, though his voice sounded distant to her. "It's good to see the process from the other side. It makes you better at working with models."

Lena felt her head nodding.

"And you know we could each have a finished figure painting by the end of the summer."

Lena was alone, trapped in her head with her loud, slow-moving thoughts. He was going to pose for her for a figure painting? The dryness of the shortbread was caked and rough in her throat. She was going to pose for him? "Or a portrait," she choked out nervously.

"You can do a portrait," he said, not seeming to register what this meant. "If you want."

Lena simply could not swallow the cookie. It sat there, choking her. She knew that prudishness had no place in the training and career of a figure painter, but still.

She tried once again to swallow. Maybe her father was right after all.

In the depth of winter,

I finally learned that

within me there lay

an invincible summer.

—Albert Camus

The next morning Carmen unearthed a pair of red flared pants she hadn't worn since the end of last summer. She'd worn them to Target, where she'd gone shopping for college supplies with Win. She'd also worn a bandana, do-rag style, and he'd kissed her massively in the parking lot.

God, that felt far away.

She put on a sexy black tank top and big silver hoops. She wore a shade of red lipstick that she knew looked good on her. She let her long, unruly hair out of its ordinary clip. She felt like a completely different person as she walked out of the dorm and into the sun. But like a familiar person.

She wanted to make her way slowly to the theater lobby. She wanted to keep the motor running low, to keep her expectations in check. The chances of seeing her name on the cast list were small, she knew. One out of seven under the best of circumstances, and she knew she wasn't as prepared or as capable as the other six.

Two days ago, she was in Judy's office trying to get out of it. Now . . . what?

Now she wanted it. She had stayed up all night working and thinking and studying, and it had culminated in her wanting it.

As she walked into the theater, she felt the mad walloping of her heart in her chest, so strong it seemed to shake her entire body. In some ways it had been easier not wanting it.

But the wanting felt good. Even if she didn't get it. Wanting was what made you a person, and she was glad to feel like a person again.

The scene in the theater lobby was dreamlike. It seemed that all seventy-five of the apprentices were standing in there. But instead of noise and chaos, Carmen had the strange impression that they were waiting for her.

So strange it was, she thought her imagination must be firing in step with her perceptions, but this was how it seemed to her: It seemed like the crowd parted for her and made a path to the spot on the board where the cast list was posted. And it seemed like they were all urging her forward to look at it. And when she stood in front of it, it seemed that one character and one name were bigger and bolder than all the rest.

Perdita, it read. And next to that it said *Carmen Lowell*.

❈   ❈   ❈

She hadn't said yes, Lena said to herself as she got out of the shower the morning after her dinner at Leo's loft. Maybe she had indicated assent, but she hadn't said the word *yes*.

He would be so disappointed if she backed out.

She looked at her naked self in the steamy mirror. The mirror was too small to see all of herself, which was just as well.

She was a prude. She had to admit it. She was modest. Overly modest. She was Greek. Her parents were traditional. She couldn't even look at herself without feeling embarrassed.

She tried to imagine Leo seeing her like this. Just the thought flooded and fizzled her circuits. How could she actually do it?

She was uptight. She wished she weren't so uptight. What was the problem, anyway? Her body was fine. She wasn't overweight or awkwardly built. There were no major patches of cellulite, as far as she knew. She didn't have hair in unexpected places. Her nipples went in the right direction. What was the big problem?

She wished she were more like Bee. Bee showered in the staff locker room at soccer camp next to guys she barely even knew. When Lena gawped and stuttered in disbelief at this revelation, Bee just ignored her. "It's not that big a deal," she said.

She thought back to Kostos and the swimming episode in Greece the summer they'd met. For a girl who liked to keep covered, fate had played a couple of pretty mean jokes on Lena.

To: Carmabelle@hsp.xx.com
From: Beezy3@gomail.net
Subject: YAAAAA!!!

Carma! I screamed so loud when I read your message my co-digger almost called an ambulance.

I am so proud of you!

Set builder turned star. You can't keep your darn light hidden, can you?

If it didn't come on Tuesday, Tibby would buy a pregnancy test.

If it didn't come on Wednesday she would buy a pregnancy test.

If it didn't come on Thursday.

If not by Friday.

Tibby stood in Duane Reade on Saturday morning. She studied the box as though it were a cobra. Aptly, it was kept behind the counter, behind Plexiglas. You couldn't just snatch it from the shelf and toss it facedown on the counter. They made you ask for it. How could she ask? She tried the question in her mind. *Can I have the blllllllll? One of the rrrrrrr, please? The box with the mmmmm?*

If she couldn't think it, what were the chances she could say it?

The nearest salesperson was a man with extravagant sideburns. She couldn't ask him. She'd come back.

She touched her belly. Her fingers related to it differently than at other times.

She walked outside. She looked up. The sun carried on its serene business of exploding, unmuffled by a single cloud. She had a free day, a blue sky, but she felt a throttling sense of claustrophobia. There was nowhere to go where the worry wouldn't go. Not even sleeping gave her respite.

Her legs went along and she found herself in Washington Square Park. Clumps of friends hung by the central fountain. A man and a woman kissed on a bench. Tibby wondered if part of what she felt was loneliness.

She thought of her friends. She felt a melting sensation in her muscles begetting a looser kind of sadness.

Oh, you guys. I had sex! I'm not a virgin! Can you believe that? I did it. We did it!

But then there was the other part of the story, inseparable from the first. Tibby was a natural believer in the other shoe dropping, and this time it had really clobbered her. It had turned happiness into agony, love into umbrage.

Wasn't that just how the world worked? You had sex for the first time with a person you really loved and the condom broke, leaving you most likely *prrrrr.*

Cynicism was a great hedge, of course. When the bad thing came true, at least you had the pleasure of being right. But that pleasure felt cold today. She didn't want to be right. For the first time in her life, she longed to be wrong.

"Do you know what time it is?" a young man in a corduroy cap asked her.

"I have no idea," she replied. She could have looked at her cell phone, but she didn't.

She couldn't make herself sit down anyplace. She walked past Duane Reade again.

Did she really have to buy the test? She couldn't. Did she have to find out? Maybe she could just play dumb for the next nine months. How far could she take the denial? She could be one of those girls who gave birth in the bathroom between classes.

She walked downtown. She crossed Houston Street and headed into deepest SoHo, packed as it was with shoppers. Tourists flocked here for the supposed urban grit, but all they found was each other.

She walked all the way to Canal Street, dipped briefly into Chinatown. She passed the stairwell to a second-floor restaurant where she'd once eaten gelatinous, scary, and delicious things with Brian and two of the girls from her hall. They'd sat at a table by the big picture window and watched the snow fall that night. Now it was ninety-five degrees. That night she'd been happy and now she felt miserable. Tibby turned north again. Her legs led her, without asking, back to Duane Reade. She paced in front of the store. She couldn't go in and buy the thing, but she couldn't do anything else. Denial could be very absorbing.

She walked past a homeless woman for the third time. She reached into her bag and found a five-dollar bill. As the puffy-faced woman graciously accepted the money, Tibby wondered what had happened to this woman. Why had she ended up like this?

Tibby put her head down and walked on. Probably all started with a teenage pregnancy.

Peter was as crazy about the dirt floor as she was. Usually Bridget was attracted to people who were more solid than she, but in this case it was the feeling of finding a soul mate that really got to her.

It was Sunday. Everyone else had gone to the beach. Bridget and Peter were left at the site, working on their floor.

"You two are crazy," Alison had commented before she left. They had both nodded acceptingly.

They were more than two-thirds done. They had cleared and exposed a generous square room, a source of excitement to everyone at the site, finding two perfectly beautiful and intact late-sixth-century Attic pots and the pieces to comprise at least five more. It had turned out to be a bigger find, a more prosperous house, than even the director had imagined. Other members of the team had worked on the walls, exposing patches of plaster and the suggestion of a fresco.

"I don't know what I'll do with my life after we finish this thing," Bridget said musingly, her hands alive in the dirt.

"I know what you mean," Peter said.

"I love it. I'll miss it. I think my life's meaning will be gone."

He nodded. He didn't act like this was so strange. He was as consumed, moment by moment, as she was.

"This is a satisfying way to dig, you know?" he said. His voice was a bit lazy under the hot sun. "It's not always like this."

"I'm spoiled."

"You've had a lucky start," he agreed.

"I am lucky," she heard herself say.

"Are you?"

"Yes. In all but the important ways."

He stopped and sat back. "What does that mean?" For days he'd been disinclined to look right at her, but now he did.

She put both hands flat on her dirt floor. "My mom died when I was pretty young." It was always clarifying to get that out there. She always knew she was somewhere once she'd said it out loud. It was like her version of scent marking.

"I'm sorry."

"Yeah. Thanks." The fact of her mother's death seemed to connect to her dirt floor, but she wasn't sure how.

"That's why you don't like to talk about your family."

I don't have a family to talk about, she was going to say, but she realized that it wasn't true. She did have a family. They were all under twenty and none of them related to her by blood, but they made her who she was. They represented the best of her. "I have an unconventional family," she told him.

He left her alone with the digging for a while. She appreciated that.

"These people lived big, I think," he said, after the sun had begun to dip. "They painted their pots, they painted their walls, they made their sanctuaries and told their stories on every surface they had."

"They did, didn't they?" she said wistfully. She was starting to feel tired.

"That's why I picked this specialty, instead of something closer to home, as I probably should have done. These people left so much of themselves for us to find."

She nodded and yawned. She sat back against the wall to rest in the shade. In these long days outside, the sun had turned her skin brown and her hair a whiter yellow.

She thought of her own house, where she lived as small as possible. What could an archaeologist ever find of her? Of her mother? They told their stories nowhere. What about the old photographs, their old things? Where were they now? Had her father thrown them all away?

She crawled back on her hands and knees to where she'd left her love, the floor. She'd go slower. She'd make it last.

"Hey, what are these?" she asked. She rubbed off the dirt and passed the heavy pieces of metal into Peter's hands.

He studied them carefully. "You know what they are?"

She shook her head, even though it was a biding-time kind of question.

"I think they're loom weights. I've seen pictures, but I've never found any before." He seemed excited about them. "Make sure you record the location."

She nodded. She wiped her hands on her shorts and took the digital camera out of her pocket. She took out her Sharpie to make the label.

"You know what this makes me think?"

"No," she said.

"It gives me an idea of this room, what it was. The orientation of it, away from where we think the road was. The kind of pots we've found. Now these."

She waited patiently. She let him think and talk.

"I'm guessing it was the gynaikonitis. We'll talk to David when he gets back. He'll be thrilled with this."

"What do you call it?"

"It means the women's quarter. Big houses had them. Men didn't like to let women be seen in public or even in their own homes. Women usually stayed in a remote part of the house where they wouldn't be seen."

"Why?" Bridget asked.

"Why? Because—" He paused to think. "Because men are jealous, I guess. What else is there?" He looked at her with a certain frankness. Maybe too much frankness. "We are jealous, fallible creatures. We look in our hearts and that's what we see."

"Hello?"

There was one reason Tibby picked up the phone Sunday evening and one reason only: She was waiting for a soup delivery and she thought the security guard was calling her room to tell her to come down to get it.

"Hello? Tibby? Are you there?"

She never would have picked up if she'd known it was Lena.

"Tibby? It's me. Please talk to me. Are you there?"

At the sound of Lena's voice, Tibby felt the long-suspended tears take position. Up came the worry, the misery. Up, up, and over. Tibby tried to keep her noises to herself. She held the phone away. A tear made a dot on the thigh of the Traveling Pants. One dot and then another. Her body was shaking. A sob made it out.

"Tibby. I'm here. I'm not in a hurry. Just say something so I know you're there."

Lena's softness opened Tibby up in a way that sharpness never could. She tried to suck in enough air to make a word. Her nose was full of snot and tears. Her hand was wet from wiping it. The thing that came out was more of a gurgle than a word.

"Okay, Tib. That's good. I hear you. You don't have to say anything if you don't want."

Tibby nodded and cried. Discordantly she remembered how she once yelled at her little sister, Katherine, for nodding into the phone rather than saying yes.

"I'll just hang out here for a while," Lena said.

"Okay," Tibby gurgled.

Tibby thought of the times in middle school, before IM'ing really caught on, when they would hang around for hours on the phone playing songs for each other, watching TV shows together.

She thought of the nights she would stay on the phone with Carmen when Carmen's mom had to work late and Carmen thought she heard noises in the apartment. More than once Tibby had fallen asleep with the phone beside her on the pillow.

Tibby struggled to make some words, if only not to be

spooky. "I'm scared — I could be — I might be — " The critical word drowned in salt water. She couldn't get it out.

Lena hummed in sympathy. Most people when they sensed a crisis got despotically curious, needing to stake out the far boundary of trouble. Tibby appreciated that Lena wasn't doing that.

Lena was patient while she cried. It took a long time.

"Lenny. I'm a mess," Tibby said finally. She laughed and accidentally blew her nose at the same time. She was a mess, but even so, she felt a tiny bit closer to sane for admitting it.

"I'm coming, okay?"

"You don't need to."

"I want to. It's easy to."

"Are you sure?"

"Yeah."

Tibby sighed.

"Is there anything I can bring?" Lena asked.

Tibby thought. "Actually, there is."

"What?"

Tibby tried to clear her throat. "Do you think you could bring a pregnancy test?"

"I thought I was going to be working on sets, actually," Carmen said to the loosely assembled group drinking iced coffee together on the steps of the theater Sunday evening.

"I heard you didn't even try out for the other two plays," said Michael Skelley, a guy from the floor below her.

A certain myth was developing around Carmen's ascent,

she recognized, and she was trying to both cultivate it and set the record straight at the same time. "Only because I didn't think I was going to try out for any of them. I was watching auditions and Judy told me to read Perdita. That's kind of how it started."

Many heads nodded.

"So what's Ian O'Bannon like?" Rachel asked.

He was the well-known Irish stage actor playing Leontes.

Carmen laughed. "I'm still getting up my nerve to say something to him. At the first read-through you would have thought he'd been playing Leontes for the last twenty years."

It was strange having all these people look at her, after having almost no one look at her for months. They didn't know she was adrift in the world, standing outside the current and watching it go by. They didn't know it, maybe, because she didn't feel that way right now.

These people were excited for her. They had all made a point of congratulating her. They didn't know that she was lost and undeserving.

There was really only one person who hadn't congratulated her and did not appear to be happy for her. That one person did know she was lost and undeserving, and unfortunately, that one person happened to be her friend.

Julia had been cast in the Community Stage production. A choral bit called "Winter" at the very end of the play, wherein she was supposed to dress up like an owl.

Carmen wondered if Judy harbored a certain vitriol for girls she had seen too many times a day.

One must have a good

memory to keep the

promises one has made.

—Friedrich Nietzsche

Tibby cried into her soup when it finally came. "I'm scared I'm pregnant," she told it. The carrots and peas made no reply, but she felt better for having told them.

She fell asleep in her clothes. In the morning she changed into her pajamas. She waited for Lena in her pajamas. And then she got too impatient for the sight of Lena's face, so she waited in her pajamas in the lobby instead.

Her underwear felt damp. She registered this almost absently, but she was now too fixed on Lena's coming to go up and check.

Tibby was standing at the glass door when Lena turned the corner. Tibby went out to the sidewalk and nearly mowed her down. She wasn't sure if Lena looked more surprised by her clobbering hug or the sight of her pajamas on the bright New York City sidewalk.

Lena held her hand as they went up in the elevator.

"Can you hang on a minute?" Tibby asked when they arrived on her floor.

"Sure."

Tibby went into the bathroom and came out again less than five seconds later.

"Guess what?" She felt as though her whole body had come undone.

"What?"

"Something got here right before you." She wanted to keep from smiling, but she couldn't help it.

"Really?"

"Yeah."

"I guess we don't need this, then," Lena said happily, holding up the plastic drugstore bag.

Tibby took the box out and studied it. It had struck such terrible fear in her in the store. Now it wasn't scary. "Man, these are expensive."

"Do you think it will stay good for a decade or two?" Lena asked.

"You keep it," Tibby said. "I don't think I could." She suddenly felt so tired, as though she hadn't a bone in her body. She fell onto her bed.

"So," said Lena. She couldn't be expected to hold off forever. "Are you ready to tell the tale?"

Tibby was. She lay on her bed while Lena sat in the chair by the window. Tibby talked and Lena took out her sketchbook and drew Tibby's bare feet while she listened. Tibby rode every cramp with the pleasure of a surfer after a hurricane.

What relief. *I will remember this feeling,* she promised herself, *I really will. I won't take anything for granted again.*

On Thursday Nora began a new four-week pose. They drew numbers to pick their spots and Lena got third. She tucked herself up close. She worried through the rest of the picks about another student encroaching on her space. She felt like a bullfrog, swelling up to look as big and dangerous as possible every time a classmate came near.

Leo had the fourteenth and last pick. He set up, to Lena's astonishment, on a low stool right at Lena's knees. She thought he was kidding at first. She would have been furious had it been anyone else, but when the pose began he started broadly blocking out the figure, and she was electrified.

Lena could see the model without any obstruction. She could also see the whole of Leo's back and hands and canvas. She could watch him work. Had he any idea how much she wanted this? How much she knew she could learn from him?

She watched him breathlessly at first. And when she began to paint, she drew such intensity from his work, she felt as though she had connected her mind to his by a broadband cable and she was conducting a download.

Yes, she was impatient with her old work and her old standards. She was full of self-criticism. But she wasn't pessimistic. She hadn't known the possibilities then. Now she was seeing them right in front of her.

They worked straight through the breaks, both she and

Leo. By four o'clock Lena's arm was aching and her legs were asleep, but she didn't care. The rhythm of her painting life was marked by breakthroughs, and she'd had more today than in the course of the entire school year.

She and Leo packed up silently and walked out together. It was hard to come down. She was speechless with stimulation and gratitude and excitement. She was like a closet packed too full. If you pulled one thing out, the rest would tumble after.

He seemed to know how she was feeling. He put a hand on her arm by way of good-bye. "I'll see you Saturday," he said.

That night as Lena lay in her bed, her body and her head were achingly full. She wasn't sure under what categories to store these different feelings.

There was desire. Maybe love. Or lust. There was the excitement of the breakthrough. The visitation of the art spirit. How these things fit together she didn't know.

In rare nights of swollen-hearted yearning (as painful as they were sweet), she allowed herself to fall asleep to amorous thoughts of Kostos: the things they had done, the things she fantasized they had done, the things she imagined they would do if they ever had the chance to be together again, impossible though that was.

Tonight she let the amorous images roll. But tonight she thought of Leo.

Bridget sat in the field laboratory doing some cursory recording and paperwork. She stamped and mailed a letter

177

to Greta and waited to use the computer. She hadn't checked her e-mail in four days. Eric was probably wondering what happened to her.

She let big parts of days, whole days, go by without thinking of him. How could she let herself do that? Well, she was occupied with her floor, of course. But more worryingly, whenever she was around Peter, she let herself forget about Eric. That was wrong.

Almost since the day Eric had left for Mexico, she had been unable to picture his face. It was puzzling. She could sort of see the outline of his head, the general shape of his hair, but the middle was a blur. Why was that? She could picture people she didn't care about. She could easily picture the fat-faced bursar at school. She could picture her roommate Aisha's older sister, who had visited once. Why couldn't she picture her own boyfriend? Why couldn't she hold Eric in her mind when he was not with her? She knew intellectually that she loved him, but she couldn't find a way to *feel* it just now.

And why not? Why couldn't she reconstruct feelings that were so powerful when she was in his presence?

Because he wasn't in her presence.

Was there something wrong with her heart? Was it failing to function? Did nothing get to her?

She thought of Peter and felt her heart kick up. No, it was working. It was working all too well.

But it was a limited heart, she realized, a literal heart that seemed to beat only in the present tense. Like desert air, it couldn't hold on to heat once the sun was gone. Like a sluice, it seemed to work in one direction—forward, not back.

What would she write to Eric? What would she say? Would he detect that her tone was forced or evasive? Was he jealous? Was he fallible?

A guy named Martin came out of the office as she stood up to go in. "Don't bother," he said. "The satellite system is down."

"No e-mail at all?" she asked.

He shook his head.

Guiltily, she felt happy to have the excuse rather than sad to have the problem. She passed Peter on her way out. "Is the hookup still down?" he asked her.

She nodded. "I hadn't realized."

"Since this morning," he said. "We're cut off, I'm afraid."

On her way through the lab she checked the mortuary section. "How's my girl Clytemnestra?" she asked the main biologist, Anton.

He seemed to enjoy the fly-by visits from Bridget. "We've got all of her. We're doing some good work."

"Like what?" she asked breezily.

"How old she was, what she ate, how she died."

"Really. How did she die?"

"In childbirth."

Bridget felt her face changing. "You can tell that?"

"Not with certainty. But it's likely."

She nodded. "How old was she?"

"Probably around nineteen or twenty."

Bridget's step was heavier as she left the lab than when she'd entered. She found herself wondering whether Clytemnestra's baby had lived. What if they found a tiny skeleton as well? Would they call the fearless Bridget over for that?

Bridget bowed her head low passing the gravesite. Clytemnestra was thousands of years old, but it occurred to Bridget that she would always be nineteen or twenty.

Oh, Lordy, Bee.

I've got a lot of stuff to tell you. I think your e-mails might not be getting through. I can't write it in this letter, but call me soon, okay?

Have fun with these here Pants and don't do anything I wouldn't do. Which should severely limit your options. But, ahem, may include one thing you might not THINK you could do but which I might in fact be capable of doing or even have done. Hint, hint.

Did I just write that sentence?

Love you,
Tibby

❁   ❁   ❁

"Maybe not this weekend," Tibby found herself saying to Brian over the phone.

"I could come just for Sunday."

"I have to work on Sunday. And also, I have to get my stuff ready for classes starting on Monday."

"Oh. Right."

She could hear Brian walking around his room. She knew the tread of his shoes, the creaky sound of the floor, and the particular ratio of carpet to wood.

"I could just come for the night on Wednesday," he suggested.

Why couldn't Brian see that he should let it go for a while? Why was he so obtuse?

"Midweek isn't good," she pronounced. If he was going to be obtuse, she wasn't going to bother with intricate excuses.

"Next weekend, then."

"Maybe."

She heard him pacing. "Tibby?"

"Yeah?"

"The thing we were really worried about . . ."

He wanted her to interrupt him, to put words in the blank, but she did not oblige.

"You said before . . . you're not . . . worried anymore?"

"No. I told you. I think it's okay."

She'd been so joyful at this news on Sunday. Why couldn't she let him be a part of it? She was stingy with the bad news and even stingier with the good.

She hung up the phone and sat on her floor, wondering. Why was she annoyed at him? Her period was full force; she was no longer afraid of pregnancy. No foul, no fault. (Or how did that go?) Why couldn't she go back to feeling happy? She'd thought the single red spot on her underwear would put everything back to right, but it hadn't. Why not?

It was as though something inside Tibby had gotten turned in the wrong direction.

The uncertainty in his voice, the number of times he called, his desperate desire for reassurance. Why did this bother her so much?

But strangely, this question she meant to ask was undermined by a deeper question she didn't mean to ask: Why hadn't it bothered her before?

Leo appeared, as a good model should, at exactly the designated hour of nine o'clock.

Lena opened the door to her tiny dorm room and let him in. She'd been sitting on her bed in her quiet room for the preceding twenty minutes, hands sweating, mind blank.

She could not hide her nervousness. There was no point.

"You ready?" he asked. Was his voice pitched slightly higher than usual?

"I think so," she squeaked. She gestured toward her French easel, upon which was perched her freshly gessoed eighteen-by-twenty-four-inch canvas. Her palette was ready. Her paints were assembled.

With him inside it, her room was almost comically small.

How, exactly, was this going to work? How could she get far enough away to see more than three inches of his rib cage? She hadn't thought this through very well. (She couldn't even manage to think about it.)

"Should I be . . . on the bed?" he asked. He was uncertain too. His uncertainty made her both more terrified and slightly more in control. Somebody had to steer the ship.

"I thought . . . yes. Only—"

"Yeah, you can't exactly—"

"Yeah, it's pretty close."

"What if I . . ."

He tried lying across the bed a few different ways, clothes blessedly on. Each time she found herself staring directly, and at close range, into his crotch.

Somewhere deep inside, Lena knew this was funny, but so panicked was she, she could no more access a laugh than if she were in the middle of a plane crash.

He seemed to recognize this. He sat up. "What about a seated pose?" he said.

He tried a few of those.

Lena backed up as far as she could. With his help she moved her dresser and sat with her back pressed against the wall. She shook her head. "I think this only works if we cut a hole in the wall and I paint you from Dana Trower's room."

He shrugged. "Dana might not go for it."

Was it too soon to give up? They'd given it the old summer-school try. Maybe they could just go have another iced coffee.

"I think I know the answer," he said.

Iced coffee? She cleared her throat. "What's that?"

"Foreshortening."

"Yeah?"

He dragged her bed to the end of the room. "I'll show you."

He positioned her easel in the corner. Then he lay on the bed, his head closest to her, his feet farthest away.

She stood at her easel and looked at him lying there. It was a strange angle. She would have to paint his shoulder and his head very big and his feet very small. His shoulder was like giant Greenland in one of those projected world maps, and his feet were way down there, little, like the Cape of Good Hope. But then again, his private areas would be somewhat less apparent in this pose. Like maybe Ecuador.

This was about as good as could be hoped for.

"I think this will work," she said.

"Okay. Good."

"Okay."

"Okay, so I'll just . . ."

"Okay." She looked down at her paints, her cheeks flaming. She was such a baby. What would Bee say?

He sat up and pulled his T-shirt over his head. She kept her head down. "I've never done this before. It's kind of strange."

She couldn't even make a noise come out.

"It seems so ordinary for the models in the studio, you know?"

She nodded, still staring at her cadmium red.

"I mean, it's just a pose. It's for a painting." He talked himself through the unbuttoning and removal of his jeans.

"Yeah," she attempted to say, but it came up more phlegm than word.

Was he really going to take off his underwear? Arg. She was such a baby.

"Hey. It's not like there's something else going on here...." His voice faded uncertainly. He tripped out of his underwear and was lying on the bed in under one second.

How could she look? How could she concentrate on painting?

He didn't think there was anything going on here? She thought there was something going on here!

Her face was sweating. Her hands were sweating and also shaking. She tried to hold the brush. If she lifted the brush, he would see how badly her hand was shaking.

He said there wasn't anything else going on here. Hey. What was that supposed to mean?

"All set," he said. "Can you time the pose?"

No. She couldn't. She couldn't do anything. She couldn't even make her eyeballs move in their sockets.

"Are you okay?" he asked. She registered that his voice was actually quite sweet.

She tried to shift her weight. "I'm Greek," she said finally. Her catchall. For garlic, for shame.

"Oh." There was some understanding in the way he said it. "Can you try to think of me as a regular model in class?"

She made her eyes shift upward slowly. His shoulder,

his face. His face was flushed, like hers, though not sweating as profusely. Their eyes met for a moment, which was not what she intended.

He didn't think there was anything else going on here?

This was not how she felt when Nora posed. This was not how she felt when Marvin posed. Not even a twenty-millionth of this.

Her indignation kept her eyes up, though her pupils did not focus. She clamped her fingers around her brush and aimed it at the canvas. It was not a good technique. She made some clumsy strokes.

Too flustered to look at her canvas, she looked at him. Frying pan to fire. She looked down his body, down all the golden skin. Oh, my. She saw what was there. How could she not? It wasn't Ecuador. It was more Brazil.

She looked away quickly. There was too something else going on here.

She let her brush rest on the palette.

"Let's take a break," he said.

And if the blind lead the

blind, both shall fall into

the ditch.

—Matthew 15:14

"You'd be so lean, that blasts of January
Would blow you through and through.—Now, my fair'st
     friend,
I would I had some flowers o' the spring, that might
Become your time of day—"

C armen looked up, caught her breath.

In spite of the fact that Polixenes was played by an
actor Carmen had seen in at least four movies, he bore an
almost uncanny resemblance to her uncle Hal. As she stood
across from him, she tried to pretend he was Uncle Hal, because otherwise she felt too nervous. He nodded at her to
keep going.

"That wear upon your virgin branches yet
Your maidenheads growing:—O Proserpina,

For the flowers now, that, frighted, thou lett'st fall
From Dis's waggon!"

She was addressing herself now to Florizel, her supposed love interest. He was at least ten years older than
she, wore cakey makeup, and seemed frankly more interested in Polixenes.

She was relieved when they finally got to take a break.
They were now in rehearsals almost ten hours a day and
costume fittings at other times.

She saw Leontes where he'd been watching from the side
of the stage and nervously attempted to swing wide around
him. He was so magnificent that she had not yet drawn up
the courage to say a word to him that wasn't one of Perdita's.

The swing did not work. He was looking directly at her.

"Carmen, that was absolutely lovely," he said to her as
she scuttled along like a baby turtle racing for the sea.

"Thank you," she squeaked in response, perspiring from
every one of her pores.

But outside, she couldn't keep down her joy. "Lovely,"
he had said. "Absolutely lovely."

"Absolutely lovely." That was what he said. She laughed
to nobody. The armpits of her T-shirt were soaked through
in a way that was not absolutely lovely.

It was astounding to her. It really was. She had never in
her life felt like she was naturally gifted at anything. In the
past she had felt like she'd worked, willed, begged, bossed,
or stolen everything she'd ever gotten.

She was good at math because she spent twice as many

hours on it as the people who weren't. She scored well on her SATs because she studied vocabulary lists and took practice tests every week for two years. She got an A in physics because she sat to the right of Brian Jervis, an overachieving lefty who never covered his test paper.

And now here she was, managing with little discernable effort to be absolutely lovely.

The joy of it. The loveliness.

Prince Mamillius came out the side door. When he saw her he sat down next to her. She couldn't remember his actual name. Though he was technically her brother in the play, he died before she was born, so they didn't share the stage.

"How's it going?" he asked.

When he was the prince, he spoke in pristine Shakespearean English, but when he wasn't, she was amused to hear, his accent was more like central New Jersey.

"Good," she said. He had a tattoo of a badger on his ankle. He was actually very cute.

"Nice flowers," he said.

Carmen lifted her hand to her ear. Andrew Kerr had asked her to wear flowers in her hair during the romancing scene to prepare for her elaborate costume as Flora. "Oh." She felt stupid, and then she decided she didn't.

He leaned over, very close to her, and smelled them. "Yum," he said. She could feel his breath on her hair.

"Can I get you a lemonade?" he asked, standing up again. He was a jumpy sort of person.

She thought of saying no, but then she said yes. "I'd love that," she said.

He raised his eyebrows at her before he turned to walk away. She realized in slow motion that Prince Mamillius, her own brother, had most likely just flirted with her.

Three hours later, Lena had squished several dollars' worth of paint around on a perfectly well-made canvas. She had wasted both, as well as Leo's time. Her painting wasn't even a painting. Her sister, Effie, would have made a better painting.

For the third hour, Lena's cheeks smoldered deep purple. There was no way she could let him look at her so-called painting.

"Let's call it quits for the day," she said defeatedly.

"Are you sure?" He didn't sound opposed.

"Yeah."

He was undeniably awkward too. "Sorry I'm not a better model."

"No. No, you're fine. It's just."

She washed her brushes in the bathroom while he got dressed. When she came back they sat side by side on her bed.

"That didn't go quite as well as I'd hoped," he said.

She breathed out in relief. That he was dressed. That she wasn't trying to hold a paintbrush.

"It's my fault," she said.

"No, it's not."

They were quiet for a while.

"Are you a virgin?" he asked.

She looked at him in surprise.

"Sorry. That's getting kind of personal, I know. Don't answer if you don't want."

She didn't want to answer at first. But his face was nice. He looked at her intently. He wore his own version of disarray, and his was beautiful.

"That's okay. God. Is it so obvious?"

"No. And anyway, it's nothing to be sorry for."

He put his hand over her hand. Not holding hers, quite, just lying there.

After he left, Lena fell into her bed in a heap of exhaustion and didn't move for an hour. Somewhere in the back of her mind pressed the knowledge that in the pose-trading bargain, today was the easy part.

Bridget had spent all day Saturday touring Halicarnassus, now a city called Bodrum. In the van she'd nearly made herself sick to her stomach reading books that Peter had lent her, gobbling up information spanning the time from the first settlements of the Greeks in Asia Minor all the way to the Persian invasion that nearly destroyed them.

Once inside the ruins of the city, she'd darted around to every column, every path, every step of the ancient stadium. She'd loved it, but she was happy to get back to the site, where a package from Tibby that contained the Traveling Pants was waiting for her, as was her floor.

Now she was sitting on the floor in her Pants, glad to think that they would forever harbor a few particles of this old dirt. She savored her time with both of them. And with

Peter, too. The fact that it was just her and Peter, and the satellite was still down, made her feel that much more insulated from the regular world.

There were only a few feet left to clear. They were both going slowly now.

"What time is it?" he asked. The sun had set hours before, and they'd spent a long, meditative stretch of quiet digging and sorting.

"I don't know. Do you want me to find out?"

He nodded. "Would you?"

She stood up.

"Hey, I like your pants," he said. It was like him to notice.

She went closer to him and stood in the light so he could see. "These belong to the unconventional family I mentioned."

He nodded, studying some of the pictures and inscriptions on the front. Then he grabbed her by a belt loop and slowly rotated her to look at the rest.

You are looking at my Pants, she told him silently, but she also suspected that he was looking at the shape of her underneath.

Self-consciously she climbed out of the room by the makeshift wooden stairs and went to the embankment party, which was just winding down. "Does anybody have the time?"

Darius had a watch. "Twelve-forty," he told her.

She went back down into the room to tell Peter.

193

"Guess what?" he said.

"What?"

"I'm thirty."

"Right now?"

"Forty minutes ago."

"No way! Happy birthday! That's a big one."

"Thanks." He sat back against the wall. He dusted off his hands. Suddenly he looked suspicious. "If you tell anyone I'll kill you."

"That would be kind of an overreaction."

He laughed. "You're right. But don't anyway, okay?"

"Okay." It seemed perhaps too natural that he should be sharing his secrets with her. She studied his face. Thirty didn't seem very old on him now that she knew him.

"You've got to have a cake or something, don't you?"

"I think I'll manage without it. I have a childhood fear of being sung to by strangers."

"Interesting."

"Yeah. Anyway, I'm happy to become thirty with just the floor." He stopped and looked at her. "And you."

She tried to shrug it off, but her face burned. "Thanks. I'm honored." She felt his mood wavering between heavy and light. She wasn't sure how to read him.

"Me too," he said. They didn't need to pretend they hadn't become close these weeks. That was undeniable.

She had an idea. "Okay, then. Hold on a minute."

The kitchen area of the big tent was empty, but she found a flashlight and, with the help of that, a half tray of baklava, a votive candle, and a bottle of wine. She found matches and two plastic cups and took the stash back to Peter.

Sitting across from him on their smooth floor, she poured two cups of wine. She lit the candle and set it next to the baklava. "I don't think you want me to sing," she said. "But happy birthday, my friend." She said it seriously and she meant it. It was a big deal, a big day. She glanced down at the floor as he blew out his candle and made his wish.

Because he was her friend and she felt solely responsible for bringing him into a new decade of his life, she lifted her cup to tap his and at the same time she leaned in. She wasn't sure what she meant by it. Maybe she thought she'd hug him or kiss his cheek, the way she did with lots of people.

But he misinterpreted her closeness, or maybe she did. Her cheek pressed against his cheek and then her mouth pressed against his cheek. And then he turned, whether to get closer or farther away she couldn't be sure. But the effect of it, accidentally or on purpose, was that her mouth touched his mouth.

The first touch was bumbling and awkward. The second touch was almost certainly on purpose. She felt herself pulled into the heat and smell of him. She touched his face, which you don't do with lots of people. She kissed him purposefully and she felt his purposeful hand on the back of her neck.

"That was a happy birthday kiss," she said, forcing herself to pull away. She was dizzy. She was not quite in her mind. She needed to keep alive the possibility of turning back. Did he need that too?

He stood up quickly and she followed. "Do you want to walk?" he asked her.

They both needed that. A walk, a breeze.

They walked toward the sea, up to the top of the hill and over it to a nice perch of soft brown summer grass laid out under a trillion stars.

She had the urge to run all the way down to the water and jump into it and swim for another shore. She had the urge to kiss Peter again, to throw herself against him and bury her face in his neck.

She was still wearing a filthy white tank top from the morning. She might have been cold but she couldn't feel it.

Peter took her hand in his and put them together on his thigh. "Bee."

"Yes."

"I have to confess to a very monstrous addiction to you." He said it slowly and with some deliberation. "I was hoping it wouldn't get to this, but I'm also hoping it might help to say it out loud."

She rested her cheek on her hand, looking across at him. "I have that kind of addiction too," she said.

"To the floor."

"To the floor. To you."

"To me?"

"To you." It did feel good to say it. *But will it really help?*

"I shouldn't be happy about that," he said, appearing to defy his words as he said them.

"No. And I shouldn't either."

She felt her hair fluttering in the light wind, tickling his arm, working its magic. She wasn't sure she wanted more magic right now.

"It's very tricky . . . ," he began slowly, his speech punctuated by consideration and a few uneasy breaths, "not to feel like I'm falling in love with you now. It's such a strong feeling and a good feeling having you right here like this. Looking at you, it's hard to keep in my mind the reasons why I can't."

"Do you want to talk about them?"

He looked genuinely unhappy for a moment. "No."

She looked at him with the hint of a challenge in her eyes. "Then what do you want?"

The reckless happiness was creeping back. He couldn't help himself. He was like her. He couldn't keep it down. "Do you really want to know?"

She nodded, knowing she shouldn't. She shouldn't have asked. She shouldn't want to know.

"Here's what I want to do. I want to pull you on top of me and roll you down this hill. Then I want to take off your clothes and kiss every part of you. And then I want to make passionate love to you on the grass right there." He pointed to a place near the bottom of the hill. "And then I want to fall asleep holding you. And then I want to wake up when the sun is rising and do it all again."

She kept her eyes closed for a minute. These were dangerous places they were passing through. How could she not picture it and feel it and want it the way he said it?

"And what will you do?" she asked, her voice hardly above a whisper.

She could practically see the opposing forces duking it out in his head. She wasn't sure which side was winning or even which side she was rooting for.

A weariness came into his eyes, giving her a clue. "We'll kiss, because it's my thirtieth birthday and it's what I've been wishing for. And then I'll walk you to your cabin and say goodnight."

"Okay," she said, happy and sad.

He did kiss her. He rolled her over onto the grass and kissed her passionately. His hands reached under her shirt to press against her naked back. She felt the strength of his longing and it made her woozy.

She sat up before they could be sucked into the next phase of what he wanted.

They held hands on the way back to camp. He kissed her on the cheek at the entrance to her cabin.

"You better get out of here before this thing goes the other way," he whispered in her ear. "You know, the rolling-down-the-hill way."

She nodded against his cheek. "Happy birthday, mister," she said out of the side of her mouth as if she were Mae West.

And so she lay on her crappy metal cot in a cloud of desire. But even in her cloud she perceived a buffeting sensation, a brooding feeling of discomfort beneath her.

They had withstood this night for the most part, but what about the next one and the one after that?

She had the taste of him now. She had the feel of his

body. They had said things you couldn't forget and couldn't take back. All the ordinary boundaries between them lay in ruins. What was going to keep them apart now? She feared they had both seen the place where they could have turned back and, knowingly, they had passed it by.

Experience is a hard

teacher because she gives

the test first,

the lesson afterward.

—Vernon Law

Leo looked surprised to see Lena at the door of his loft on Sunday morning. She was surprised to be there.

"I wasn't sure you'd come," he said.

"I wasn't either."

"I'm glad you did," he added. He did look happy, and also uncertain. He was looking at her in a different way.

"I'm nervous," she said honestly. "But fair is fair."

His eyes on her were different. She couldn't say why. "You are fair," he said. "But you don't have to do it."

She smiled nervously. "Thanks."

"Do you want a cup of coffee?"

"Sure." She considered the state of her nervous system. "Maybe tea," she mumbled, following him into the kitchen.

He put the kettle on and sat down. Northern light—artists' light—fell all around them from the high windows.

"Where's your mom?" Lena asked.

"She volunteers all day at our church," Leo said. "I thought the privacy might make it easier."

She nodded.

"But I understand if you don't want to."

"Okay."

She sat and thought.

He looked at her, his elbow resting on the table, his chin in his hand. When she saw him looking, he smiled. She smiled back.

She thought of drinking her tea and going back home. She thought of staying here and taking off her clothes and letting Leo paint her. The second alternative didn't seem possible, but in a strange way, neither did the first. She had the odd sense of pushing off the edge into unknown territory. She had already let her mind travel. There were possibilities now. It wasn't enough to go back and forget. She wasn't the forgetting type.

"I think we should try it," she said.

"You do?"

"Do you?"

"I do."

"So let's."

"If you're uncomfortable, we'll stop."

She shrugged with a laugh. "I will be uncomfortable. We'd have to stop before we start." She breathed deep. "But I think we should try it anyway."

Leo's bedroom was spacious and skylit. He had dragged a

small ruby-colored couch into the center and draped a pale yellow sheet over it. His easel was folded in the corner.

"I was thinking of here," he said a bit sheepishly. She could tell he'd made the effort to set it up more like a painting class, not just put her in his bed. "We could do it somewhere else, though."

The colors glowed. The light dusted over the drapery in a beautiful way. She could almost see the painting. "No. This is good."

He disappeared for a moment and came back with a robe, probably his mother's. He handed it to her with a question on his face. *Do you really want to do this?* "I really won't be upset with you if you don't," he said.

"I think I might be upset with me," she said.

He nodded. "It's just a painting."

It wasn't just a painting for her. She needed to do it anyway.

"I'll give you some privacy," he said.

"Not for long," she joked nervously. It was like when the doctor left the room as you undressed and dressed again. As if the nakedness weren't embarrassing if you could transition into it alone.

She took off her clothes quickly, before she could think about it and stop. Tank top and loose yoga pants and flip-flops in a pile on the floor. She was too nervous to fold them. She had dressed herself like she'd observed the models did—loose clothes for easy on and easy off. No weird red marks from a tight waistband or pinching bra strap.

She'd thought to shave her stubbly parts so she was smooth and unremarkable.

She hurriedly propelled herself into the robe. To what end? she wondered. She just had to get right back out of it. But models always had the robe. Maybe it could be like Superman's telephone booth. She'd go into the robe a terrified and prudish virgin and come out of it a seasoned artist's model.

She took the robe off. She sat on the couch. She lay on the couch. She rearranged herself on the couch. Leo knocked on the door. "You ready?"

Every one of her muscles contracted. She felt her shoulders, neck, and head fuse into one ungraceful mass. Apparently she had come out of the robe the same way she had gone in.

"Ready," she whimpered.

"Lena?"

"Ready," she said a little louder. This had the quality of a bedroom farce. She wished she could find it funny.

He was nervous too. He didn't want to affront or embarrass her by looking too quickly or too much. He occupied himself with his easel as though there weren't a naked girl in the room. She said some things about how it was hot out, also pretending there wasn't a naked girl in the room.

"Okay, my friend," he said. His paintbrush was poised in his hand. He was ready to work. He looked at her through his painter's eyes.

"Okay," she breathed. This "my friend" business might

be doing it for him, she thought sourly, but it wasn't doing it for her.

He moved the easel to the left. He pushed it a couple of feet closer to her. He came out from behind it. "Head up a little," he said, coming closer.

She did.

"Perfect." He came closer still. He was looking now. "Okay, hand more like this." He did it with his own hand rather than touch hers.

She obliged. She wished she could make her muscles soften a little.

"Beautiful," he said. He kept studying her. "Legs a little . . . looser."

She let out a nervous laugh. "Yeah, right."

He laughed too, but vaguely. She could tell he was starting to really think about painting now. Why hadn't she been able to do that when it had been her turn to paint?

"Okay. Wow." He went back to his canvas. He raised his eyebrows. She could tell he was excited. He was excited about his painting.

Bridget was crouched over her cereal bowl the next morning groggily spooning in the Frosted Flakes when she noticed the unfamiliar car pulling into the makeshift parking area. She didn't make anything of it at first. Her mind was too full and unkempt as it was.

She dimly registered the slams of a few car doors and some stir at the other end of the tent. Slowly it made its way to her.

"Have you seen Peter?" Karina asked her.

She blinked and swallowed her mouthful of cereal. "Not this morning," she said. Something about the question started the slow tick of alarm. At the far end of the tent an unfamiliar woman was talking to Alison. Then into Bridget's view bounced a very small person, a little girl with a messy ponytail that had migrated to the side of her head. It was unusual to see a child here.

None of the pieces stuck together until she saw Alison marching toward her looking agitated, which doubled for excited in the case of Alison. "Do you know where Peter is? His wife and kids are here to surprise him."

His wife and kids. They were here to surprise him. The ticking accelerated into a wild knocking. His wife and kids had popped out of their theoretical ether and appeared here. To surprise him.

For his birthday, Bridget realized, her thoughts bumping and scraping along. His secret birthday, which she had somehow believed belonged to her. It did not belong to her, she acknowledged with a messy ache in her chest. It belonged to them.

Peter's wife and kids were far enough away and backed by flooding sunlight, so she couldn't really see them.

"No. I don't know where he is," she said robotically. Suddenly she felt the shame of Eve. Why did everybody keep asking her? What did they know? What did they suspect? She wished she hadn't stayed up late all these nights. She found herself wanting to be sure that her cabinmates knew she'd woken up among them every morning.

How would his wife feel with everyone seeking information about her husband's whereabouts from the tired blond girl with the kissed lips and the starry expression? She felt the urge to defend herself, but to whom?

She was stuck there in her chair, midchew, unable to swallow her cereal or spit it out, when she heard Peter's voice somewhere behind her. She realized she needed to get out of there before this reunion took place. For her sake, but even more for Peter's. She didn't want him to see her there. She crouched lower. She momentarily considered crawling under the table and hiding.

He had a wife. A *wife*. Theoretical and now real, with dark brown hair and a canvas bag over her shoulder. A wife like you had in a real family. Kids like you had in a real family. Kids who jumped around and needed things.

In her mind she switched from identifying with the wife to identifying with the daughter. A daughter like she was a daughter. A person with wishes and disappointments of her own.

These were dangerous places indeed.

Tibby finally let Brian come that Sunday, but not for the reasons he hoped.

She intercepted him in the lobby. It would be worse if he came up to her room.

"It's pretty nice out. You feel like taking a walk?" he asked her gamely, innocently.

She used to adore his innocence. Now she wondered about him. Was he a bit stupid? No, not stupid, really. She didn't mean that. He had a high IQ and all. But was he kind of like an idiot savant?

"Yes," she said dishonestly.

Maybe, Meta-Tibby suggested, she liked his innocence better when her own heart wasn't so black.

They didn't walk far. She turned on him in the middle of Astor Place.

"Brian, I think we should take a break," she said. That was the phrase she had decided upon.

He looked at her, his head cocked like a Labrador retriever's. "What do you mean?"

"I mean, I think we shouldn't see each other for a while."

"You are saying that . . ."

The sadness and surprise was beginning to wear through his trusting expression, but she couldn't feel anything for him. She saw it, but it didn't go past her eyes. There were times in her life when she felt his pain more acutely than he did. Why not now?

"But why?" he asked.

"Because. Because . . ." This was such an obvious question and she hadn't thought up an answer for it. "I just think . . . because of the long distance and everything . . ."

"I don't mind coming up here," he said quickly.

She glared at him. *Just protect yourself and go away, would you?* She felt like shouting at him. *Get mad at me. Call me a bitch. Walk away from me.*

"I don't want you to," she said flatly. "I want to be by myself for a while. I can't even explain it very well."

He was processing. His T-shirt blew against his body. He looked thin.

Brian didn't confine himself to the mirror dance. He did what he did, he chose what he chose in the bravest possible way. She used to love this about him. But now the best thing had turned into the worst thing. She thought he rejected the dance as small-minded and fearful, but now she wondered if he even knew it. Was it rejection or total ignorance? Why, for once, couldn't he just follow her lead?

There is no such thing as too much love. That was what a doe-eyed and slightly creepy friend of her mother's had once said to Tibby, seemingly out of the blue. *Well, yeah, there is,* Tibby thought now.

"Is it because of—" he began tentatively.

"I don't even know what it's because of," she snapped. "I just know that I don't want to keep going like this."

He looked up and then he looked down. He watched people cross Lafayette Street. He considered the banner snapping over the entrance to the Public Theater. Tibby was worried he would cry, but he didn't.

"You don't want me to come up and see you anymore," he said.

"Not really. No."

"You don't want me to call you?"

"No."

Had Brian ever taken a hint? Had he always required a total clubbing over the head to make him comprehend even the most obvious point?

Suddenly she felt an insidious suspicion. She saw this

version of Brian in the eyes of the world, and she saw herself, too. Did people think he was basically a moron? Did they laugh at her for being with him?

Tibby hated herself for this cruelly disloyal thought. But who in the world has a brain she can force to think only the acceptable things?

Do I hate him? she wondered about herself. *Did I ever really love him?*

On that fateful night they'd had sex, it seemed to her that she'd fallen asleep one person and woken up another. She couldn't remember the hows and whys of who she used to be. It was bewildering. Like hypnosis or a magic spell or a dream that had broken on her waking.

"Then we should say good-bye," he said.

Her head shot up. She could see by his face he understood now. She could see it in his eyes. They were no less hurt, but they had stopped questioning her.

"Y-yes. I—I guess," she stammered. If anything, he had gotten ahead of her.

She hadn't pictured him storming away, though she might have wanted that. But neither had she figured on his sticking around for a proper eye-to-eye good-bye.

"Good-bye, Tibby." He wasn't angry. He wasn't hopeful. What was he?

"Bye." Stiffly she leaned in to kiss his cheek. It felt wrong, and midway through she wished she hadn't done it.

He turned and he walked toward the subway, carrying his worn red duffel bag over his shoulder. She watched him, but he didn't turn back to look.

He walked in a way that struck her as resolute, and she recognized that she was the one left standing alone and confused.

She realized all at once the deeper thing that bothered her, the thing that made him not just irritating but intolerable: how he kept loving her blindly when she deserved it so little.

Oh, darling, let your body in,

let it tie you in,

in comfort.

—Anne Sexton

Lena realized a strange and comforting fact of life: You could get used to almost anything. You could even get used to lying naked on a ruby-colored couch under the gaze of a young man you hardly knew while he painted you. You could do that even if you happened to be a Greek virgin from a conservative family whose father would die if he knew.

For the first hour, Lena agonized.

Sometime in the second hour, her muscles began to un-kink, one at a time.

In the third hour, something else happened. Lena began to watch Leo. She watched him paint. She watched him watch her. She saw how he looked at her different parts. She kept track of which part he was working on, feeling a thrill in her hip when he painted that and along her thigh when he got there.

As much as she ordinarily dreaded being looked at, this

felt different. It was a different way of looking. He looked at her and through her at the same time. He only held any one image long enough to get it onto his canvas. It was like water through a sieve.

His intensity built and she began to relax. His relationship, she realized, was with his painting. He was relating to his version of her more than to the actual her. It freed her mind to wander all around the apartment. Were all relationships this way, to some extent? Whether or not they involved any artistic representation?

She liked the way the diffuse sun felt on her skin. She began to like the way his eyes felt on her skin as she became free to wander.

He put on music. It was Bach, he said. The only instrument was a cello.

In the fourth hour, he looked at her face at a moment when she was looking back. They were both surprised at first and looked away. Then, at the same moment, they both looked back. He stopped painting. He lost his way. He looked confused and then found his way back.

In the fifth hour, she stopped taking breaks. She was under a spell. She was languorous. Leo was also under a spell. They were under different spells.

In the sixth hour, she thought about him touching her. The blood that came to her cheeks was a different blood. It came for a different reason.

He put on more Bach. It was music for solo violin this time. It sounded raggedly romantic to her.

He was painting her face. "Eyes up," he said. She looked up. "I mean at me," he clarified.

Was that really what he meant? She looked at him.

And for the next hour, he looked at her and she looked back. And like in a staring contest, the stakes seemed to rise and rise until it was almost unbearable. But neither of them looked away.

When he finally put down his brush, his cheeks were as flushed as hers. He was as breathless as she. They were under the same spell.

He came over to her, still not breaking eye contact. He put his hand lightly on her rib cage and leaned down and kissed her.

In the past when Bee was overwhelmed or depressed she took to her bed. But this was too awful even for her bed. This was a more active misery, a hunt-you-down-and-find-you kind of pain. In her bed she'd be a sitting, lying duck.

Barefoot, she walked from the dining tent. Once in the clear, she spit her mush of Frosted Flakes into the grass. She was afraid she might throw up what was in her stomach as well.

She was so grateful she had left the Pants on her cot. She didn't want them to see her like this.

She walked from the camp and kept going toward the sun. She would just keep going. If you set out for the east, you could walk practically forever. To India, China.

She walked and walked and her feet grew sore. How sore they would be when they got to China.

Sometime later the sun passed over her head and she realized she was walking away from it now. She didn't want to walk away from it, but if she walked with it, she would have to turn back around, and she couldn't turn around. She shivered. Was it cold in China?

She felt like a reptile, relying on the sun to warm her blood. She didn't feel the capacity to generate her own warmth.

She had known almost from the beginning that Peter was married and had children. There had been nothing new divulged this morning. That wife and those children were no more real now than they'd ever been. But now she'd seen them. That was what destroyed her peace.

Out of sight, out of mind. How could she allow that of herself? That was for people with amnesia and brain damage. That was for newts and frogs. What was wrong with her? Why couldn't she hold things in her mind? There was no comfort to be taken from her inability, no excuse.

This was a different game she was playing. Not a playground challenge or a warm-up or a scrimmage. It was real and it counted. Peter was an adult. She was an adult. They had real lives to make or lose.

She could flit around and show off in front of the married man. She could kiss that married man and pretend it was all big, mischievous fun. But it wasn't.

As she walked she shuddered. It was time to grow up. She looked ahead of her and saw the crest of a hill. That crest stood for growing up, she decided as she willfully crossed it.

She stood up her straightest, to her full woman's height of five feet and ten and a half inches. If she didn't take her life seriously, who would? She was becoming the person she'd be for her whole life. Each thing she chose contributed to that person. She didn't want to be like this.

Carmen liked being in the theater. Even the longest, crankiest late-night rehearsal was preferable to being in her dorm room. Andrew Kerr could take her down with a look, but even at his scariest he was friendlier than her roommate.

Carmen had transformed from invisible to visible in the eyes of everyone on campus except for one person. For two long weeks, even though they shared a small room and slept within five feet of each other, Julia had acted like Carmen wasn't there.

Which was why it surprised Carmen in the third week of rehearsals when Julia turned to her and said, "How's the play going?"

Carmen was pulling off her socks at the moment it happened, exhausted but also excited at having tried on her costume for the first time.

"It's going pretty well. At least, I hope so."

"How is it working with Ian O'Bannon?" Julia asked.

She asked this like they'd been having friendly chats night and day. Carmen was scared to believe it was actually happening.

"He's . . . I don't even know what he is. Every day I think I can't be more amazed and then I am."

"Wow. Lucky you, you get to work with him."

Carmen sifted through these words, girding herself for jeering or sarcasm, but she didn't hear it.

"It is really lucky," Carmen said warily.

"It's like . . . the experience of a lifetime," Julia said.

Again Carmen weighed these words, studied Julia's face. Julia's face, which had seemed so beautiful and commanding at one time and now seemed furtive. The qualities Carmen had most admired in her seemed extreme now. She was too thin, too poised, too careful.

"I think it is," Carmen said.

Carmen fell asleep that night wondering what had brought about the thaw, scared to trust it, but more than anything, grateful that it had happened.

So that when she woke up the next morning, she was still doubtful, though still hopeful.

"You should wear those green pants. They look really good on you," Julia said when Carmen was rummaging through her drawer.

Carmen turned. "You think so?"

"Yeah."

"Thanks." Carmen put on the green pants even though she didn't think they looked so good.

"What are you rehearsing today?" Julia asked.

Carmen counseled herself to take the friendliness at face value and just be glad for it. "I think it'll be Leontes going bonkers for the first part. Perdita doesn't even come in until act four, scene four, but Andrew wants me to watch. 'Watch and absorb,' he always says, and he shakes his fingers over my head. He thinks that's entertaining for some reason."

"He's kind of an oddball, isn't he?" Julia said.

"He is," Carmen said, though she suddenly felt protective of his oddness. "I have no experience or anything, but I think he's a good director."

Julia could easily have said something cutting then, but she didn't. "He's got a huge reputation," she said.

"Does he?"

"Oh, yeah."

"Huh." This was enough pleasant conversation to last Carmen for the week, but Julia kept going.

"I can read with you if you ever want some extra practice," she said.

Carmen looked at her carefully. "That's nice. Thanks. I'll let you know."

"Seriously, any time," Julia said. "My part in *Love's Labour's* is not exactly consuming, you know?"

Carmen didn't want to be caught agreeing. "You have the last word, though. That's a big deal."

"As an owl."

"Well."

Julia's expression was openly rueful. "R.K., our director, asked me if I'd give a thought to helping with sets during my downtime."

Carmen tried to keep her expression neutral. "What did you say?"

"I said that sets really aren't my thing."

Carmabelle: Wow, Leo's black?
LennyK162: Yeah. Half, anyway.
Carmabelle: You really are trying to kill your father.
LennyK162: Pretty much any color boyfriend would do it.
Carmabelle: Does Leo identify more with his black side or his white side?
LennyK162: What?
Carmabelle: I'm a woman of color. I'm allowed to ask these things.
LennyK162: I still don't know what you're talking about.
Carmabelle: Okay, does he listen to U2?

Bridget ended up that evening not in China, but on her dirt floor with a bad sunburn stinging her shoulders.

She was glad to have her floor again. She had worried that the joy of her floor somehow depended on Peter, but she now realized it didn't. It was her own separate joy and could not be taken away.

She was glad to hear that Peter had gone with his family into town for dinner. She wanted to skip dinner, but she didn't want to skip it on his account.

She continued this busy overthinking, feeling it an annoying by-product of adulthood. Were people in her work team treating her too carefully?

At least her hands still knew how to seek out the floor. She was down to the final couple of feet left over from last night. She couldn't draw it out much longer.

She dug and sifted and sorted. At the final edge, her finger touched something hard. She was used to that by now. She assumed it was a piece of terra-cotta, like so many of the other bits were. She shook if off and held it up, but the sunlight was too faded to help. She felt it between her fingers. It was tiny. It wasn't porous like clay. It wasn't heavy like metal.

She recorded its provenience and hopped up the stairs to find a flashlight. Holding the little thing under the light, she felt her heart begin to thump.

She took it to the lab, glad that Anton was working late.

"What've you got?" he asked her.

She handed it to him. "I think it's a tooth." She was shaken by it. She felt a shaky chill in her abdomen.

He looked at it. He held it under magnification. "You're right."

"A baby tooth."

"It certainly is."

"Can you tell who it belonged to? I mean a boy or a girl?"

He shook his head. "You can't discern gender from any of a child's bones. Before puberty, boy skeletons and girl skeletons are exactly the same."

Why was Anton looking so jovial about this when she felt sickened by it?

"I found it in the house," she said. "In the new room." Her breathing was moist and a little bit ragged. "I expect to find this kind of stuff in mortuary, but not in the house." She really did not want to cry.

Anton looked at her carefully. "Bridget, it wasn't in mortuary because the kid didn't die."

"It didn't?"

"Or I should say, its death was not related to this tooth."

"It wasn't?"

"No." Anton smiled, apparently wanting to cajole her out of her somber face. "The tooth fell out, Bridget. It got lost on the floor. Maybe the kid's mother saved it."

Bridget was still nodding as she walked back to her floor, almost wanting to cry with relief. This person, whoever he or she was, had long, long since died. But the person hadn't died with a baby tooth. The little tooth did not represent death. It represented growing up.

I have drunk, and seen

the spider.

—William Shakespeare

"Do you miss him?" Carmen asked.

"I don't think so. I'm not sure," Tibby said, holding the phone with her shoulder and picking her big toenail. Some of the summer students were crowded around a portable video game in the hall. It was too noisy for a serious conversation.

"You're not sure?"

"No. I don't know. I was pretty sure of needing to break up with him. I don't want to see him, but I do sometimes think about whether he's going to call or something."

"Uh-huh."

"I kind of think he will, but also that he won't. Does that make any sense?"

"Uh." Carmen's voice was high in her throat. "I think so."

Tibby could tell it didn't make sense to Carmen at all, and that furthermore, nothing Tibby had said about any part of the relationship since the summer began had made one bit of sense, but that Carmen was hanging in there nonetheless.

"Do you want to talk to him about anything in particular?" Carmen asked. Carmen's patient voice was among her least convincing. Tibby found it surprising to think that she was having so much success as an actress this summer.

"No, not really," Tibby said wanly, purposeless. There was an explosion of hooting out in the hall.

Most conversations, particularly with the Carmen of old, had some storyline, some momentum. Going toward intimacy or coming away from it. Achieving agreement on some subject or unearthing a probable conflict. Giving succor or getting it. This conversation had nothing. Tibby knew that was her fault, but she didn't feel motivated to take the steps to fix it. She felt tired. She was supposed to work on her script. She needed to take a shower. What was she going to eat for dinner?

"It's really noisy here. I'll talk to you later, okay?" she said to Carmen.

"Okay," said Carmen.

There was no satisfaction in being on the phone or in hanging up.

Tibby sat at her desk and pulled up the document on her computer that supposedly contained the script for her intensive screenwriting class. The document was eagerly titled "Script," but it didn't actually contain any scriptlike writing. She'd been in the class for almost three weeks and all she had was a page of notes, randomly spaced and ordered. Not one of them seemed to have anything to do with another. She couldn't even remember writing half of them.

She let her computer fall back to sleep. She flicked on the TV. She could live a full life just going from one screen to another. Everything she needed was inside an electronic box.

She waited for her favorite newslady, Maria Blanquette, with the big nose and the laugh. An authentic island in a sea of fake. But Tibby was too late. The newscast had already moved on to the weather.

She wondered again about Brian calling. He would probably call her as he made his plans for the fall. He would call her with a good excuse—advice about housing or requirements, or meal plans or whatever. He was almost certainly expecting that once he got to NYU in September, they would go back to being friends, at least.

And what would she do? And what would she say? Should she help him? Should she encourage him, or was that a mistake? Would that just make it harder for him to get over it?

Bridget still felt weepy when she called Tibby from the empty office late that night, deeply grateful that the satellite service was back up and running. She knew the call would cost a bundle, but she didn't care. She hadn't told any of them the truth about Peter, but now she needed to.

"I feel so stupid," she said. She let herself weep. She was a walking wound and she needed to get the fluid out.

"Oh, Bee," Tibby said soothingly.

"I knew he was married. I knew he had kids and I let it happen anyway."

"I know."

"I saw them this morning and I felt so disgusted with myself. But why weren't they important before?"

"Mmm," said Tibby to indicate she was listening and not judging.

"He's part of a family, you know? They depend on him. They belong to him. I'll never belong to him."

With that said, Bridget took a long break to cry. And as she did, she realized she had been more honest with Tibby than she'd intended.

"Beezy, it's okay. You belong to other people," Tibby said, her heart in her voice.

Bridget thought of her father and felt an overwhelming sense of despair. She thought of Eric and felt no right to his love. She thought of her mother and ached for the things she hadn't left behind. "I belong to you and Lena and Carmen, Tibby," she said through her tears. "I don't think I belong to anyone else."

On Monday morning, Lena got to the studio first. Leo got there second. He came over to her immediately. She was shy again.

"I've been too excited to sleep," he told her.

He did in fact look both very excited and very tired. Was it the painting? Was it her?

"I brought it," he said. He lifted the thin box. "Can I show it to you?"

"Not right here," she said. Already other students were wandering in.

"I know. But later. We'll go somewhere private."

"Okay," she said. She was nervous to see it.

She tried to concentrate on her painting. She tried to get into the trance of watching and working. It took a while.

He packed up fast after class. She had to hurry to catch up to him. He found an empty studio on the second floor and closed the door behind them.

He leaned the painting in its box against the wall. He drew her to him and kissed her. He pressed his face into her cheek.

"Nora's a great model," he said. "But now I just want to paint you."

He kissed her more until she was out of breath, furry headed, and furry limbed. "I never kissed a model before," he said. "I never painted a girl I kissed."

"You could try kissing Nora."

He made a face.

"Or Marvin."

He made a worse face.

"Okay. I'll show you," he said. He took the painting out of the box. He did it gingerly because it wasn't entirely dry.

It was hard to make herself look. She took it in one bit at a time, trying to think of it as just another student painting of a female figure. This building was loaded with such paintings.

But no. This was her. It was hard to set her appreciation

for Leo's work apart from her own self-conscious judgment. It was hard to look at it without distortion.

But when she could relax a little, she could see that it was beautiful in some objective way. And it wasn't a school painting either. There was something different about it. It was more intimate. It was a painting set in his room in the house where he had grown up. And it was of her, and she had belonged to him alone for those hours when he painted it.

She realized something else. Most school paintings were purposefully desexualized. This one was not.

"It's sexy, isn't it?"

His smile was inward and outward, too. "Yeah."

"Boy, I hope my parents never see this."

"They won't."

They were still awkward together. At a few different places in the relationship at the same time—seen each other naked, didn't know each other's friends.

When the pose had ended the day before, what if she hadn't put her robe on? What if she had let his kiss develop? She could tell it was what he wanted. She'd had all those thoughts too. But the sheer heft of the sexual energy between them had been too much for her.

"You did a lot better than I did in this trade," she said.

Leo looked genuinely regretful of that. "You were a better model."

"You were a better painter."

"Less inhibited, maybe," he said.

She could still feel the place on her ribs where his fingers had lain on her skin. "That's fair," she said.

"Maybe we could try it again."

"I don't know."

"Please?" He had a slightly desperate look. "Because if you don't paint me, I can't ask you, can I? And I *really* want you to pose for me again."

Was it just a painting he wanted from her? What would happen if she agreed? "You can ask me," she said.

"Will you? Please? I'll beg if you want me to."

"You don't have to."

"Sunday?"

It wasn't so bad being wanted. "I'll think about it."

"Say yes."

"Okay."

"Do you want to have dinner tomorrow?" He was happy. He packed up the painting. She knew he had to get to work.

"At your house?" she asked.

"We'll go out," he said as he led her down the hall. "I don't think I can kiss you in front of my mother."

Julia was waiting at the back entrance of the Main Stage when the cast broke for lunch. Carmen was taken aback, but pleased that Julia was looking friendly and ostensibly waiting for her.

Prince Mamillius, who was also called Jonathan, was walking next to Carmen, so Carmen introduced him to Julia.

"Are you coming to the Bistro?" Jonathan asked Carmen when they reached the split in the path. The Bistro was what they called the smaller, nicer dining room, which was reserved for the professional actors. Bistro people never went to the canteen and vice versa, Carmen understood, although Ian and Andrew and especially Jonathan tried to persuade Carmen to eat with them.

"No," she said.

"Oh, come on."

She was tired of having this argument. "I'm not supposed to."

"Shut up, miss. You know you are."

"Jonathan."

"You can bring your friend."

Carmen turned to Julia, who looked unmistakably excited by this idea. "Do you want to?" Julia asked Carmen.

Carmen didn't, actually.

"I just think it would be fun to see it," Julia said.

Carmen gave Jonathan a look. "It's supposed to be reserved for Equity actors," she said. "But if the prince here is so eager to eat with us, he can get takeout and bring it to the lawn."

Jonathan shook his head. "I am overmatched," he said. "Fine, Carmen, I'll meet you on the lawn."

"Give those apprentice girls a thrill," Carmen said wryly.

To Julia's delight, Jonathan did meet them on the lawn, the grassy area beyond the canteen where all the apprentices hung out. He brought three turkey sandwiches that tasted to Carmen exactly the same as the ones you got at the canteen.

His presence there did cause a stir. It seemed most of these people were more up to date with his filmography than Carmen. Julia chatted happily with him, discussing each thing he'd acted in.

Watching Julia, Carmen felt a certain mystery being solved, and she was relieved by it. Julia had become friendly again, Carmen realized, because she believed Carmen could connect her to real actors.

Carmen could have been annoyed by it, but for some reason she wasn't. So Julia was using her. So what. It was much better than the silent treatment.

Only in the last couple of days had Carmen acknowledged to herself just how painful it was to live with someone who wouldn't speak to you. She thought with earnest regret of the times she'd doled out that particular punishment to her mother.

Carmen had been unhappy with the fraught silence, but she'd also been uneasy about Julia's recent turnaround. Now that she understood it, she felt much better.

Later she saw Jonathan backstage and she thanked him. "The sandwiches stank, but I think my friend really appreciated your eating with us."

He laughed. He'd taken to touching bits of Carmen when he could, and he did it now, pulling on the end of a curl of her hair. "No problem, sister."

"Only now she wants to know what you're doing for dinner tonight."

Jonathan laughed again. "Yeah, well. Your friend is what we call a striver. You see a lot of that type in L.A."

❖   ❖   ❖

Well, Bridget had dug down to the bottommost thing. The most crushing thing. It was good to know where the bottom was, she thought, lying in her cot that night. She was a lying duck, lying at the bottom and letting the agony come for her. She was accepting it.

Peter had said she could learn a thing or two from the Greeks, and he was right. The Greeks knew about cycles of misery. They knew about family curses passed down through long generations. Even seemingly forgivable infractions started wars, infidelities, the sacrifice of children. They also ended in wars, infidelities, the sacrifice of children.

No—in fact, they didn't end that way. They didn't end at all. In the stories, the destruction kept on going, propagated by the blind bungling of human failure.

And that was the course she was setting for herself. Her family was unhappy. No family was allowed to be happy. On some level she didn't want Peter—or anyone—to have what she didn't have. She didn't even want his children to have it.

Now she wondered. Did the fact that Peter had a family dampen her interest in him? Or did it inflame it? How chilling that her most destructive impulses should mask themselves as romance.

Those blind, bungling Greeks always seemed to make the same mistake. They failed to learn from the past. They swaggered onward. They refused to look back. That was what she did too.

A child of five would

understand this.

Send someone to fetch a

child of five.

—Groucho Marx

Tibby cut back her work hours. Or Charlie recommended she cut back her hours, more accurately. He thought if she worked less, she might be more patient with the customers. He hired a girl who wore scented lip gloss and tiny pants and didn't care about which movies were good or bad. Charlie was too nice to fire Tibby outright.

Tibby didn't mind that much. She didn't have anyone to go out to dinner or to the movies with these days, so she didn't need the money as much. It gave her more time to work on her script. Or at least to open the file named "Script."

In late July she went home for a long weekend. Katherine and Nicky were doing a variety show at their day camp, and she thought she'd surprise them.

Would she see Brian? That was what she wondered as her train chugged southward and still wondered later as she waited for her mom to pick her up at the Metro station in Bethesda.

She would see him. She felt sure she would. How could she not? Brian loved her family. In fact, he appreciated them much more than she, an actual member of it, did and was appreciated much more in return. How was she going to feel about that now?

Indeed, on Friday morning, Brian appeared in the kitchen when Tibby was eating her Lucky Charms.

"Hi! Hi!" Katherine danced around him excitedly. "Are you taking us today?"

Was Brian surprised to see Tibby? She wasn't sure. At first she'd assumed he'd shown up with the idea of seeing her, but now, judging by the look on his face, she wasn't sure he'd known she'd be there.

"Hey, Tibby," he said.

"Hey." She kept her eyes on the little marshmallows. She wanted to be friendly, but she didn't want to lead him on.

"Brian takes us on Friday sometimes instead of Mom," Katherine explained happily. She had completely abandoned her own cereal in favor of Brian.

Tibby heard her mother upstairs yelling at Nicky to stop playing on the computer and get dressed. "Well, that's really nice," Tibby said stiffly. "You should eat your breakfast, Katherine," she added. She couldn't imagine volunteering to take her brother and sister to camp, and she was the one who supposedly shared their DNA.

But then, Brian didn't have any brothers or sisters. Desire came from deficit, and Tibby had a surplus.

"How come you're not hugging anymore?" Katherine asked, looking from Brian to Tibby and back.

Moments passed. Brian let Katherine stomp around on his shoes but did not answer the question. Tibby kept her pink face turned to her cereal bowl.

"Are you in a fight?" Katherine persisted. Now she appeared at Tibby's leg, both hands on one of Tibby's knees, leaning into her.

Tibby clutched her teaspoon and stirred. The combination of the pink hearts, yellow moons, blue diamonds, and so on turned the milk a sickly gray hue. "Not in a fight," she said. "Just . . . doing different things this summer."

Katherine did not immediately accept this answer.

"Do you want to come?" Brian asked Tibby politely.

"To . . . ?"

"To take us to camp!" Katherine got right on board. "Yes. Can you come?"

"Well. I guess I could—"

Minutes later, Tibby found herself in the passenger seat of her mother's car with her ex-boyfriend, who was driving her brother and sister to camp. But the true awkwardness began once the two noisy passengers had gotten out of the car.

"How's it going?" Brian asked into the silence.

He seemed more comfortable than she felt. But he wasn't the guilty one, was he?

"Pretty good. How about you?"

"Doing a little better, I guess. I'm trying to." He was

willing to be honest and she wasn't. That was why she didn't want to have a conversation with him.

She couldn't think of anything to say. They were stopped at the longest red light on record. She had always hated this light on Arlington Boulevard. Why had Brian gone this way?

"How's it going with school and everything?" she asked finally.

"What do you mean?" he asked. At last they were moving again.

"With financial aid and that stuff."

"I probably won't need it."

"Really? But I thought—" She was inside the conversation now.

"At Maryland, it's—"

"No, at NYU, I mean," she said.

He didn't say anything for a while.

She wished she could take back her words, remove herself once again from the interaction at hand.

"I'm not planning to go to NYU anymore," he said slowly, just as they were turning onto her block. "I withdrew my acceptance a couple weeks ago."

She was opening the car door before it had fully stopped. "Right. Sure." She forgot for a moment it was her mom's car and Brian would be parking it in her driveway. "That makes total sense. Of course," she said. She was flustered, spasmodically waving to him from the sidewalk on her way into her house.

He was looking at her, but she wasn't sure of his expression, because she wasn't really looking at him.

"I hafta run. So I'll see you later!" she declared as she disappeared into her house.

She walked up to her room and sat stiffly on her bed. She looked out the window but saw nothing.

Of course Brian wasn't going to NYU! He was only going because of her, and she'd broken up with him!

Brian, it seemed, had accepted the reality of their breakup. That much was suddenly clear.

But had she?

When Carmen got home after rehearsal ended that night, she was struck to see that Julia had left a stack of books for her on her bed.

"That one is about the Elizabethan stage in general," Julia said eagerly, pointing to the first one Carmen picked up. "The big one under it, that's about language and pronunciation. That will be really helpful. Then there's that one, which is just an analysis of *Winter's Tale*."

Carmen nodded, studying them. "Wow, thank you. These are great."

"I think they might be useful," Julia said.

"Right. Definitely," Carmen said. The books struck a certain chord in Carmen. She wondered why she hadn't thought of going to the library. She, a girl who trusted herself to beg, borrow, study, and steal more than she trusted herself to be naturally good at something.

She was exhausted, but instead of going straight to sleep, she left the light on for a while and confused herself about the different kinds of verse.

The following night Julia coached her about looking through the text and beyond the text. And then Carmen read the passage Julia recommended about Leontes as self and antiself while Julia feverishly wrote something at her desk. Around midnight, when Carmen was getting ready to turn off the light, Julia presented it to her.

"Here, I marked this up for you."

It was a half inch of photocopied pages from the script, marked up with a dizzying number of symbols and annotations.

"I wrote the meter out for you," Julia explained. "I tried to put the beats in the way you're supposed to."

"Really."

"Yeah. It seemed like you could use some help with that."

"Okay. Yeah."

Julia pointed to the first line and started reading it, exaggerating the rhythm.

"I get it."

"Do you?"

"I think so."

"Do you want to try it?"

Carmen didn't want to try it. She didn't really get it at all and she felt stupid and she wanted to go to sleep.

"Just try a line or two," Julia prodded.

Carmen tried.

"No, it's like this," Julia said, demonstrating.

And so it went until Carmen was doubly exhausted and also had a headache.

On Sunday of that weekend, Tibby went to see Mrs. Graffman, mother of her old friend Bailey. Tibby was going back to New York by train that night, and she wanted to make some effort to see her before she left.

"Do you want to meet for coffee or something?" Tibby asked when she called.

"That's fine. Let's meet at the place around the corner on Highland."

"Perfect," Tibby said, relieved. She preferred not to go to the Graffmans' house if she could avoid it.

Tibby had tried to visit Mrs. Graffman, or at least call, the few times she'd been home in the last year. Usually she wanted to, but today it felt more like an obligation.

Tibby gave Mrs. Graffman a brief hug at the entrance where she was waiting. They got their coffee at the counter and sat down at a tiny table by the front window.

"How're things?" Mrs. Graffman asked. She looked relaxed in her yoga pants and slightly muddy gardening sneakers. She was more robust-looking than she'd been six months and a year ago.

Tibby considered neither the question nor her answer. "Pretty good, I guess. How about you?"

"Well, you know."

Tibby nodded. The "you know" meant that she missed Bailey and that life was only good or remarkable in a very limited context when you'd lost your only child.

"But work is fine. I switched firms, did I tell you that?"

"I think you had just switched last time," Tibby said.

"I redid the downstairs bathroom. Mr. Graffman is training for the Marine Corps Marathon."

"Wow, that's great," Tibby said.

"We try to keep our sense of purpose, you know?"

"Yes," said Tibby. Mrs. Graffman looked sad, but to Tibby's relief, she didn't look urgently sad in a way that needed tending.

"What about you, my dear?"

"Well, I'm taking this intensive screenwriting course. We're supposed to have a full-length script done by mid-August."

"That's exciting."

Suddenly Tibby realized that Mrs. Graffman was going to want to know what it was about.

"What's it about?" she asked cheerfully, right on schedule.

Tibby sipped her coffee too fast and burned her tongue. "I'm kind of working with a bunch of different themes, still. I'm kind of gathering images, you know?" She had heard someone say that once, and she thought it sounded cool. But in the air between her and Mrs. Graffman it sounded like the fakest thing ever.

"Interesting."

Which is another way of saying I haven't started, Tibby should have said, but didn't.

"And how about our friend Brian?" Mrs. Graffman asked with a smile. She was another one of Brian's many ardent parent-aged fans.

"He's . . . well. He's good, I guess. I haven't been seeing him as much."

Mrs. Graffman had a question in her eyes, so Tibby kept talking so she wouldn't get to ask it. "It's just been so crazy, because I have a job and school and he has two jobs and we're in different cities, and so . . . you know."

"I can imagine," Mrs. Graffman said. "But next year you'll be together?"

"Well." Tibby wished she could leave it at that. She wanted to go back to her tiny dorm room, hours from home, and watch TV. "I don't know. It's kind of tricky."

You see, I broke up with him. And now, oddly enough, it seems that as a consequence, we are not together anymore and our future is no longer shared. How mysterious. Who would have thought?

Mrs. Graffman was too sensitive to push into places Tibby didn't want to go. Which left them almost nothing to talk about.

"You're coming to my parents' party in August, right?" Tibby asked, gathering her things.

"Yes. We just got the invitation in the mail. Twenty years. Wow."

Tibby nodded blandly. She never wanted to do the math

as far as her parents' wedding was concerned. Here was yet another blocked conversation.

Tibby realized why she found comfort in simpler, more one-sided interactions, like with, say, the TV.

Lena had forgotten about forgetting about Kostos. That was how she knew. When you remembered to forget, you were remembering. It was when you forgot to forget that you forgot.

The thing that reminded Lena about Kostos came not from any movement in her brain (which would have constituted a failure to forget) but from a knock on her door on a hot Thursday afternoon at the very end of July.

It was simple. When she saw Kostos, she remembered him.

Why, what could she have

done, being what she is?

Was there another Troy

for her to burn?

—William Butler Yeats

I t was after class that it happened. Lena had kicked off her flip-flops and fallen asleep on her bed in her shorts and T-shirt, her hair falling out of its ponytail. The knock came in the first deep part of sleep. She was groggy and disoriented and sweaty before she even opened the door.

When she saw the dark-haired man standing there, she only half believed that he could be Kostos. Even though he had Kostos's face and Kostos's feet and Kostos's voice, she persisted in thinking that maybe he was somebody else.

Why was this man, who looked so strangely like Kostos, standing in the doorway of her dorm room? Disjointedly she thought of calling Carmen and telling her that there happened to be a guy in Rhode Island who was almost identical to Kostos.

Then she remembered what Carmen had said about when Kostos would come, and she remembered about the forgetting.

She felt suddenly jolted and afraid. Like she'd woken up in the middle of her SATs. Did that mean it could be him?

But it was impossible, because Kostos lived on a Greek island thousands of miles away. He lived in the past. He lived unreachably inside the walls of a marriage. He lived in her memory and her imagination. That was where he spent literally all of his time. He existed there, not here.

He could not be here. Here was the leftover turkey sandwich from a hurried lunch in the studio and the ratty drawstring sweatpants she'd cut into shorts, and the mosquito bite on her ankle she'd ruthlessly picked, and the charcoal drawing she'd Scotch-taped to her wall two Mondays ago. Kostos did not live here or now. She'd question her eyes and ears faster than she'd question that.

She almost told him so.

"It's me," he said, sensing her confusion, faltering in his certainty that she would recognize him.

Well, she did recognize him. That wasn't the point, was it? She was hardly convinced. So what if he was me? Everyone was me. She was me. Who else was he going to be?

Just because he was Kostos and appeared at her door and said "It's me" didn't mean he was occupying space and time in her actual life. She thought of telling him so.

She had that frustrating dreamlike confusion of racking her brain for the answer and then forgetting what the question was. There was a question, wasn't there? She thought of asking him.

"I should have called first," he murmured.

She recognized that her heart was beating either many

247

more times or many fewer times than it was meant to. She considered. Maybe it would stop altogether. Then what was she supposed to do?

For some reason she pictured her chest opening like a cupboard door and her heart sproinging out at the end of a coil.

Was she awake? She could have asked him, but he was the last person who would know, having no place in reality himself.

"I think I might sit down," she said faintly. She was like a corseted girl in an old movie, taking the big things sitting down.

He stood in her doorway with the question on his face of whether he should come in. He looked worn out and rumpled. Maybe he really had come all the way here.

"Maybe you could come back later," she said.

He wore the look of being tortured. He didn't know what to make of her. "Can I come back this evening? Maybe around eight?"

She found herself wondering, did he mean eight her time or his time? She only confused herself. "That would be fine," she said politely. Could they really be in the same time?

If he came back at eight, she decided, listening to the door close, tipping over onto her pillow, that would strengthen the case for his being here.

On that same scorching Thursday at the end of July, the security guard called up to Tibby's room and told her she had a visitor.

Immediately she thought of Brian, even though she hadn't seen him or spoken to him since she'd returned from Bethesda. She felt her heart quicken. "Who is it?" she asked.

"Hold on." Tibby heard muffled conversation. "It's Effie."

"*Who?*"

"Effie. Effie? She says she's your friend."

Tibby's heart changed its stride. "I'll be there in a minute," she said.

She wet her hair down and pulled on a tank top and a ragged pair of shorts. Suddenly she was worried something might be wrong with Lena. She flew down the hall to the elevator.

Effie was practically in her face when the elevator door opened in the lobby. She backed up quickly, stumbling as Tibby burst out of it.

"Is everything okay?" Tibby asked.

Effie raised her eyebrows. "Yes. I mean, I think so."

"Where's Lena?"

"She's in Providence." Effie acquired that subtly damaged look she got when confronted with the reality that Lena's friends were not equally her friends.

"Oh. Right." Tibby realized it might sound mean to say *So what are you doing here?* Rather, she waited patiently for Effie to explain what she was doing there.

"Are you busy right now?" Effie asked.

"No. Not really."

"You're not like, rushing off anywhere or anything."

"No." Tibby was imploding with curiosity, with the sense that something was afoot. She'd been alone a lot.

"Do you want to go get a cup of coffee? Is there a place around here?"

Effie looked a bit nervous, Tibby decided. She was jumpy. Of her total of four hands and feet, not one was staying still. She was wearing a short strawberry pink wrap dress, which revealed an impressive amount of cleavage.

"There are a million places around here." Tibby counseled herself not to be impatient or mean. It was actually really sweet that Effie had come all the way here to see her. Did she want advice on something? Was she suddenly interested in film as a potentially glamorous career? Did she hear there was a disproportionate number of cute boys at NYU maybe? Not that there were. "We can get iced coffee at a place on Waverly."

"That sounds great," Effie said. She wiped a coat of sweat off her upper lip.

"Are you in New York for a while?" Tibby asked as they walked along, fishing for clues.

"Just the day," Effie said.

At last, equipped with a two-dollar iced coffee for Tibby and a five-dollar raspberry white mocha frappuccino for Effie, they sat at a dim, cool table in the back of the café. An opera in Italian was playing over the speaker to the left of Effie's head.

Effie's drink was so thick she had to really suck to get any of it. Tibby watched and waited.

"So you and Brian broke up," Effie said finally.

"Right."

"I couldn't believe it when I first heard it."

Tibby shrugged. Was this the preamble? Where was it going?

"Do you think you'll get back together?" Effie asked. Her expression was not demanding. In fact, she mostly fiddled with the paper from her straw.

"I don't think so."

"Really?"

Tibby tried not to be irritated. Was Effie just trying to make pleasant conversation? Because it wasn't all that pleasant.

"Really."

"Huh. Do you think you are over him?"

Tibby looked at her carefully. "Do I think I am over him?"

Effie opened her hands as though to show there wasn't anything in them. "Yeah."

"I'm not sure I would even know."

Effie shrugged lightly. She sucked on her drink. "I mean, like, would you be upset if you found out he was going out with someone else?"

As Tibby replayed those words, she felt her brain turning inside out like a salted slug. Her vision grew distorted and she blinked to get it back into focus. She tried to keep her face on, to remain calm.

What did Effie know? Had she seen Brian with another girl? Was Brian fooling around with some girl all over Bethesda? What had Effie seen? What was going on?

Tibby drank her coffee. She breathed the air. She listened to a tenor hollering just over Effie's head. She could not lose it in front of Effie. Effie, no matter what her cup size, was still a little sister.

She desperately wanted to ask Effie what she knew, but how could she without seeming like it bothered her? Like she was upset and disturbed and blindsided by the thought of it? She couldn't.

"You would be upset," Effie concluded.

Tibby had her pride, if nothing else. "No," she said finally. "I would be a little surprised, maybe. But look. I was the one who broke up with him, right? It wasn't like I didn't know what I was doing. I totally did. I didn't have any doubt that it was time for us to break up and that, for me, it was the right thing to do." Suddenly Tibby realized that talking felt better than thinking.

"Really?"

"Sure. I mean, it was really over. For me, it was over. Brian should do whatever he wants to do. He's totally free to go out with anybody he wants. Really, he probably oughta go out with somebody else if that's what he wants to do." Tibby felt like her head was teetering slightly on her neck. Like one of those dumb bobble-head figures people put in their car.

Effie nodded and sucked on her so-called coffee, her eyes wide, listening intently. "Would it matter if it was someone you knew?"

Never had Tibby imagined pure torture in the guise of Effie Kaligaris in a wrap dress sucking a pink drink. Someone Tibby knew? Who was it? Who was Brian with? Someone she knew? Brian was hooking up with someone she *knew*? Who was it? How could he do that to her? Tibby racked her brain to think of who it could be.

How could she ask and not betray her abject misery? How could she not ask and continue to suffer like this?

"It would," Effie proposed solemnly.

Once again, Tibby gathered herself. She could fall apart later. She could call Lena and get the truth. She could even call her mother if it came to that.

"Why should it?" Tibby said, tapping her fingers in a poor facsimile of nonchalance. "Why should it really matter if I knew the person?"

Suddenly every damn singer in the opera seemed to be screaming at the top of their lungs. "The point is that Brian is no longer my boyfriend and I am not his girlfriend." Tibby was almost shouting. "Who he goes out with is totally his business. Who I go out with is totally mine."

Effie nodded slowly. "That makes sense."

Tibby was actually quite proud of her answer. It sounded like exactly the right thing, even if it bore no relation to how she felt. She tried to catch her breath. She wished the opera singers would take it down a notch.

"That makes a lot of sense." Effie sucked more on her drink.

"So then . . ." Effie put her drink down and readjusted herself in her chair. Her eyes were now locked on Tibby. "You wouldn't mind if . . ."

Effie uncrossed her legs under the table. Tibby realized

she too felt the need to put both feet on the floor. For mysterious reasons, Tibby held her breath.

"You wouldn't mind if I went out with Brian?"

Things like this should not happen to Lena, Lena decided, looking at the bricks outside her window and then the gaps between them where the mortar had mostly worn away. They should happen to other people, like Effie. Effie, who, for instance, was more skilled at being a person.

The light got old and the bricks turned dark. The only concessions Lena made to the possibility of eight o'clock were putting on deodorant and brushing her hair.

In the latter movement was a memory, because she had also brushed her hair for him on the day of her bapi's funeral. That was two years ago.

The feelings of loss from that time were multiple: Bapi's death, her grandmother's agony, her father's harsh rigidity. And finding out about Kostos, of course. All of them had crashed together like malevolent winds. They had created a storm strong enough to suck in all the incidental qualities of that moment, however innocent: the particular pattern of clouds and the buzz of a certain kind of airplane, the smell of dry dirt and the feeling of having brushed your hair especially for a person you loved.

The storm had even sucked time into it—hours and days and weeks that didn't rightfully belong to it, so that the time before it struck was freighted with the knowing sorrow of inexorability, and the time after it bore the bleakness of wanting things she could never have.

Within the memory of brushing her hair for him hovered the foreknowledge that Kostos would abandon her.

She remembered certain things he'd said. They kept at her all this time, like a talk radio station turned very low at the bottom of her consciousness.

"Don't ever be sad because you think I don't love you," he'd said. "Never think you did anything wrong." "If I've broken your heart, I've broken my own a thousand times worse." "I love you, Lena. I couldn't stop if I tried."

The most haunting thing was not that he didn't love her anymore. She could have accepted that eventually. The most haunting thing was that he did. He loved her from afar. (Sometimes that was the way she loved herself.) He loved her in a way that was preserved in time, that couldn't be sullied. And she tended it in her careful, curatorial way.

She was lovable. She clung to that. She was worthy of being loved. That was what mattered, wasn't it? Even if he had married someone else? Even if he had wrecked her hopes?

She was lovable. It was what she had. In her dreams, she heard him say he still loved her, that he didn't forget her any hour of any day. She was unforgettable. That was the most important thing. Better, even, than being happy.

And where did that leave her? Alone on her Greek urn. Lovable but never loved.

She was free of risk. Bold within her limits.

It was the same old hedge.

❀ ❀ ❀

It reminded Tibby a little bit of the child-catcher's scene in *Chitty Chitty Bang Bang* where his candy truck is suddenly revealed to be a cage.

Sitting there across from Effie, her cup of melted ice sweating on the table, Tibby watched the four solid walls turn into the bars of a cage. She was trapped. She had walked right into it, pleased with her own cool, lying head.

What could she do? What could she say? Effie had played it masterfully. Suddenly Tibby understood everything Effie had intended, every question she had asked. Effie did not hail from the land of Socrates for nothing.

Tibby couldn't think anymore. She couldn't hope to combat Effie. Her head bobbled.

"You would mind," Effie concluded quietly, but Tibby could practically see the smugness peeking through. Effie looked ready to fly, to take her victory and run with it.

"No. That's fine," Tibby mumbled. What else could she say?

Up stood Effie. That was good enough for her. "Oh, my God. I am so relieved, Tibby," she gushed. "You don't know how worried I was. I couldn't do anything until I knew you'd be okay."

They were already on the sidewalk, Tibby following numbly.

Brian and Effie? Effie and Brian? Effie with her Brian? Was that what he wanted? He wanted to be with Effie? She thought of Effie's cleavage.

"I'm just so glad it's okay. Because Brian and I are like

the only two people left at home this summer, you know? And I've— Well, anyway. But I wouldn't even think of doing anything without making sure you would be fine."

"I'll be fine," Tibby managed to say, just to finish the charade properly. Then she went home and fell apart.

You shall know the truth,

and the truth shall make

you mad.

—Aldous Huxley

The alleged Kostos did come at eight.

Lena hazarded a touch to his wrist before she submitted to the belief that he was three-dimensional. He was too warm to be a ghost, figment, or hologram. He had eyes and lips and arms that moved. He was in her time, in her doorway. She had to accept him.

And so she stepped back, considering him silently and without regard to her own presence. She was a pair of eyes, not a person to be interacted with. If he insisted upon being present, maybe she could disappear.

So he was Kostos. She thought her memory of his face should certainly have diminished the reality of his face, but it hadn't. His face still had its power, she recognized, but as though from a distance.

He put out his hand and held hers, earnestly but without expectations. She stayed too far away to be read as wanting to embrace.

So he was Kostos and she was Lena, and after all this time and misery they were facing each other in a doorway of a student dorm in Providence, Rhode Island. She was watching it more than experiencing it. She was keeping track so she could tell herself about it later and brood appropriately.

There were people who lived in the moment, Lena knew, while she lived at a delay of hours or even years. And with that knowledge came the familiar frustration of wanting to club herself over the head with a combat boot if only to be sure of experiencing and feeling something in unison for once.

"I won't stay if you don't want me to, Lena." Tentatively he took one step into the small room. "But there are a few things I want to say to you in person."

She nodded, her mouth clamped and pointy like a bird's beak. The sound of her name in his voice was jarring.

They should walk, Lena decided. Walking was easier because they didn't have to look at each other. "We should walk," she said.

In single file they walked down the hallway and three flights of stairs. She led him out of the building and toward the river. The air had grown kind, warm but not steamy.

She had the vague thought that they would walk along the place in the river where fires burned in the middle of the water on summer nights. It was one of the few tourist attractions of Providence, but she was too disoriented to remember what time they were lit or even quite where they would be.

"I didn't know how you would feel," he said, walking beside her.

She didn't know how she would feel either. She had absolutely no idea. She waited to know as though someone might tell her.

She took him the wrong way. They wound up walking past a gas station and a 7-Eleven and picking their way along a busy road in the dark. She hadn't the gifts of a tour guide.

She thought of Santorini and how it was beautiful and how Kostos knew the way. The thought struck her heavily, almost like a boot, making her eyes sting.

"I'm not married anymore," Kostos told her between speeding cars. He looked at her and she nodded to show that she had at least heard him.

"I became officially divorced in June."

She was not freshly startled by this. Once she'd accepted his presence in her doorway, a part of her brain seemed to know he was no longer married.

With his solemn face he stood as they waited for a line of cars to pass. He was patient about it. They were both patient, perhaps overly so. They had that in common.

She steered them back in the direction of campus to a quiet bench in a green and dimly lit patch of garden between two administrative buildings. It was no olive grove, but they could talk.

"There's not a baby," he said gingerly. He seemed to have considered his phrasing in advance.

"What happened to it?" She felt bold to ask, but reasonable, too.

He looked at her openly. He hadn't the anger or guard-edness she'd seen two years ago. It was easier to talk about a baby that he didn't have.

"Well." His sigh indicated complexity. "Mariana said she miscarried. But the timing of it was hard to explain. Her sister told me privately that she hadn't been pregnant, but had wanted to marry and figured a baby would come in due course."

"But it didn't," Lena said.

She could tell by his gaze that he was measuring how much was the right amount to say. "I was angry in the be-ginning. I wanted to find out the truth. I refused to live . . . as a husband with her."

Lena wondered at the meaning of all of this. What American man would talk this way?

"We lived separately after the first half year, but stayed married. I thought I couldn't dishonor my grandparents by divorcing. It's not accepted among the old families. It's something that the newcomers and the tourists do."

Lena recognized how deep in Kostos's character was the need to please. The desire not to disappoint. It was an-other thing they had in common. He was the darling of all the families in Oia. He wanted to be lovable too, even if it meant setting happiness aside. His happiness and hers, it seemed.

What was this compulsive need to be lovable? They both had it, were driven by it, bound by it. They would even sacrifice each other for the sake of it.

But she sensed they were afflicted differently. He wanted

to preserve his worthiness in the eyes of other people. It was because of losing his parents; it had to be. Parents were the only ones obligated to love you; from the rest of the world you had to earn it.

And what about her? Whose love did she so compulsively doubt?

She knew without thinking. From her earliest memory she had perceived the chasm between how she looked and how she felt. She knew whose love she doubted. It wasn't her parents' and it wasn't her friends'. It was her own.

"And so what happened?" she asked dully.

"It was really my grandparents who mattered the most to me. You know they are old and very traditional. I held off doing what I had to do. I dreaded telling them."

He had thought about this part too, she knew. He had planned this speech. She nodded.

"When I finally told my grandmother, I thought she'd fall apart."

"She didn't," Lena guessed.

Kostos shook his head. "She told me she prayed every night I would have the courage to do it."

She pictured their two grandmothers, Valia and Rena, two old ladies full of surprises. How much did Valia know?

"Valia didn't say anything," she said.

"I asked her not to. I wanted to tell you myself."

Lena studied his calm face and suddenly felt affronted by it.

"I would be furious if I were you," she said.

"But who does that help now?" he asked.

She felt furious even though she wasn't him. She felt furious *at* him for having granted himself the right to dispense with her grievances too. "I would want to know what really happened," she said hotly.

Kostos looked pained, but he shrugged. "I had to let it go. What did it matter? What would it help to give out blame?"

What did it matter? Kostos could decide that it didn't. It was, technically speaking, no business of hers. And yet, in another bootlike strike, she felt quite sure, looking back on the past two years of her life, that it did matter.

That was the stupidity of loving someone from a different planet, wasn't it? You didn't just give yourself away to him. You put yourself in the path of crazy girls who made up babies, and strangling customs you didn't even care about.

That wasn't what she wanted for her life, was it? She had enough to stifle her without that. She thought bitterly of her father. She had enough of those old customs as it was.

And then, abruptly, she thought of Leo. Of his loft. Of his ruby red couch and the feeling of lying on it.

She lost her breath for a moment. It was almost intolerable to think of Leo in the same brain where she thought of Kostos. She felt unnerved, disassociated, as if she were living in two universes, being two people at the same time.

She had forgotten about Leo. The possibility of Leo. It came back to her like another kick.

Was she really so bad at forgetting? Maybe she was better than she thought.

There was the boot yet again, and it hurt. But wasn't that what she wanted?

No. It wasn't. *Leave me alone*, she felt like screaming. She didn't want the boot. She didn't need another crack over the head. She didn't want Kostos. She didn't want any of it.

"Carmen, what the hell are you doing?"

Carmen tried to be impervious to the devil glare coming from Andrew.

"I'm saying my line," Carmen said.

"What's the matter with you? You sound like a robot. You sound worse than a robot. I *wish* I could listen to a robot instead of you."

Carmen made herself stand firm. This wasn't Andrew's first tirade, though it was perhaps the first aimed so directly at her.

"Try it again," he ordered.

Carmen tried it again.

"Bleep. Bleep," harangued Andrew. "Robot."

She took a deep breath. She would not cry. He was tired. She was tired. It had been a very long day. "I think maybe I'll take a break," she said tightly.

"You do that," he said.

You are horrible and I hate you, she said to Andrew in her mind, although she knew he wasn't and she didn't.

She staggered to the back door and pushed it open. The air was hot and sticky and it offered no relief.

She sat down and rested her head in her arms. Andrew was being hateful, but he wasn't wrong. The lines had grown stilted in her mouth. She was thinking about them too much. Or more, she was thinking about the technicalities of saying them too much.

Some number of minutes later, Carmen looked up and saw Julia.

"Carmen, is that you?"

"Hey," Carmen said, sitting up straighter.

"What's the matter? Are you okay?"

"I'm having a bad rehearsal."

"Oh, no. What's wrong?"

"I think all the working on meter is just confusing me," Carmen said truthfully.

"Really?" Julia looked genuinely worried. She sat on the step next to Carmen. "That's no good."

Carmen closed her eyes. "I can't believe I have to go back in there."

"You know what the problem is?"

"What?"

"This always happens. The first time you learn the structural stuff it confuses you. Totally standard. The thing you've got to do is just keep going with it and then you get it. It becomes natural as soon as you get a handle on it."

"You think so?"

"I'm almost sure of it."

After Carmen was released from her rehearsal of pain, she went back to the room, where Julia was waiting.

"Here, I tried marking it in a new way," Julia said. "I think this will make it easier."

Carmen looked at Perdita's familiar words and they looked distant to her. Now that she was considering them in a different context, she couldn't access them in the old way anymore. She couldn't re-create the simplicity. She couldn't seem to go backward. So maybe Julia was right. Maybe she had to go forward.

She appreciated Julia's patience in staying up with her almost until dawn to make sure she worked through it.

Lena was angry. She couldn't sleep.

She'd been accepting, she'd been numb, she'd been sad, now she was angry. She was cycling through the stages of grief, but on fast-forward and in jumbled order.

In the middle of a night long ago, she'd gone to Kostos full of ardor, wearing her vulnerability in the form of a fluttery white nightgown. Tonight she knocked on his door at the Braveside Motor Lodge battened down in a slick black jacket held tightly closed against wind and rain.

He'd put on pants by the time he opened the door. She looked past him to a familiar bunch of suitcases, a familiar mess of clothes, familiar shoes. It all carried a familiar smell that hurt her. Why had he brought so much stuff?

"You shouldn't have come here," she said, noting as she did that she was the one knocking on his door at two in the morning.

Surprise, pain, defensiveness took turns on his sleepy

face. The creases of his pillowcase were still pressed into his cheek.

"Anyway, what are you trying to do? What did you think would happen?"

"I—" He stopped. He rubbed his eyes. He looked as though his own dog had bitten him.

"I just want to understand!" she exclaimed.

That was a lie. She didn't just want to understand. She wanted to catch him and punish him.

Maybe he didn't do that kind of thing. Maybe he was too good for it. Maybe blame didn't matter and people who ruined your life didn't matter to him. But maybe she couldn't get past it.

"I wanted to tell you what happened. I thought you had a right to know."

"Why? What business is it of mine?" she snapped. "You were married. Now you're not married. That was years ago. Why should it mean anything to me?"

Another lie. Far worse than the first. Even as she said it, she didn't know if she wanted him to believe her.

From the look on his face, he did believe her. "I—" He stopped himself again. He looked down. He looked at the night sky past her head. He looked at the few cars parked in the motor court. He did what he could to contain himself.

She clutched her jacket so tight around her middle she thought she might break a rib.

"I'm sorry." He did look sorry. He looked sorry in numerous ways. She wanted him to continue, but he didn't.

She felt like shaking him, screaming at him. *What are you sorry for?*

For coming here?

For thinking I'd care?

For caring yourself?

For breaking my heart?

For choosing other people instead of me?

For knowing how badly I want to hurt you right now?

For knowing I do care and that I hate you for it?

For having to see that I'm not who you thought I was?

She gritted her teeth so hard her ears ached. "Was I supposed to rush into your arms?" she asked derisively.

He looked taken aback. He was still believing she would be lovable. "No. Lena. I didn't expect that. I just . . ."

"Anyway, I have a boyfriend," she said conclusively, meanly, dishonestly. "Your timing is pretty terrible. Not that it matters."

There was something horrendously liberating about lying. It was an experience she'd never known before this.

He pressed his lips together. His body began to close in. It took a lot to make him distrust her.

A part of her wanted him to get mad, to prove himself as nasty and as unworthy as she was. Could he even do it?

She wanted an inferno. She'd preserved their love so carefully in her mind these years, but now she wanted to burn the thing down. She wanted every part of it broken and burned and wronged and done.

No, he couldn't do it. His stance was no longer open.

269

His face was shutting down. He was silent as she smoldered.

"I'm sorry for everything," he said at last.

She wanted to punch him, but instead she strode away. She turned the corner and listened silently for the click of his door.

On the way back to her dorm her walk turned into a run. She let go of her coat, let it flap heavily around her. She ran as fast as she could until she was out of breath and her heart was shuddering.

She realized later, shaking under the sheet in her underwear, that she'd never really gotten mad at anyone before.

Illusions are art, for the
feeling person, and it is
by art that you live,
if you do.

—Elizabeth Bowen

When Lena awoke early the next morning, she was no longer angry. She was astounded. What had she done? How could she have done it?

A fearful, reckless energy prompted her out of bed and into clothes. She walked back to the motel, the scene of the crime, as if to prove to herself that she had actually done what she thought she had done. That it had really happened.

Had it really happened? What could she say to Kostos? Was she apologetic? She checked her heart.

She didn't find an apology there exactly. She couldn't quite define what was there: a strange brew of stridency and terror. What should she do?

As she walked along the open corridor, she was scared to see the remnants of the mess she had made.

She prepared herself to knock, but she saw when she got close that the door was already open. She thought of how much stuff there had been in the room, the number of suitcases and the piles of clothes. Now she looked past the housekeeping cart into a room clean and empty.

Tibberon: Oh, Len. Carmen told me what happened. Are you okay?

LennyK162: I'm okay. A little dazed maybe.

Tibberon: Do you want company?

LennyK162: I love your company, Tib, but I don't need you right now. I'm not really even sad. I'm relieved it's over. It's been over for a long time.

Love was an idea. Nothing more or less.

If you lost the idea, if you somehow forgot it, the person you loved became a stranger. Tibby thought of all those movies about amnesiacs where they don't even know their own spouse. Love lives in the memory. It can be forgotten.

But it can also be remembered.

Early in the summer, Tibby lost the idea of loving Brian. Because of the sex, because of the condom breaking, because of her worst fears seeming real. She couldn't know exactly why. But she knew the darkest parts of growing up had become linked to him that night. Those dark parts had attached to him and somehow overwhelmed the fragile idea of love.

Tibby distinctly remembered the strange sense that night that her idea of love had vanished. It was a spell broken, a dream ended, and reality took over. She had come to her senses and realized that she didn't love Brian, that his best qualities were actually his worst ones, and that furthermore, the fact that Brian inexplicably loved her was stupid and intolerable. She had awoken from a dream of love.

And yet.

Now it was all different again. Her dream had come back, and she didn't know if she was waking or sleeping, what was real and what was illusory.

She called Lena even though Lena had her own things to worry about.

"Do you have any idea what's going on?" Tibby raved. She was done with playing proud.

"With what?" Lena asked.

"With Effie and Brian!"

Lena was silent. Not for more than a second, but long enough for Tibby to know she knew something.

"Well." Lena sighed.

"What do you know?" Tibby practically exploded.

"I don't know anything for sure." Lena's voice was slow and steady. "I mean, I know Effie's had a crush on Brian. But that's been going on a long time. Everybody knows that."

Tibby felt she might swallow her tongue. "They do?"

"Oh, Tib. Just a crush. You know, a juvenile kind of crush. Brian is very good-looking, obviously."

"He is?" Tibby wasn't breathing at all anymore.

"Tibby! Come on. You know what I mean. I'm not trying to torture you. I'm just stating the facts of the case."

Tibby sat on her hand. "Okay," she squeaked.

"Do you want to talk about this?"

Did she? No! But there was nothing else in the world to think of or talk about. "I have to know," she said.

"I don't think there's much to know," Lena said, and her voice was pitched for comfort. "Effie has a crush on Brian, Brian is miserable over you. I think they've talked on the phone a few times."

"They have?" Tibby's hand was asleep. Her ear was hot from the phone.

"Tibby, I don't want to be in the middle of this. But I do want to be honest with you."

"They haven't . . . gone out together or anything."

"I don't think so."

"You don't *think* so?"

Lena sighed again. "It's the kind of thing Effie would mention. Trust me."

"Do you think Brian likes her?"

"I have no reason to think so. But I do think he's had a pretty lonely time."

"Because of thinking I broke up with him?" Tibby asked vacantly.

"Because you did break up with him."

"Oh."

"Hey, Tib?"

"Yeah?"

"I don't mean to bug you, but you really should have told Effie the truth."

"Gee. Thanks."

After she hung up with Lena, she sat at her desk and tried to unscramble her brain.

Effie wanted Brian. Brian was a dreamboat. Duh. Everyone knew that. Everyone wanted him. In fact, it so happened that he was way way way too good for Tibby.

It was base and painful how these things mattered.

Yes, Tibby had once forgotten how to love Brian, but her memory was now effectively jogged. Oh, how painfully she remembered.

Of course Brian was gorgeous! It wasn't like Tibby didn't know that! That wasn't even what mattered!

But all the other stuff did matter—that he was confident and good and that he was an optimist and could whistle Beethoven and didn't care what other people thought. That he loved Tibby! He knew how to love better than anyone. Or at least, he had.

Now the idea of loving Brian was back. Now she couldn't remember the idea of not loving him. When she thought of Effie and Brian, she wished she could remember the idea of not loving him.

A spell broke again, a dream ended, but this time in reverse. Now not loving him was the spell. Not loving was the dream she woke up from. That was how it seemed to her. But how confusing it was! How could you even know what was real? Or what would be real tomorrow? She was so scrambled she couldn't keep track.

Who was she that she could change her mind, her very reality, so completely? Could she ever trust herself again?

Over the next few days she wished she were working more at Movieworld. With her hours so much reduced, she had endless time to stare at her "Script" and wonder about these things. The more she wondered, the less she knew.

She tried to write her script. She had the idea it would be a love story. But she couldn't hold on to any thread. All she could think about was love's intermittency, and that made for no story at all.

Peter came to see Bridget in the lab a few days before she was set to leave for home. She had labels in her pockets, stuck all over her clothes. She had three different-colored Sharpies in her left hand and one in her right.

She'd avoided her lab responsibilities for almost the whole program. She knew she had won the notice of David, the director, for her work in the house, so she could get away with it. She liked being outside in the sun. She liked having her hands in the dirt. She did not like this part. So she'd saved her dues-paying until the end of the trip. She thought of Socrates before the hemlock. You had to pay up eventually.

She saw Peter and she removed the label she was holding in her mouth to say hello.

"How's it going?" he said. They were much changed since the kiss on the hill, both of them chastened.

She shrugged. "Okay."

He looked around to make sure they had privacy. "I didn't want you to go without saying good-bye."

She nodded.

"I feel bad about what happened."

"Probably not as bad as me," she said. She cringed inwardly. What a weird thing to be competitive about.

"Hard to imagine feeling worse," he said.

God, they were alike. Going overboard even at this stage.

"It makes me realize what a mistake it is for me to be away from my family for this long. I lose sight of what they mean to me, you know?"

She did know. She knew exactly. He was canny and he was hungry in all sorts of ways. He lived in the present just as she did.

"You're probably right about that," she said, also knowing that he was missing the deeper solution.

He grinned at her. "It could have been worse."

She raised an eyebrow. "You think so?"

"We could have rolled down the hill."

At that point, it would have just been gravity, but she didn't say so.

"I think back on that night. I feel like we dodged a bullet," he said.

She looked at him without saying anything. No, they hadn't. They hadn't dodged a bullet. The bullet had dodged them.

She thought of Eric, and for the first time in a long time she could actually begin to picture him. The set of his mouth when he concentrated on something. The crumple of his forehead when he was worried. The slightly jaunty overlap of his front teeth when he smiled. He came to her in little bursts, and she could feel, achingly, what it was to miss him.

278

She had gone to some lengths not to feel this, she realized. In spite of the sweetness and reliability of his e-mails, she had guarded against her feelings for him. She had long ago instituted a personal policy against missing people, based on the fear that you would spend your life missing people if you really got going on it.

The time had come to rethink that policy. You blocked the pain and you blocked everything.

Eric loved her. She trusted him more than she trusted herself. She appreciated the wisdom of loving someone built so differently than she was. She was stupid to let him go, even in her mind, even for a day. It was her loss.

As she said good-bye to Peter, she suddenly felt sad for him. He would do this same thing again. At some other place with some other misguided girl. He was already looking forward, shaking off the past—a past that now included her.

She made a vow to herself not to do that.

Tibby called her mother. Sad but true.

"Have you heard anything?" she asked. She had no pride. None. This would be unthinkable if she had any.

"Honey, no."

"Have you seen them together?"

"No."

"You know something. I can tell."

"Tibby."

"Mom. If you know something you have to tell me."

Her mother sighed in exactly the way that everybody

Tibby had talked to had sighed. "Your father saw them at Starbucks."

"He *did*?"

"Yes."

"Together?"

"Seemed like that."

"Brian doesn't like Starbucks!"

"Well, maybe Effie does."

That was the worst possible thing to say. Tibby felt the need to pout for a while.

"Tibby, sweetie. You sound like you are really upset about this. Why don't you tell Effie to lay off? Why don't you tell Brian how you are feeling?"

Typical her mom. These were the worst and least practical suggestions Tibby had ever heard in her life.

"I have to go," she said sullenly.

"Tib. Please."

"I'll talk to you later."

"You know what your dad said?"

"No. What?"

"He said that Brian did not look happy."

Tibby breathed out. That was the first and only good thing her mother said the whole time.

She cannot fade, though

thou hast not thy bliss,

For ever wilt thou love,

and she be fair!

—John Keats

"Hey, Carmen?"

"Yes, Andrew."

"What's going on?"

It was just the two of them in the empty lobby of the theater. Andrew Kerr seemed to have recognized that public humiliation didn't work, so he was trying to reach Carmen privately.

"I don't *know*." She put her face in her hands.

"Carmen, darling. Just relax. Just tell me what."

"I don't know what."

"You were doing so beautifully with this role. Even Ian said it. 'She's a miracle,' he said, and do you know what I said?"

Carmen shook her head.

"I said, 'Let's not jinx it.' "

"Thanks a lot, Andrew."

"Carmen, I know what you are capable of. I believe in you. I just want to know why you are not doing it."

"I think I'm thinking too much," she said.

Andrew nodded sagely. "Ah. Very bad. Don't think too much. Don't think at all."

"I'll try not to."

"Good girl."

Ten minutes later she was back onstage with flowers in her hair, trying to say the line about hostess-ship.

"Carmen!" Andrew thundered. "I hope you are not thinking again!"

"Are we on for Sunday?" Leo left the message on her answering machine.

"Are you there? Are you okay? Do you want to have dinner? What's up?" was his message on Saturday.

"Please, please call me, Lena," he said on Sunday morning.

So she did. When he asked her how she was, she couldn't quite figure out what to say.

"Can you pose today?" he asked hopefully.

Could she? An echo of the old terror sounded at the thought, but it was far away, more like a representation than the real feeling. "Okay," she said. She didn't have the stamina to think why not. "I'll be over in half an hour," she said.

She took a shower. Her skin felt cool and clean, a strange coating for her strange soul. She didn't try to organize her impressions or her anxieties. She just walked to his building and rang 7B.

Upstairs at the door he pulled her into the loft and hugged her and kissed her as though he'd been starved of love for his entire lifetime. Failure to return calls was a depressingly effective aphrodisiac, she thought fleetingly, even among decent guys.

She felt her body curve into him, her lips respond instinctively. Maybe she was starving too.

Leo was a little bit self-conscious when he drew her into his room. He closed the door behind him, which he had not done the week before. She sensed he didn't want the common rooms bearing witness.

The robe was ready. His bed was carefully draped. The little red couch was pushed against the wall.

"I was thinking . . ." His feet shuffled in a winning way. "You could be on the couch again if you want. Or . . ."

"Or?"

"Well, I was thinking maybe . . ."

She pointed to the bed. She could tell it was what he wanted.

"Right. Because. Well, I've sort of been envisioning this painting." He could not stand still. He was practically bouncing.

She could see how much he wanted it. Whether for her or for art she didn't know.

"Do you mind? If you are uncomfortable I totally understand." As he said it, his eyes pleaded with her to get on his bed.

"I don't mind," she said. For some reason, she didn't. The way he'd set it up was lovely. She could see how he wanted the painting to be. She was happy for him.

He politely disappeared and she shed her clothes, not bothering with the robe. She lay on her side on the bed. She laid her head on her arm. She loosened her hair over her shoulder and back and let it fan out behind her on the sheet.

Leo knocked timidly. He came in with the close-held expression of a man who didn't expect his desires to work out. But his face changed when he saw her.

"That's exactly, exactly what I imagined," he said, awestruck. The energy in his long limbs made him seem young to her. "How did you know?"

"This is how I would want to paint it," she said honestly. She wondered where all her millions of layers of self-consciousness had gone. It was strange. Where were the coiled muscles, the purple cheeks, the inability to follow a single thought?

Maybe it was depression. Maybe after the horrible incident with Kostos, she'd lost her will. Maybe she'd held the old hopes so tight that once they were gone, nothing much mattered anymore.

But she didn't feel sad, exactly. She would probably know if she were truly sad. She'd certainly known in the past.

She felt old, she realized. She felt tired. She felt like she'd lived a long time and could see her coquettish self of last week from a very far distance. She felt she hadn't the same things to hide. Or maybe she just lacked the energy to try.

Maybe she cared less. She looked at Leo gazing at her, poised with his brush. Maybe she cared differently.

Maybe it was just a relief to know that the epoch of Kostos was finally, finally over.

"Beautiful," he murmured.

She wasn't sure if he meant her or the painting. Maybe it didn't matter. In a strange way she felt as though she was off the hook.

She watched him paint. She listened to the music he'd put on. More Bach, he said, but this time orchestral and choral. She almost felt like she might fall asleep. Her mind unwound into drowsy thoughts about the sea and the sky as it looked outside her grandmother's kitchen window in Oia.

She might have fallen asleep, because when she opened her eyes the light was different. Leo had put down his brush and was studying her.

"I'm sorry. Did I fall asleep?" she said.

"I think so," he said. His eyes were intense, but in a way particular to painting. He was gathering his impressions, transferring them to his canvas without holding on to them.

"How's it going?" she asked.

"It's — I don't know. I'm afraid to say."

That meant it was going well, she understood. "I think I should take a break for a couple minutes," she said. Her arm was prickly all the way down to her fingers. She sat up and moved to the edge of the bed before he could put down his brush and his palette.

He paused halfway to the door. "Do you want me to go?" he asked.

"You don't have to," she said.

Leo watched her stretch and yawn on the edge of his bed. He was as unfamiliar with her behavior as she was. He drifted back to his canvas in some disbelief.

"What time is it?" she asked, shaking out her sleeping arm.

There was a clock on his desk. "Almost four."

Her eyes opened wide. "God. I really did fall asleep."

He nodded. "You sleep very still," he said.

Silence had fallen over Tibby's life. Lena claimed to know nothing. Tibby's mother claimed to know nothing. Carmen claimed to know nothing. Bee claimed to know nothing, but Bee was in Turkey. Bee was the only one Tibby believed.

In a low moment Tibby found herself on the phone with Katherine. She couldn't help herself.

"So have you seen Brian lately?" Tibby asked casually, hating every word as it came out of her mouth. And also hating her mouth and the weak body to which it was attached.

"Yes," said Katherine. Tibby suspected she was watching cartoons.

"Did he take you to camp on Friday?"

"Uh-huh." Now Katherine was chewing on something.

"Did you see Effie?" Oh, the shame.

"Huh?"

"Did you ever see Effie with Brian?"

"Effie?"

"Yes, Effie."

"No."

Tibby felt the relief flood through her body. Maybe Lena and everybody else were telling her the truth after all. Maybe there really wasn't anything going on.

"But she picked up Brian in her car," Katherine mentioned over the opening song of *Blue's Clues*.

"She did?"

"Two times."

What? What? "Are you sure?"

"Yeah. You know what I think?"

"What?" So intense was Tibby she had practically shoved the phone into her ear cavity.

"She has big boobies."

In the last hour of his light, Leo grew agitated.

"When's your mom coming home?" Lena asked, moving her mouth but not her head.

"Not till tomorrow. She went to the Cape with friends this weekend."

"Oh," Lena said. She began to consider a different explanation.

When the music ended, Leo put down his brush and stowed his palette. He walked over to her, and the fading light showed only half of his face.

"Are we done?" she asked.

He didn't answer, but he touched her calf lightly with his fingers. He put the palm of his hand against her hip. He waited to see if she would protest or move away, if she would feel around for the robe as she had done before.

She considered doing all of these things, but she didn't. She liked the feel of his hand on her skin. She wanted to know what came next.

He sat on the bed and leaned over her, kissing her. She drew in her breath as she felt his hand find her breast. She resumed the kiss as his hands explored her body, finding out a few things his eyes couldn't tell him.

He lay next to her and she unbuttoned his shirt. She recognized her own clumsiness, but it didn't register as shame.

She wondered at the intimacy of the sounds in his throat, the smell of his neck and his chest. She pushed her body against his wide, muscled expanse of skin. It was intimate, but not like what she'd had before. Her mind was peaceful. Her body was stirred and it was curious. She wanted to know how it would go.

This wasn't like it was with Kostos: the fierce want bordering on anguish, the longing intermingled with ache. It was something else. It was a simpler pleasure. Maybe you didn't have to go around feeling that much.

Two years ago, she'd stopped when she'd wanted desperately to go. Why not let it unfold? What was she waiting for?

She'd had enough dreams, enough fantasies. She'd read and she'd heard and she'd imagined. She knew what this was about.

"I have something," he murmured. She realized that he meant he had a condom and that he was asking her if she was ready, if this was what she wanted.

She paused, but only for a moment. "Okay," she whispered back.

Leo wanted her to sleep over, but Lena realized she wanted to wake up in her own bed. He was sorry to walk her home, she knew. He walked her upstairs and to her door, and kissed her until she playfully shut the door in his face.

"We'll have lunch before class tomorrow," he said to her before he left. "I'll bring the sandwiches."

She sat on her bed for a long time without turning on the light. She considered the different parts of her body and how each of them felt. People said that the first time often hurt or felt bad. It didn't for her. She'd been lying naked in his bed for many hours, drowsy and stirred among his sheets and his pheromonal boy smells. She was ready when it happened. Her pleasure was tentative and new, but she was also able to take joy from Leo's more complete rapture.

She was his muse, he told her. The combination of the erotic and artistic had been a revelation to him. She was happy with that. Especially as she thought of her own painting and knew that he was a muse for her too.

Does he even know there is more?

Lena checked herself. She stopped her thinking and went back over the question, unsure of what she'd meant by it. More what? More sadness? More tragedy? More ragged exposure, like you had turned yourself inside out? Was that more?

What if Leo didn't know? What if he never knew? Maybe that would be a piece of good luck.

With Leo she didn't feel turned inside out. She was happy about that. She put on an old pair of pajamas, feeling very much outside in.

But when she woke up sometime in the early morning, she was crying. Her face and hair were soaked, her pillow was damp. How long had she been crying?

The crying kept going as she sat up and wondered about it, not seeming to will it. But she knew what the trouble was. She knew her dream self was permitting a sadness her waking self hadn't allowed.

All this time she'd been waiting for Kostos. She'd always thought her first time would be with him.

Remember to let her into

your heart.

—John Lennon and

Paul McCartney

Tibby tortured herself for the days leading up to her parents' anniversary party. But there was a strange comfort in the fact that at least she deserved it.

Brian and Effie were acting like a couple. No one was even denying it anymore.

"They are the only ones left at home," Bee said.

"Maybe they're just friends," Carmen said.

"Brian's lonely. He misses you," Lena said.

Tibby didn't believe any of it.

If Effie had used even half of the tactical brilliance on Brian that she'd used on Tibby, there was no hope. Effie would probably be wearing an engagement ring the next time Tibby saw her. It wouldn't even matter whether Brian liked her or not.

Silly old Effie, clueless little sister who couldn't tell time without a digital clock. Ha. In Tibby's mind, Effie had transformed into the devil herself.

Tibby's subconscious produced a new anxiety dream just

for the occasion. Tibby dreamed it night after night, all night long: Effie doing various bold things while wearing the Traveling Pants. Only once in all those dreams did Tibby get to wear them herself. And when her big chance came, Tibby somehow ended up with her whole body stuffed into one leg.

"Do you want me to disinvite Brian to the party?" her mother asked the week before Tibby was set to take the train home.

"Let me think about it."

Tibby called her mother back an hour later. "No, he should come. It would be wrong to tell him not to. Anyway, I'm going to have to see him sometime."

They were quiet for a minute.

"I can't exclude Effie," her mom said, naming the very thing Tibby was hoping for.

"You can't?"

"Honey, they're all coming. They are like our extended family. I couldn't think of not having Ari and George. And Lena? That's not a question. I can't exactly say everybody come but leave Effie home."

"Why not?" Tibby said sourly.

"Tibby."

"So would you mind disinviting me?"

More and more, Tibby spent her time watching TV. She'd given up on the computer and her "Script." She watched all the murder shows. All the makeover shows. All the soap operas. All the cooking shows. Even the bug shows and the history shows. She blew most of her savings buying a TiVo on eBay. With the rest she bought a used PlayStation. Everything she needed was right there in that little TV. She watched for Maria Blanquette, but she never came on anymore.

There were quiet moments, though, maybe in the middle of the night or the very early morning, when the countless hours of TV sanded her brain down so that she could see life's bigger patterns. And then Tibby had the sad thought that while she was staring at the screen, Brian, former Dragon Master, was being with a girl and living a life.

To: Tibberon@sbgnetworks.com; Carmabelle@hsp.xx.com; Beezy3@gomail.net
From: LennyK162@gomail.net
Subject: It

I truly cannot believe I'm writing a shotgun e-mail to tell you this, but I couldn't tell one of you without telling the others.

I did it. It it. Or we did it, I should say. Me and Leo.

Bee, I think it was you (was it not) who bet a dozen crullers it wouldn't happen before I was twenty-five. Ahem.

It's not that I was in a hurry or anything. I really wasn't. I would have forked over the donuts. I think I just realized that I was waiting for something that wasn't even real.

I'll have to give you the details in person when we are together. (Carmen??)

I'm suddenly picturing my dad seizing my computer and reading everything I write.

Love, love, love, love, love,

Your Loving Lena

(Lover of Leo)

Originally, Bee's return trip took her from Izmir to Istanbul to New York and ended with a short flight to Boston. Her plan at the time was to end up in Providence with a week and a half to get in shape for preseason soccer training camp.

But at the airport in Istanbul she switched the flight to Boston to a flight to Washington, D.C., instead.

And what made her happy, after a disorienting number of hours in transit, was seeing Tibby and Lena at the very front of the baggage area waiting for her. She ran at them, almost flattening them in her joy.

"I'm so glad you are here!" she shouted at them.

"We missed you," Lena said as Bee hugged and hugged them.

"I missed you," Bee avowed.

There was too much to say, so they didn't bother quite yet. They drove to Angie's downtown and stuffed their faces with pancakes and bacon even though it wasn't breakfast time, and felt happy to be together. Bee realized they were good at trusting that the moment would come when all would be shared and all would be known. They would wait until Carmen was with them for the true unburdening.

Bridget was lucky, she really was. In the ways that counted.

"I've got to take care of some things at home," Bee said as Tibby pulled her mom's car up to Bee's house. "But I'll come by your parents' party later, okay?"

"Good. It'll be you, me, Len . . . Brian and Effie," Tibby said darkly.

"Oh, no," said Bee. "Really?"

"Yes."

Bee looked at Lena, who shrugged. "Has Effie ever done what I wanted?"

"I'll bring my riot gear," Bee said.

Bee realized after she'd waved good-bye and watched them go that she did not have the key to her house. She didn't feel like knocking. She left her bags in front of the door and went to the back of the house. She still knew the tricks of the kitchen door. She jimmied it patiently and it opened for her. She walked purposefully inside.

Her dad was still at work, she guessed, and Perry would be in his room. She got her bags from the front of her house. She marched them upstairs. Without stopping to think too much she unzipped her duffel bag and began putting her things in her old, emptied drawers.

She opened a window in her room. When she was done unpacking, she walked down to the kitchen and opened a window there, too. She made a quick circuit around the small and overgrown backyard, stopping briefly to pull a few hydrangea balls from the neighbors' bush. She put the blue flowers in a glass in the middle of the kitchen table.

She looked in the refrigerator. There wasn't much there. A bottle of ginger ale. A half-full carton of milk. Some take-out boxes. A wilting bunch of celery in the bottom drawer.

In the cabinet were various cans, who knew how old.

Then she remembered the cereal. She opened the pantry door and saw the impressive lineup of boxes. Both her father and her brother were big on cereal.

She found a bowl and a teaspoon. She poured herself a short layer of cornflakes and added some milk, pleased that it had not yet expired. She sat herself down at the little kitchen table. She wasn't hungry and it didn't taste particularly good, but she ate it.

She left her bowl and spoon in the sink. She left her purse dangling on the chair.

For better and worse, this was her home, and she would remember how to live in it.

The magic had worn off. The loveliness had vanished absolutely. She was back to sweatshirt Carmen, though it was too hot to actually wear one.

She stayed in her bed, trying to sleep through rehearsal. She felt the old Destructo-Carmen impulse, and she tried to work it.

Julia was sympathetic. She brought her cookies and tea from the canteen. She brought her bags of salty Fritos and let her borrow her iPod. She promised they would never talk about meter again if Carmen felt like it was making it worse.

"Thanks," Carmen said tearfully.

She would have stayed in bed all day, but opening night was now four days away, and Carmen knew if she missed the afternoon part, Andrew would maim, mangle, dismember, and also kill her.

She dragged herself miserably to the theater. She was

slowly turning invisible again. Jonathan wasn't even bothering to flirt with her anymore.

She was unfortunately still visible to Judy, who was waiting stage left to pounce on her.

"Carmen, c'mere," she said, walking briskly out back.

Carmen felt herself suffocating, even apart from the ninety-five-degree heat and one-hundred-percent humidity.

"I don't like to think I have made a mistake."

"Me either," Carmen said dolefully.

"I'm trying to figure out what's wrong with you."

"Where to start," Carmen said.

Judy looked at her sharply. "You're wallowing."

"I know."

"It's too late to get someone else to do this."

Carmen felt the thud of her pulse in her head.

"And yes, I have thought about it."

Carmen was done with being smart. She had nothing to say.

"You know, Carmen, the great majority of people achieve real quality in acting by work and study. There are a few people who have very strong natural instincts, and for them it sometimes makes sense to just get out of the way and let it happen. Do you know what I'm saying?"

Carmen nodded, though she didn't fully know what Judy was saying.

"So you go home and figure out what the trouble is and come back tomorrow for dress rehearsal and do your job."

Carmen gazed at Judy without confidence.

"One last thing."

"Yes."

"Trust yourself. Don't listen to anybody else."

Carmen tried not to roll her eyes, but it seemed to her a laughable command at this point.

Judy shrugged. "That's all I'm going to say."

"So look what I bought," Bee said to her father when he got home from work.

He was surprised to see her, first off, let alone the array of vegetables, fresh fruit, and pasta she'd bought at the new Whole Foods and left on the counter. "I'm only home for a couple of nights, so I thought we could make dinner together."

Once upon a time her father had enjoyed cooking. He used to listen to Beatles songs in the kitchen, and he played them loud, so the words made their way onto Bridget's sheets of homework.

She pushed him gently and amicably on the shoulder. "What do you think? You know how to make pesto, don't you?"

He nodded. He looked strained, shell-shocked, slightly frightened.

"Good. I'll get Perry. He can make the fruit salad."

This was an absurd notion, but Bee was ambitious tonight.

She dragged Perry downstairs, blinking like a mole pulled from the dirt. "You can go back to your game after dinner," she told him. She set him up at the counter next to her with a paring knife, a pile of fruit, and a blue bowl. "Cut off the peels and cut everything more or less into squares," she explained.

He was so startled he just did what she said.

She started chopping garlic for the pesto. "Like this?" she asked her dad. He looked up from washing basil.

"A little smaller," he said.

She plugged in the long-unused kitchen radio, an artifact of sorts, and tuned it to an oldies station. She bounced around a little as she grated the cheese.

"Penne or linguine?" she asked Perry, making the boxes dance in front of him. "You get to choose."

"Uh." Perry looked from one to the other. He seemed to take his job seriously. "Penne?"

"Perfect," she declared.

They worked in silence but for a dumb Carpenters song on the radio.

"Did you get pine nuts?" her father asked her.

She was so pleased that she had. "Here," she said, plucking them from behind a loaf of bread.

"Some people use walnuts," her father told them, "but I prefer pine nuts."

"Me too," said Bridget earnestly.

Perry nodded.

After she'd set the little kitchen table and lit a candle and helped Perry transfer his burgeoning salad to a bigger bowl, she heard "Hey Jude" come on the radio. She felt a sad and strange sort of exultation. She turned her face away from them for a moment and closed her eyes, caught in the grip of remembering how it used to be in this house, in this kitchen.

To her right, over the sound of water running in the sink, she heard her father sing along to two words of the song. Just the two, and yet it brought her a joy she could hardly contain.

Bouncing is for balls.

—Tibby Rollins

Tibby's parents' twentieth-anniversary party was for her, in a way, like a traffic accident taking place in slow motion over a long period of time. Sometimes she was in the accident and sometimes she was watching it.

It also had the feature, for Tibby, of having been foretold. And as with an accident, Tibby didn't dare look, but she couldn't not look either. Her better angels told her to look away. And she told those better angels to take a hike.

Lena brought her the Traveling Pants to wear. Lena and Bee hovered so close to her she felt like she'd grown two more heads. She finally told them they had to go away.

Tibby talked to various family friends. She acted like she was writing a real script, being a real film student, and not just playing one while watching TV.

The first time she saw Brian he was eating hummus. The next time he was eating shrimp dumplings. The third time he was eating stuffed grape leaves. How could he eat so much?

The fourth time, he was with Effie. It had to happen eventually. Tibby watched while Effie, in a fit of lurid effrontery, touched Brian on the back. In front of everybody. Tibby felt sick. Both Lena and Bee magically reappeared, each at one of Tibby's elbows.

Effie looked beautiful. She really did. Her cheeks were pink and her legs were tan and her breasts looked like they were ready to take over the room. To be fair, Effie wasn't overdressed. She wasn't overly made up. Effie was happy. That was the thing.

And by that standard of beauty, Tibby was a pure fright. A Boo Radley spooking around her parents' happy party.

Tibby spent some of the time in her room. At one point she went into the backyard and found Bee teaching soccer moves to Nicky and Katherine. Tibby tried to be zany and get up a game of spitting watermelon seeds, but who was she kidding?

"Can this just be over?" she asked Bee before the cake was even presented.

At last, in a blur of warm tidings and well wishes and drunken neighbors, it really was over. She ended up saying good-bye to Effie and Brian in order. She could tell it wasn't what they'd intended. Everyone looked embarrassed at the way it had fallen out.

Tibby kept her face on. And yes, there was Effie, close enough to smell. Tibby moved her mouth and formed words in the generally appropriate category. "Thanks. Great. Yeah. Blah, blah blah." Effie moved on.

Now it was Brian's turn. Tibby said the same robotic

and stupid things, but Brian didn't say anything stupid or robotic back. He just looked at her. Tibby's spirits were fried, but even so, her brain carried on. It continued to perceive things and have thoughts.

Yes, Effie was glowing. Effie was a goddess. But when Tibby looked with honest eyes she could see that Brian, all handsomeness notwithstanding, didn't look so happy. He was a second Boo Radley, but with a fuller stomach.

Tibby stopped whatever stupid thing she was saying in the middle of a sentence. Enough already. Brian held her hand. He held it and he looked at her straight on, eye to eye. She didn't look away. It was the first brave thing she'd done in three months.

There was the natural rhythm of things you knew without knowing. The natural rhythm dictated that Brian let her hand go now, but he didn't. He kept on and so did she. Before he got shoved along by a paralegal in her father's firm, Brian squeezed her hand. But so quickly and subtly she wasn't completely sure it was on purpose or actually that it had even happened.

She watched him go with a sad, slow feeling, as though she saw close things from miles away. She went up to her room without saying good-bye to anyone else.

She climbed into her bed and looked at the place by the window where Mimi's cage used to sit, where Mimi had lived her soft, simple guinea-pig days among her wood shavings and her pellets. Tibby wished she could go back to when Mimi was still alive. To when Bailey was still alive.

She thought about the first time she met Brian. It was Bailey, of course, who thought of it, who put them together. Bailey was uncanny in that way. Before Bailey died, she basically set Tibby up with everything and everyone she would need for a happy life. And Tibby mostly lost or forgot them.

It was so hard to live the right kind of life, even if you knew what it was.

Tibby wished she could at least go back to the night in June when she'd lost the idea of love. She didn't wish she could take back the sex. She used to wish that, but not anymore. She and Brian loved each other. They were old enough to know what they were doing. She wanted to be with him in every way, and that was one of them.

As she thought about it, she realized she wouldn't even change the condom breaking or her fears about pregnancy. If she really got a wish, she wouldn't want to be greedy or impractical. You couldn't turn back time or bring the dead to life. If she got a wish, she would hope to be more modest with it.

She remembered when she was around four or five asking Carmen if she believed the wish Tibby had made over her birthday candles would come true. "Yeah, if you wish for something that could actually happen," Carmen had said philosophically.

Tibby's wish would be to hold on to the idea of love even in the face of darkest doubt. Because that was the way in which she failed. Not once, but again and again.

❖   ❖   ❖

That night, Carmen tried to figure out what the trouble was. She walked around the campus. She sat on the hillside where she'd first met Judy. She called Tibby, and then she remembered about the Rollinses' anniversary party and she cried because she wasn't there with them.

Why are we always apart? she wondered. A voice on the phone wasn't enough sometimes. *Why have I kept away all this time?*

Because we have the Pants, she thought quickly. *The Pants make it okay to do that.*

She went back to her dorm room, and without bothering to take off her clothes or brush her teeth or turn out the lights, she crawled into bed.

She was lying there, eyes open, a while later when Julia came in.

"Look what I have for you," Julia announced gaily. She was in her Florence Nightingale persona.

"What?" said Carmen weakly.

"Those buttermilk scones you love. They make them at night. Did you know that? I have three in the bag and they are ho-o-ot!" She drew out the *O*, trilling it in song.

Carmen sat up. Scones were, in fact, the most comforting food in the solar system.

But as she looked up at Julia's face, something occurred to her. Julia looked happy. Not just cheering-up-a-friend happy, but genuinely happy. Carmen, on the other hand, felt—and undoubtedly looked—genuinely sad.

In the next moment another thing occurred to Carmen. She remembered the time, just a few weeks ago, when

Julia was the one who looked unhappy. And it happened to be at the same time that Carmen was feeling, and undoubtedly looking, happy.

Was this a coincidence? She thought not.

Julia was happy when Carmen was unhappy. In fact, Carmen's unhappiness was the very thing that seemed to make Julia happy. And, alternately, Carmen's happiness caused Julia displeasure.

There was a notable misalignment there. A serious one. What kind of friend thrived on your unhappiness?

She knew the answer. No kind of friend.

She lay back down, her mind whirring.

She thought of her pathetic resolution to be a more worthy friend to Julia, deciding that if she lost weight and pulled herself together, Julia would like her better. How wrong she had been! Julia liked her precisely for her unworthiness. All the ways Carmen failed made Julia feel better about herself. What few ways Carmen succeeded made Julia despise her. Even sabotage her.

Julia seemed to sense the change in mood, but she didn't want to let go. "Butter or jam? Butter *and* jam!"

Even now, even amid deepest doubt, confusion and misery, Carmen didn't want to let Julia down. Too ingrained was her idea of how friendship was. "No. Thanks," she said. "I'm just really tired."

"Are you sure? They are hot. They won't be hot in the morning."

Julia made it hard not to take what she offered. "No, thanks," Carmen said again.

Julia's face got a pinched look. "No problem," she said. "I'll just leave them on your desk."

"Thanks," said Carmen, dully. She picked herself out of bed, brushed her teeth, put on a sleeping shirt, and crawled back into bed. "Do you mind if I turn off the light?"

Julia grabbed a book from the floor. "I'm going to read for a while," she said.

Carmen tried to sleep, but she couldn't. Her despair was so big that she couldn't think of a way to feel better.

And then she remembered a way.

Under Julia's suspicious frown, Carmen took her script from the end of her bed and crept out into the hallway. She sat under the good light and tried to reacquaint herself with the lost girl.

When Tibby woke up, she lay in her old bed for a while and let the waking world come back to her slowly. And she realized her breath had an echo. That was kind of funny, to be breathing in twos.

Then she realized that the second breathing was not hers. She opened her eyes and saw Lena's face where she lay across the end of Tibby's bed. Lena's small, patient face, made with more precision, more fineness than ordinary faces. Most people would tap you and wake you up, but Lena was happy to just wait while Tibby slept.

"Hey," said Tibby. She wondered at how she could love one Kaligaris sister so much and really hate the other one.

Lena smiled. She seemed pretty satisfied with lying there in the sunshine.

"When do you go back?" Tibby asked, crooking her elbow and propping her head on her hand.

"I'm going to stay here for a few days. What about you?"

"I think Bee and I are going to take a train tomorrow night."

They were quiet for a while, but companionably so.

"I think you should get back together with Brian," Lena said finally.

Tibby felt as if she could see the words floating down like feathers freed from her comforter. "I can't, though."

"Why not?"

"It wouldn't be fair," Tibby said, earnestly hoping that Lena would not agree with her.

"It wouldn't be fair to whom?"

"Well, to Effie, I guess."

Lena studied Tibby's face thoughtfully. She seemed to want to project her thoughts from her eyes as much as her mouth. "I don't think you should worry so much about Effie."

"How can I not? She asked my permission and I gave it."

Lena looked sad. "Yes. I know. And Effie's my sister. And I don't want to side with you over her. It's not like I haven't thought about all this."

"I know, Lenny," Tibby said apologetically.

"I've waited to say anything, because I don't want to hurt Effie."

Tibby nodded. She'd worn her anger at Effie like a skin, protective and irritable. Now Tibby felt herself molting, slipping out of it not in bits, but as a piece. And like a molted skin, once disembodied, it sat dry and weightless beside her. It had captured her completely, and yet it didn't belong to her.

"Effie is strong, you know? She bounces."

I don't bounce, Tibby acknowledged to herself.

"She loves Brian. But she loves him in the Effie way. It's like she's going in circles a hundred miles an hour and he's practically standing still. She only sees him when she laps him, but still she thinks they're together."

Tibby laughed in spite of herself.

"Brian wants to cooperate, but it's not right for him."

Tibby marveled at Lena's perfect recapitulation.

Lena resettled her body so she was sitting cross-legged directly across from Tibby and holding her close with her eyes.

"Here's one thing I know," Lena said.

Tibby sat up too. Lena picked the important things carefully.

"There are some people who fall in love over and over."

Tibby nodded, understanding the particular melancholy as it revealed itself on Lena's face.

"And there are others who can only seem to do it once."

Tibby felt tears in her eyes just like she saw in Lena's. She knew Lena was talking about her and Brian. And she was also talking about herself.

And maybe . . .

you are a little

fat bear cub

with no wings and

no feathers.

—Else Holmelund Minarik

Bridget coaxed Perry into going on a bike ride with her. She'd gone to some lengths to borrow Carmen's stepdad's bicycle and helmet, but she'd tried to pass it off to Perry as the lightest of impulses.

"What do you say? We'll just go down to Rock Creek Park and back."

He looked doubtful.

"Please?"

She got on her old bike, not giving him too much chance to think. She was happy when he reluctantly followed. Perry had never been athletic, but he used to love riding his bike.

It was a beautiful late-summer day, not nearly as hot as it could have been. The traffic was blessedly light, as though the cars had purposely stayed away, knowing it was a fragile situation.

By the time they'd made it to the park, Perry was riding right up next to her, coasting along.

She stopped inside the entrance as promised. "Do you want to turn around?" she asked.

He shrugged. "We can keep going," he said, making her feel happy.

They biked for an hour more before they stopped at a cart and bought ice cream bars. Perry had money and wanted to pay. They sat on the grass by the creek and ate them.

There was so much she wanted to say to him. She wanted to get him to talk about their mother and about things he remembered. But she knew she had to go slow. It would be too easy to scare him away.

Before they got back on their bikes, she put her arm around him and squeezed his shoulders. How long had it been since anyone had touched him? He was a little stiff, a little uncomfortable. It probably wasn't what he wanted, but she felt in her heart it was something he needed.

On the way home they stopped at the pet store on Wisconsin Avenue. Perry had always loved animals, but he'd never been allowed to have anything but newts, because their mother was allergic to animals with fur.

They held hamsters first, and then an obese guinea pig. Perry held a baby white mouse with utmost care. Next they each picked up a rabbit. Perry's tried to climb down the front of his shirt and it made him laugh.

Soon after they got home from the pet store, Bridget's

cell phone started ringing. With a galloping heart she recognized Eric's cell number. He didn't have service in Mexico, did he?

"Hello?"

"Bee?"

"Eric?"

"It's me," he said sweetly. "Where are you?"

It had been so long since she'd heard his voice she thought she might cry.

"I'm in D.C. Where are you?"

"I'm in New York."

"You are in New York?" she screamed joyfully. She couldn't help herself. New York wasn't right here, but it was a lot closer than Baja. "Is everything okay?"

"Everything is fine. I really want to see you." He said it tenderly.

"I *really* want to see you." Whatever had happened this summer, the way she felt now, she could not doubt that she loved him.

"What time is it?" he asked.

She walked in view of the kitchen clock. "Almost noon."

"I'll be there in time for dinner."

"Here?"

"There. You better give me your address again."

"You're coming here?" She was screaming again.

"How else am I going to see you?"

"I don't know!" she shouted giddily.

"I can't wait until tomorrow," he said.

❀   ❀   ❀

Carmen dressed that morning under the watchful eye of Julia. She forced herself to wear lipstick, even though she didn't feel up to it. Sometimes you could trick yourself.

She didn't collect any of the books she'd taken to carrying around. She didn't even take her script. She could no longer see the words for all the markings.

She did, however, pick up the bag of scones from her desk and take them with her as she walked out the door. Julia looked pleased with that, at least.

Carmen carried the scones as far as the big front doors, where she dumped them in the garbage can.

At rehearsal she kept to herself. Andrew had an eye out for her, but he left her alone. Judy left her alone. Carmen didn't feel invisible to them. She felt they were trusting her to find her way. Either that or they had given up on her, but she didn't really believe that.

She sat in the back row, in the dark, and listened to Leontes rage about nothingness. She thought of the idea she'd had on the hillside the night she'd met Judy. Where there is nothing, there is the possibility of everything. When you live nowhere, you live everywhere.

She wished she had the Pants right now, but she didn't. She had to rely on herself. You have to be like a turtle, she thought; you have to figure out how to bring your home along with you.

She saw Hermione, Perdita's lost mother, bustle down the aisle in full statue costume and makeup. That was a fantasy, wasn't it? Your mother turns into a statue. William Shakespeare knew a thing or two about wish fulfillment.

317

The statue-mother stays exactly where you left her. You always know where to find her. She doesn't move, doesn't change, doesn't even age.

Carmen thought of her mother. She was hardly a statue. She didn't stay still for two minutes. And yet, even with her new husband and her new baby and her new house—with her *happiness*—Carmen always knew where to find her.

She thought of what it was to begrudge someone their happiness, and this brought to her a stinging set of feelings. She didn't want to think about Julia. She was afraid she would begin to seethe, she'd be sucked into the maelstrom of her old temper and it wouldn't help her. She didn't have the stomach for it. She didn't have the power. She didn't have the wherewithal right now to stake that kind of claim.

Instead, she thought of Ryan's walking shoes. She touched the Pants charm dangling from a chain around her neck. For some odd reason, she thought of Tibby's old guinea pig, Mimi.

Julia was waiting for her outside the theater when they broke for lunch. Carmen saw her there waiting with a smile and two big sweating iced teas, sandwiches, and bags of chips. She beckoned to Carmen and Carmen felt the familiar reactions, outmoded and dislodged though they were. She felt the old pull of gratitude. She felt needy and uncertain. She still clung to the notion of a friend, even a crappy one.

But Carmen didn't move. "No, thanks. Not today," she said finally, and she walked right by.

❖　❖　❖

Bridget fretted out loud in Lena's bedroom. Once the euphoria of getting to see Eric had quieted a little, she'd realized she had problems.

"I told Perry we'd all have dinner together again. He actually seemed like he wanted to. I can't blow it off."

"So you can eat together," Lena said.

"Together?"

"Yeah. Why not?"

There were many reasons why not. But were any good enough to prevent her from doing it?

"Okay, so what do I do with Eric?"

"What *do* you do with Eric?" Lena smiled craftily. "Only you can answer that."

Bridget pretended to punch her. "Come on. I mean where do I put him?"

"In your house."

"In my house?"

Lena shrugged. "That's my only idea."

Bee never brought anyone to her house. Not since middle school. Not even her friends. She hardly brought herself there. Certainly not a boyfriend. It was almost too strange to imagine. Did she need to ask her father? What would he make of it?

And more terrible, what would Eric think of them? How would he feel about her if he saw her house? If he met her father and brother? She had wanted to protect him from the truth.

"Lenny, you know how my house is."

"I think Eric can handle it."

"Do you honestly think that?"

"If he's good enough for you, Bee, I honestly do."

On the walk from Lena's, Bee's adrenaline started pumping. At home, she couldn't be still if she tried. She started with vacuuming, then dusting. She sprayed Fantastik on the walls, trying to make them look a little less gray. She opened all the windows. She brought a fan down from the attic. She mopped. She found boxes in the garage and started putting the ugliest stuff in them—plates, pictures, papers, odd bits of furniture. She stuffed them all out of sight in the basement. She shook out the rugs. She tried to rearrange them to cover the vomitously ugly wall-to-wall carpets. She cleaned the bathroom tile on her hands and knees. She stole more flowers from the neighbors' yard.

When her father arrived home, he looked as though he'd found himself in the wrong place.

"Hey, Dad," she said. "My friend . . . actually my boyfriend is coming to stay for a night. Is that all right?"

Her father's confusion was almost impenetrable. She had to explain it four times before he showed any light of understanding.

"Where will he stay?" he finally asked, with his faraway look.

"In the den. On the couch."

"In my den?"

"Yes. Unless you want him in your room." She meant that as a joke, but it didn't go over like one.

"I don't think so," her father said solemnly.

330

"In the den, then? Is that okay?"

He nodded and she went back to her cleaning, getting crazier as the hours passed. At five o'clock she corralled the two of them in the kitchen.

"No headphones outside of your rooms," she commanded.

They both nodded fearfully.

"Try to circulate a little. If Eric talks to you, it's a plus if you answer."

They both nodded again. They didn't even look offended.

"We'll have dinner at seven-thirty, okay? Dad, we'll have the leftover pesto and I'll make a salad."

More nodding.

"That's it. Just . . . be yourselves," she finished, which was the least helpful thing she could possibly have said.

By seven o'clock she ran out of steam. She floated along the hallway feeling sorry and hopeless and sad. She wished Eric weren't coming to this house. She wished she hadn't bullied her father and brother into hostile resistance. She wished she lived any life other than this one. Sometimes the past and the future could not be forced together.

But when she walked past Perry's room she saw him cleaning up his desk. When she went downstairs she saw her father carefully folding sheets and a blanket onto the couch in his den.

She'd thought they had nothing to offer her, but they did. She'd thought her efforts were lost on them, but maybe they weren't. She'd thought they had no power to hurt her or make her happy, but at this moment she knew that wasn't true.

They had meager offerings, all three of them. But if they could align what little they had, maybe they could start to make it better.

Tibby called Brian late on Sunday afternoon. "Will you meet me at the picnic table?" she asked him. It was their significant place, site of their first kiss. It stood under a giant copper beech tree in a tiny triangular park equidistant from their houses.

"Okay," he said.

"Now?"

She got there first. She pointed her face in the direction of his house and watched for him. At last he came, the sun drooping faintly behind him. She felt joy spilling over in her chest. Something about his face made her stand up and greet him with her arms. She put them around him courageously. He let her.

She took a step to the side so he could sit at the end of the picnic table. She was grateful that he obliged.

The perfect thing about this table was that when he sat on the end of it and she stood between his legs, they were at the exact right height for seeing each other eye to eye and also for kissing. They had done it many times in the past. She didn't try kissing him this time. But she put her face against his so her mouth was near his ear. "I am so sorry," she said.

He pulled away and looked at her carefully.

"I got scared. I panicked. I forgot everything that was important."

Sometimes it seemed to her that he could extract everything from her mind with his eyes. Sometimes it seemed like her words just got in the way of it.

"I knew that, Tibby. I understood. Why wouldn't you talk to me?"

A blink of her eyes released unexpected tears. "Because I can't lie to you as well as I lie to myself."

He nodded, seeming to understand even that.

"I promise I won't do that again," she said. His eyes tested her words, but she wasn't scared. She knew they were true.

Softly she held his two hands in her two hands. Brutally she shoved aside her chronic instincts of pride and fear. She had no business with them now. "I missed you," she said. "I wish we could go back."

He shrugged. "We can't."

"We can't?" Her agony stretched her words out over the abyss. Had she been wrong in believing that he would forgive her?

"We can go forward, though."

"Together?" She did nothing to temper the abject hope in her face.

"I hope so."

"Really?"

He nodded. "I won't be going to NYU, though."

She winced. "Because of me. Because I ruined everything." She was prepared to eat the blame like ice cream if he'd take her back.

"It's all right. Maybe it's not such a bad thing."

"I'll make it up. I really will. I'll take the bus back every weekend."

"You don't have to do that, Tibby."

"But I want to. I will."

"Let's see how it goes."

"Okay," she said, unnerved by his reserve, his reasonableness.

She realized he was right when he said that they couldn't go back. For better or worse, it would be different now. Innocence was not one of the things you could get back.

"Maybe we can trade off," he said.

Life's a voyage that's

homeward bound.

—Herman Melville

Eric had probably hoped for a dinner alone in a restaurant where they could laugh and kiss and play romantic under-the-table foot games to their hearts' content. Instead, he got underheated pesto, a distractedly made salad, and a lot of awkward silence from Bridget's two poorly socialized family members.

He might have thought he'd get to sleep in a bed in a nice suburban house, but he got a scratchy couch in a falling-down house occupied mostly by ghosts.

He tolerated all of it bravely, and his reward did come when she tiptoed downstairs and led him by the hand into her room and shut the door quietly behind her. She knew her brother and father were happily ensconced in their headphones, and this one time it made her glad.

She sat him down on her bed and he groaned with delight as she hitched up her nightgown and sat on his lap, wrapping her tan legs around him. She kissed him long and deep, tangling him up in her web of limbs and fingers and soft hair.

"Why did you come back early?"

"For this," he whispered.

"No, really."

"Really."

"Really?"

"I missed you."

"Did you?"

"A lot."

She hugged him harder.

"I thought of you everywhere all the time. On the beach. On the soccer field. In the water. Lying in bed I *really* thought of you."

His expression was so shameless she laughed. "I mean it, Bee. Every girl I saw I wished was you."

She looked at him with wonder. He was so much better at this than she was! She felt suddenly sad for herself and happy for him. Or rather, the opposite: She felt happy for herself, getting someone as wonderful as him, and sad for him, getting someone as wretched as her.

"Did you miss me?" he asked.

She looked at him thoughtfully. She didn't want to lie. She had some complicated things to tell him and she wasn't yet sure how. "When you told me you were going to Mexico, I wasn't sure what it meant," she said slowly. "I wasn't sure if it meant you wanted to . . . go our own ways for a while."

Each one of his features seemed to grow solemn in turn. "Did you really think that?"

"I wasn't sure what to think."

"Do you think that now?"

"No." She knew her answer right away.

He put his hands on either side of her face. "I never thought of going separate ways. I never wanted that. The way I looked at it was, when you're meant to be, what's a summer?"

She felt the ache in her throat. He didn't question his love. Why had she?

"So does that mean you didn't miss me?" he asked.

"I didn't realize how much until the end," she said.

"And the beginning and the middle?"

She rubbed her cheek thoughtfully. "I think I was missing the idea of missing," she said. "But I think I might have figured it out now."

He let her pull his T-shirt over his head. He let her kiss him. He obliged when she pulled at the waist of his boxers, and he seemed eager to get her out of her nightgown. He was going to trust her and she was going to be worthy of it.

It was maybe strange to want to make love to your boyfriend in your old bedroom after such a summer. But it was undoubtedly what she wanted.

Maybe it was her need to connect old and new. Maybe it was her desire to put a happy memory, an act of love, into this house that had seen so few of them.

*   *   *

Carmen wore Perdita's flowers in her hair and she kept quiet. She spoke when she was onstage and otherwise she floated around in the state of a dream. For three days, she didn't look at her script.

The hardest part was the few hours in the middle of the night spent in her room. It was hard to be impervious to Julia's overtures. It was perhaps harder to be impervious to Julia's silent rage.

You don't want me to be happy, she said to herself to ward off Julia's poisonous spirit.

She wore her costume. She mused on the warmth of her skin and the sensation of new textures against it. She listened to Leontes. She listened to Polixenes and Autolycus and Paulina. She bathed her brain in luxurious language and mostly forgot about thinking.

She said her lines, but she did not look at Andrew and he said nothing to her. *We're trusting me to figure this out,* she knew.

In the morning Eric had to leave, he said. Maybe he just wanted to leave. But he promised Bridget he'd meet her in Providence in a few days. That was a relief. She wanted to practice being better at missing him, but not quite yet.

Before she left home she had a number of things to take care of. The last was retrieving the boxes of stuff she had shoved into the basement in her apoplexy of cleaning the day before.

She sensed that her dad and Perry were happy with some of her alterations, but she didn't want to go overboard. If

Perry needed to keep his Lord of the Rings calendar from 2003, then so be it.

She walked down to the basement and hauled up the boxes one at a time. Going down for the last load, she finally thought to turn on the light to make sure she wasn't forgetting anything.

Her eyes caught on a shelf holding a series of neatly placed boxes. She didn't remember them—neither the shelves nor the boxes. How long had it been since she'd looked around down here? She walked over to study them more carefully.

Each of the boxes was labeled with a name and a year or, in a few cases, a span of years. The writing was all capitals, but she recognized it as her father's.

In a state of breathlessness she took down *Bridget* from 1993. Was it kindergarten? Maybe first grade? Inside, carefully stacked and piled, were artworks, clay pieces, efforts at writing and tracing. There were pictures, some with notes on the back in her mother's handwriting. There was a card from Greta. A necklace she remembered beading. There was a photograph of her with Tibby and Lena and Carmen. There was a crayon drawing she'd made of Perry with a tiny head, holding a newt.

She took down the box that said *Marly, 1985–1990.* There were pictures from her parents' wedding, her mother's journals, pictures her mother had drawn, the beginning of a baby book for her twins. Bridget never knew that her mother had drawn pictures.

She took down another of her boxes, *Bridget 1994.* Here were many more photographs of the Septembers. Here was the first of her soccer trophies. Bridget picked up a tiny cardboard box, the kind you got when you bought a piece of jewelry. She shook it, and she knew without looking what it was. She remembered the celebration of little teeth tucked under her pillow, expecting money and usually getting it.

She put it back without opening it. She put the boxes back in place on their shelves and sat down on the dusty floor.

She thought about the vast amount of work her father had put into saving these things, the care with which he had preserved every single object. Out of sight, but still here. Her mother was here too. They didn't live big, maybe. But they lived.

She put her arms around her knees and hugged herself and let herself cry.

Lena extended her time in Bethesda by a few days because she sensed she might be needed there. Effie was leaving for a ten-day trip to Europe the following week, but until then, Lena sensed her sister might need some girly distraction. Lena was mentally preparing herself for round-the-clock manicures, pedicures, and home facials. One nice thing about Effie: There were few reversals in her life that a manicure couldn't fix.

Lena had the idea of calling Leo and telling him where she was and why. But when she actually got him on the phone she decided not to. He was happy to hear from her and eager to tell her about a new painting he had started, but he didn't need to know where she was or when she'd see him. That wasn't the way it would go between them. She knew that and she wasn't sorry.

Was she? Honesty required that she ask that question of herself a second time. No, she wasn't, she decided, trailing her hand over her bedspread, still looking at the phone. She would be happy to see him again. She admired him, she was attracted to him. But she wasn't sorry to let it go. The interlude in Leo's bed had been exciting and it had been clarifying for her, but even as it had unfolded she had sensed it was more like the end of the story than the beginning.

Lena went by Tibby's and Bee's houses that afternoon to say good-bye. Not long after she returned, she heard a knock at the door and Brian's voice downstairs and understood that he and Effie had gone for a walk.

She closed her door and sat on her bed and waited patiently for the noise to start. Within forty-five minutes it did. First Lena heard the front door slam. Then she heard the pounding on the steps and the slam of Effie's bedroom door.

She knew better than to relax. Minutes after Effie's door slammed the first time it slammed again, and then Lena's own door flew open.

"I cannot believe her!" Effie's face was red and her eyes were smeared with black. It had to have been an ambush of sorts, because Effie had an almost unerring instinct for when to wear waterproof mascara.

Lena deliberated with herself as to how much knowledge

to convey. She decided to be quiet. When it came to Effie, quiet usually worked best.

"Why did she tell me it was over? I gave her the chance! Why did she lie?" Effie's gestures were big with indignation.

Lena tucked her hands under her.

"Brian is an idiot! Why would he go back to her? After what she did? She doesn't care about him! She doesn't *love* him!"

Lena opened her mouth even though she shouldn't have. "How do you know that, Ef?" Instantly she regretted the mistake.

"What?" Effie came in closer, bearing down. "Are you saying she does?"

Lena kept her voice low and uncommitted. "Don't you think it's possible?"

"No! It's not! Do you know how she treated him?" She shook her hands emphatically. "You don't treat someone like that if you love them!"

Lena felt her own face warming. *Oh, but sometimes you do.*

"Lena? Lena!"

Lena looked up.

"You are siding with her, aren't you? I knew this would happen! You are taking Tibby's side, even after what she did!"

"Effie, no—"

"You are! Just admit it. Tibby lied to me, she treated Brian like *crap*, she betrayed me even after I went to New

York to get her *permission*, and you are still siding with her against your own *sister!*"

"No, Effie—" This had taken a wrong turn. The path to manicures had been forsaken.

"It's true!" Effie was really crying now, and Lena's heart felt frail. These were not histrionic tears, but sad, uncontrollable ones.

And Lena knew they had gotten to a deeper, harder thing, even harder than losing the boy you thought you loved.

"You always do that! You do! You always have. You know that?"

Lena felt the dull ache in her throat. "Effie—"

"You do. You do, Lena. I am your only sister, but you always choose them over me."

"Effie." Lena stood up to try to comfort her or touch her or even block her way, but it was too late. Sobbing, Effie fled.

Lena wished for a hearty door slam, but that wasn't what she got. Her door swayed quietly so that she could still hear her sister's tears. She minded them more than all the shouts and slams put together.

She tried to go to Effie's room a while later, but Effie wouldn't answer. The next day, Effie wouldn't open her door at all.

Lena left for a few hours in the late afternoon, and when she came back, Effie's door was still shut. She still would not answer.

Lena spent most of the evening hours quietly in her room, wondering whether she'd done the wrong thing. Had she really chosen Tibby over Effie? It didn't feel that simple. In a way that was almost more troubling, she felt like she'd chosen one way of being over another. She'd chosen Tibby's agony over Effie's joy. In a weird way, she'd chosen herself.

Before Bridget left home she went to the pet store and came home with a rabbit and a hutch.

"It's for you," she said to Perry, presenting it to him in the backyard.

He was startled and he didn't want to accept it at first, but as he held the little creature she could see his mind changing.

He began to get excited as they set up the hutch under the dogwood tree. He held the rabbit in his arms and fed it a stalk of wilted celery.

"I'll have to get a water bottle," he noted to himself and to her. "And carrots and lettuce and stuff."

"You can borrow my bike if you want," she said.

He nodded. How nice he looked with a little sun on his face.

She would come back home again in the next few weeks. She promised herself she would. And in the meantime Perry would have the company of this warm-blooded and furry thing. A reason to get out of his room and out of the house. Something to take care of, something that needed him. Something to nuzzle his neck and crawl down his shirt, to get him back into the practice of loving another soul.

She suspected that what he really needed were anti-depressants, but until she could rally herself for that effort, a baby bunny rabbit was the next best thing.

He named it Barnacle. She had no idea why.

"She's got to come out eventually, right?" Lena said to her mother the next morning in the kitchen.

"Effie?" her mom said.

"Yeah. Have you seen her?"

"She left early this morning. Daddy drove her to the air-port."

"What? You are kidding me! Where did she go?"

"She went to Greece."

Lena was stunned. "She went already?"

"She called Grandma last night and asked if she could stay in Oia for the week. Grandma was delighted. She wants Effie to help her paint her house. Your father changed the ticket on the computer."

How had she missed all of this? "She left this morning?"

"Yes."

Lena scratched violently at a bug bite on her wrist. She needed to think for a minute. "Did she seem okay?"

Her mother gave the first sign of knowledge. "Depends on what you mean by okay."

"Will she talk to me if I call her?"

"Maybe you should give her a few days."

Lena felt stricken. "That bad, huh?" She kept her eyes down.

"Lena, honey, she feels betrayed," her mother said, perching on a tall kitchen stool. Ari rarely gave in to a true sit.

Lena put her arms on the counter. "Brian didn't love her, Mom. She was going to have to notice that eventually."

"I think you're right. And I think Brian basically told her that as gently as he could," Ari said.

"You do?"

"I do. But I don't think it's Brian's love she's missing."

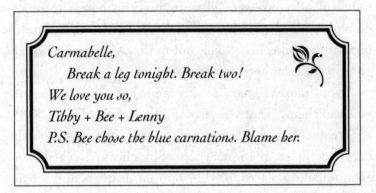

> Carmabelle,
>   Break a leg tonight. Break two!
> We love you so,
> Tibby + Bee + Lenny
> P.S. Bee chose the blue carnations. Blame her.

Lena had thought she'd be needed here at home. Now she wasn't. She couldn't reach Effie on the phone to make anything right, and she was too guilty and fitful to hang around sidestepping conversations with her father about her plans for the future.

So she came up with an even crazier idea.

She fooled with the phone in her father's office until she managed to get Tibby and Bee on at the same time. Within two minutes she'd presented her crazy idea and they'd both agreed to it.

Once she secured the borrowing of her mother's car, she went upstairs to pack her bag.

"Hey, Mom?"

"Yeah?"

"Have you seen the Traveling Pants?" Lena went down to the kitchen to ask the question rather than just shout it.

"No. I don't think so."

"I thought they were in my room." She began to feel a touch of nervousness. "Was anybody in here cleaning or doing laundry yesterday?" She trusted her mother and the regular housekeeper, Joan, not to do anything insane, but once in a while there was a substitute.

"No. Joan was here on Friday. That's it. Are you sure you had them? That you brought them from school?"

"Yeah. I'll go back and look more," Lena said, darting back up the steps to her room. She checked everywhere, even hopeless places like her bottom drawers and a trunk she hadn't opened in months.

She knew she had brought them home for Tibby to wear to the party. Tibby had worn them and then given them back. She *had* given them back, right?

Lena thought she had, but there was enough doubt to provide modest comfort for the moment.

crazy is what crazy do

—The Black Eyed Peas

Opening night arrived, and Carmen's stomach somehow climbed into her neck. She might have thrown it up, but luckily, it stayed attached.

There were photographers, critics, hundreds of people. Andrew was trying to protect her. She could feel that. He held her hand and walked her around backstage.

Jonathan kissed her and pulled her hair.

"Lovely." Ian nodded at her decked out in her flowers. He kissed her head and she thought she might cry.

Could she do this? Did she know how? She tried to swallow her stomach back down to her stomach again.

From where she sat backstage, she listened to the first act and let the trance begin. She heard the words more clearly than she ever had before. She heard more in each word, more in each combination of words, and exponentially more in each line of words.

These were real performers. Her heart swelled to know

them. They had given so much in five weeks of rehearsals, she would have thought they'd given everything. But now she knew that they had saved something for this.

During intermission she peeked out at the theater, watching it refill. When it was almost full and the lights blinked on and off, she saw three people file in through the center door and her breath caught. Time lapsed as they walked down the center aisle: three teenage girls all in a row.

They were so big, so bright, so beautiful, so magnificent to Carmen's eyes that she thought she was imagining them. They were like goddesses, like Titans. She was so proud of them! They were benevolent and they were righteous. Now, these were friends.

Lena, Tibby, and Bee were here, in this theater, and they had come for her. Her big night was their big night. Her joy was their joy; her pain their pain. It was so simple.

They were absolutely lovely, and in their presence, so was she.

In the presence of her friends, Carmen rediscovered the simplicity she had lost. They enabled her to find the voice of Perdita as she had first understood it. It felt good to be able to go back.

But the greater miracle was her understanding of the last scenes in the play: the reunion, the end of estrangement, the end of winter. She had understood from the beginning the feeling of the girl who was lost, and now she also understood the girl who was found.

In front of six hundred and twenty souls, three of them

most precious to her, Carmen's winter ended and she felt the return of her own extravagance.

Lena was singing along to an old Van Morrison tune on the radio, driving along the New Jersey Turnpike. She'd dropped Bee off in Providence and Tibby in New York, and now she was heading back to D.C. to return her mother's car. It was four o'clock in the morning and she needed to do something to keep herself awake.

Her cell phone began buzzing in the front pocket of her skirt. That worked too.

"Hello?"

There was no connection at first, and then she heard an urgent though distant voice. "Lena?"

"Effie! Is that you?"

"Lena, are you there?"

"Yes, it's me. Are you okay? Are you in Greece?" She jabbed the radio button off. She was relieved and grateful to get to talk to Effie so much sooner than expected.

"Yes, I'm at Grandma's," Effie said, muffled, but crying openly.

"Ef? Effie?" For several seconds Lena heard sobs but no voice, and she agonized. "I am so sorry, Effie. Please talk to me. Are you okay?"

"Lena, I did something really terrible."

Even over a cell phone connection, Lena suddenly sensed that these were a different kind of tears than the ones Effie had left with. "What? What is it?" Lena tried not to drive off the road.

"I can't even tell you."

"Please tell me."

"I can't."

"Effie, what could it be? How could it be that bad?"

"It is. It's worse."

"You're making me nervous, you know. Just tell me or I'll drive into a ditch."

"Oh, Lena." More sobs.

"Effie!"

"I—I . . . your pants."

"What? I can't hear you!"

"I took your pants."

"The Traveling Pants?"

"Yes." Crying. "I took them."

"To Greece?"

"Yes."

"Effie." Now she knew where they were, at least.

"I was mad and I just—I was mad at Tibby and you and everybody and—"

"Okay, I get it," Lena said, disoriented by the rapid reallocation of guilt between them.

"It's worse than that, though."

Lena felt the bang bang bang of her portending heart. "What?"

"I wore them on the ferry and they got wet."

"Yes."

"I hung them on the line on Grandma's terrace to dry. I never thought—"

Bang bang bang. "You never thought what?"

"It was windy. I wasn't thinking that it could"—several words were lost in tears—"or that I would lose them."

"What do you mean, Effie?"

"I went to get them and they were gone. I've looked everywhere. For the last three hours I've looked." Another crash of sobs. "Lena, I did not mean to lose them."

Effie had taken the Pants. Now Effie couldn't find them. But she had not lost them. They were not lost. "Effie, listen to me. You cannot lose them! Do you hear me? You have to find them. They have to be there somewhere." Lena's voice was as hard as she'd ever heard it.

"I've tried. I really have."

"You keep trying!" There was static on the line. "Can you hear me? Effie? Effie?"

She was gone. Lena threw the phone down on the passenger seat and clutched the wheel. She felt like she could crush it in her hands.

The Pants could not be lost. They had magic to protect them. They were not the kind of thing that could be lost. They were there, and Effie would find them. Anything else was not a thing she could think.

It had been hard for Carmen to see it end. The honors, the admirers, the catered parties, the champagne, the little egg rolls. Her singular pride in introducing her friends to the cast. But the evening had eventually come to an end.

It had been hard to say good-bye to her friends as they piled into Lena's mother's car to drive through the night and be back by morning in time for their obligations.

Walking back from the parking lot, Carmen had passed the theater again to savor the taste of the night.

Judy and Andrew had still been there, sleeves up and hair down, going over the points of the evening one more time. It had been hard not to cry when they hugged her.

"You did me proud, sweetie," Judy said in her ear.

"I'm not going to jinx it," Andrew said. But when Carmen let out a few tears, she saw that he had some too.

Hardest of all had been ending up back in her dorm room.

Thankfully, Julia was asleep when Carmen crept into her bed. Carmen slept a long and virtuous sleep. But as does tend to happen in the morning, Julia woke up.

"How did it go?" Julia asked pointedly.

"Weren't you there?" Carmen asked.

"No, I had other plans."

This was strange, because during one of the many curtain calls, Carmen had actually seen Julia in the audience. She knew she had, because she had been struck at that moment by the contrast between the three beacons of friendship burning like suns in her eyes and Julia, the cheapest, scrawniest, chintziest ten-watt bulb of a counterfeit friend.

"That's weird, because I saw you there."

Julia was again looking couched and furtive. "No, you didn't."

Carmen could have summoned her towering anger at this moment. She thought of it. Her power was restored enough that she could have taken on Julia as the rock-hurling Carmen of old, and Julia would have suffered for it.

Carmen could have, but she didn't. Julia had once seemed too valuable to cross. Now she didn't seem valuable enough.

She began getting dressed as Julia looked on sourly.

"I don't know what your problem is," Julia snapped before Carmen could get out of the room. "I thought we were friends."

Carmen turned. She towered a little in spite of herself. "We weren't."

"We weren't?" Julia echoed, surprise and sarcasm mixing.

"No. You know how I know?"

Julia looked heavenward, the same kind of petulant expression Carmen herself used to make. "How do you know?"

"Because you wanted me to fail. But I didn't. Too bad for you. That means we were not friends."

Before Carmen left, she thought of one more thing.

"You know what the sad thing is?"

Julia's jaw was locked now. She wasn't saying anything back.

"The way you are going, you will never have one."

As Carmen walked away, she felt sorry that she'd been taken in by a snake like Julia. But in some strange way she felt appreciative that it had happened. In friendship terms, she'd lived her life in the Garden of Eden. Her bond with her friends was so powerful, so supportive, so uncompetitive, she'd thought that was how friendship worked. She'd been spoiled and she'd been innocent. She hadn't recognized how good she had it, or how bad other alleged friendships could be.

Now she knew.

If she could go back, would she do anything differently? She thought about that.

No, she probably wouldn't. It was that old idea—better to put your heart out there and have it abused once in a while than to keep it hidden away.

But jeez, a little judgment wouldn't hurt.

Poor empty pants

With nobody inside them.

—Dr. Seuss

From the moment Bee learned the state of the Pants, time had ceased flowing in its normal way and instead proceeded in nervous jolts.

"Should I call Lena again?"

"You talked to her ten minutes ago," Eric said from the back of Bee's neck, where he'd been kissing her.

"I know, but what if she heard something? What if she talked to Carmen?"

She and Tibby and Lena had done almost nothing but call each other since Lena had set off the alarms.

Bee's phone rang before she could decide. It was Carmen. "Oh, my God."

"Lena told you." Bridget's agitation was big and her dorm room felt tiny.

"Yeah." They had deliberated waiting until after Carmen's last performance on Wednesday.

"What are we gonna do?"

"What can we do? Hope Effie isn't blinded by anger and jealousy."

Bridget paused. "I kind of wish we had someone else looking."

"Yeah. But who else have we got?"

"Grandma."

"Ugh."

Lena called Effie every hour for twenty straight. Grandma was getting annoyed, but what could she do? She let Effie take the blame.

"I'm trying. I'm trying everything." That was all Effie would say.

Lena even wished she could call Kostos to see if he was there and could help. But unfortunately, that was a bridge she had burned.

"I think I know what the problem is," Tibby said to Lena on the phone from her room in New York.

They called each other so often, they hardly bothered hanging up anymore. "What?"

"The Pants don't want Effie to find them."

"Oh, my gosh. You could be right."

"They're scared of her." Tibby suspected that she was possibly overidentifying with the Pants, but still.

"Maybe that's it."

"So what should we do?"

❀   ❀   ❀

Lena waited for twenty-two more hours and made another uncharacteristically rash decision.

"I'm going to go," she said to Carmen on the phone.

"What?"

"I'm going to Greece. I'm online as we speak. I'm buying a ticket."

"No."

"Yes." She had made up her mind. It was her fault, really. The Pants had been in her possession. It was her lunatic sister who had taken them. She was the one with the crabby grandma in Oia. Who could find them but her?

"When?"

"Thursday is the soonest I could get."

"Whoa."

"I just pressed the button, Carma. I bought it."

"You are fearsome. With what?"

"A credit card."

"Whose?"

"My mother's."

"Does she know?"

"Not yet."

"Oh, Lenny."

"You can't put a price on the Traveling Pants."

"Yeah, but maybe your mom can."

Lena started to get suspicious when Bee called on Tuesday and asked her for her flight number for the third time. "What's up?" she asked.

"Nothing," Bee said.

When Lena arrived at the gate at Kennedy Airport in New York for her flight to Athens on Thursday, she was surprised to see Bee standing there with her duffel bag over her shoulder, but she was not stunned. She was stunned to see Tibby and Carmen standing beside Bee.

She laughed out loud. The first time in days. It was cathartic. "Did you come to say good-bye?" she asked, full of happy suspicions.

"No, baby, we came to say hello," Carmen said.

Bee said she'd borrowed the money for her ticket from her dad. According to Carmen, David had about a billion frequent flyer miles, so he gave her some when she pleaded. Tibby's parents had given her an open ticket voucher for her graduation present last June. They'd also loaned her a hundred bucks to get an expedited passport, which was going to be hard to repay since she'd given notice of exactly one hour at her job.

"Call us Beg, Borrow, Steal and . . . ?" Bee looked at Tibby.

"Use," Tibby said.

"I wish I was Steal," Carmen said.

"I wish I was Borrow," Lena said.

"Nobody wants to be Beg," Bee pointed out.

They had to argue at the ticket desk to get their seats together, but when the plane took off for Greece, all four of them were sitting side by side.

Lena looked right and looked left and laughed again. How

much it sucked to be traveling under these circumstances. But how exquisitely great it was to be doing it together.

"Are you worried they're going to kick you off the team?" Tibby asked.

As the plane soared through space, as their reckless energy dissipated and the hours stretched, they began to calculate the number of things they had blown off and people they had upset by doing this.

"Not unless they can do without a center forward." Bee explained that the coach would be furious and threaten her a lot, but then he would forgive her in time to start her in the first league game.

Tibby realized they could not talk about the length of this trip. They couldn't cast their minds forward to an outcome other than finding the Pants and bringing them home, and who could say how long that would take? But they were heading into the third week in August. It was hard not to recognize the fact that most schools started in a week and a half.

"I'm going to take an incomplete in my screenwriting class," Tibby said. In the three days she'd spent in New York since her reunion with Brian, she'd made gigantic strides on her love story, but she hadn't quite gotten to the end of it.

"I was supposed to pack up my room this week. My mom and David are moving into the new house the day after Labor Day. I'll just have to do it later."

"Eric said he'd forgive me for leaving if I wore a burka and promised not to flirt with any Greek boys," Bee said.

"Greeks do like blondes," Lena said.

"Brian offered to come and help us search," Tibby said.

"How about Leo?" Carmen asked.

"He called last night," Lena said. "I think he's going to Rome for most of next semester."

"That's sad," Carmen said.

Lena shrugged. "It's not, really. It's all right. I kind of knew it wasn't going to turn into a long-term thing."

Tibby noticed how different Lena looked from the old days of Kostos, when every time she proclaimed equanimity, she looked as if she had stolen a car.

"It's for the best," Carmen consoled her. "Lena. Leo. Your names don't sound good together anyway."

Tibby laughed and hugged Carmen's arm. "Well, thanks, Carma. That about settles it."

Lena laughed too.

"Have a thorny relationship problem? Just ask Carma," Bee said.

"You should get a column."

"Start a blog."

"I think I should," Carmen agreed. "Hey, did I tell you who came to the final performance last night?"

"Who?"

"Well, my mom and David . . ."

"Right," Lena said.

"And my dad and Lydia."

"Really?" Bee said. "All four of 'em."

"Yep. They were surprised to see each other at first, but they all had such a great time together I told them they should get a room."

Tibby laughed and listened to her friends laugh and then just sat back and listened to the flow of their familiar voices. As unhappy as she was about the Pants, she was joyful that the four of them were finally together. She felt a little guilty about it, like she was laughing at a funeral. And then she realized that the Pants wouldn't want her to feel that way.

"Do you guys realize this is the first time we've really been together since the beach at the end of last summer?" Tibby said, unable to keep her appreciation to herself.

"Yes, I thought of that too," Lena said a little sadly.

"How could we go so long?" Carmen asked.

"You're one to ask," Tibby said, but even as she said it she was filled with gratitude to have their regular Carmen restored to them.

"You know what?" Bee said.

"What?"

"I don't think it's just that the Pants are scared of Effie."

"Then what?" Lena asked.

Bridget looked at each of her friends in turn. "Look at us. I think the Pants are smarter than we even know."

At first cock-crow

the ghosts must go

Back to their quiet

graves below.

—Theodosia Garrison

It was late when they got to Valia's house, and the four of them were so tired and punchy, so confused as to their whereabouts in time and space, they felt like they'd been inhaling from a whipped cream can.

Lena was earnestly happy to see her grandmother and surprised not to see Effie. She had been girding herself for an uneasy reunion.

"Effie left for Athens today," Valia told them impassively, but a few minutes later she pulled Lena aside. "She tried her hardest, you know. She tried to find those pants all day and night."

"I know, Grandma," Lena said.

Tired as they were, they knew their purpose. Lena found two flashlights and they set out with them on the narrow cobblestone roads and paths beneath the perch of Valia's terrace.

"It's all up and down here," Tibby pointed out, waving her hand down the cliff to the dark water below. "No flat."

That made it harder to find things, Lena acknowledged to herself. Gravity always played its advantage here.

Valia shook her head at them, making no secret of her doubts, and after a while even Lena realized the futility of their method. Why struggle to light up tiny patches of the world when the sun would do the job so effectively in a few hours?

"We should get some sleep," Lena said. "That's the smartest thing to do. That way we can get up early and get to work."

They did get to work in the morning. And yet, preoccupied as they were by their loss and their mission, they couldn't help being awed by what the sun showed them.

"This is the most beautiful place I've ever seen. A thousand times more beautiful than the next most beautiful place," Carmen said.

Lena thought that too. She felt a great giddiness along with a deep satisfaction at getting to share it with them. Another unexpected gift, courtesy of the Pants, she thought.

She told them about the formation of the Caldera, really a giant crater left by what was possibly the hugest volcanic explosion in the history of the world. It sank the whole middle of the island, leaving sheared cliffs around a center of water.

"And what about those islands?" Bee asked, squinting over the water to three masses of land floating in the Caldera.

"Patches of lava left over," Lena explained.

Lena led them along the sloped paths where they thought the wind could have carried the Pants from Valia's patio. The whitewashed houses and crumbling churches, the dazzling blue of the domes and doors, the blinding pink of the climbing bougainvillea, all of it was so intoxicating to the eyes it was hard to stay focused on the job at hand. After a few hours in the sun, they took a break in the shade and tried to strategize.

"I wouldn't be surprised if someone found them," Tibby said.

"That's a good point," Lena said.

They went to town. Luckily, most of the shopkeepers spoke at least a little English. Lena went armed with a picture.

"We're looking for something," she explained to a man in a clothing shop. She pulled out the picture of the Pants as worn by Tibby last summer at the beach. She pointed to the Pants. "We lost these."

The shopkeeper looked alarmed. "You lost this girl?" He put on his glasses and held the photograph up close.

"No, she's right here," Bridget explained. "We lost those Pants."

They found a copy shop in town. Using the photograph, they blew up the image of the Pants, beheaded Tibby, and circled the Pants with a thick black marker. *LOST PANTS*, Lena wrote in English and Greek. The copy lady helped with the translation. Lena put down her grand-mother's address and number. *REWARD!*, she wrote in Greek.

While they waited for fifty copies to be made, Lena gave them a little tour.

"This is the forge that belonged to Kostos's grandfather. I think he sold it in the last year or two. That's where Kostos used to work," she explained. "That's where we kissed the first time," she added as an aside.

She took them down to the little harbor. "Did you ever see the picture I drew of this? It was one of the first ones I ever liked. Kostos and I went swimming here."

"There's a certain theme to this tour, I think," Tibby said.

"Ha ha," Lena said. As they stood on the dock she pretended to push Tibby into the water.

"How could you not fall in love here?" Bee asked.

Inspired by her thoughts of love and of beauty, of ancient places and dirt floors, Bee lifted her arms to the sky and did an arcing dive off the dock into the sea. It was thrillingly cold. She popped her head through the surface and screamed with joy.

Because they were her friends, and perfect friends in nearly all ways, the three of them screamed back and dove in after her.

They all shouted about how cold it was. They swam around screaming in their wet, billowing clothes. Bee hauled herself out first and helped the others, who were laughing and shivering so hard she was afraid they might drown from elation and harebrained stupidity.

They all lay side by side on the dock so the sun could dry them. The sky was the most perfect and cloudless blue.

Bee loved the sun. She loved her heavy, dripping clothes. She loved the water lapping against the pilings beneath her. She protested aloud at the encroachment of Tibby's cold toes against her shin, but she loved that, too.

She belonged to her friends and they to her. That much she knew, even if the Pants were temporarily mislaid.

"I think our copies are probably ready," Carmen pointed out dreamily.

They posted their signs all over the place. Throughout Oia and its environs.

"I think we should cover Fira, too," Lena suggested.

So they went to Fira that evening with fifty more. They were fanning out, posting them around the crowded tourist spots, when Bee came running.

"Lena! I think I just saw Kostos."

Lena felt the *zzzzt* of electrical current up her back.

"You never even met Kostos," Tibby said, appearing next to her.

"Well, I know, but I saw his picture," Bee insisted.

Lena looked around, trying to feel calm. She did a slow, calm survey. "My grandmother said he's not here. He hasn't been around all summer. Where do you think you saw him?"

Bee pointed to a corner with a café and a bike shop.

"What are the chances? You probably imagined it," Carmen said. She stood protectively by Lena.

"Carma, he does *live* here," Bee pointed out. "It's not

like I'm claiming to have seen him in Milwaukee or something."

"Whether he was or wasn't, he does kind of haunt this place," Lena said diplomatically. "I am the first to admit that. Anyway, let's keep going."

They posted their signs until it was dark, Lena distractedly imagining she saw Kostos everywhere.

"Now we'll go home and wait for people to call us," Lena said.

At home Lena stepped into the kitchen, where Valia had cooked up a huge feast. "Grandma, Kostos isn't on the island, is he?"

"I heard he's traveling all this summer. I don't see him vunce. I talk to Rena, but I don't know vhere he goes." Valia was pretending to be dismissive of Kostos. Like Lena, she'd spent too much time hoping.

They had a long, cozy night at home. Valia went to bed early but left them a bottle of red wine. They sat on the floor drinking and talking and talking and talking.

It was magical, but by the time they dragged themselves up to bed they realized that in spite of one hundred signs, not one person had called.

Lena was the only early riser of the group, and her body seemed to adjust most quickly to Greek time. At sunrise, she decided to take a walk.

She took a long, slow walk. First she thought about Effie and then about Bapi, and after that she let herself think about Kostos.

It was fitting, in a way, to walk and see all these ruins. Here, on this island, the place where she'd both given away her heart and seen it broken, there were ruins all around, though not all of them ancient.

Ruins stood for what was lost, and yet they were beautiful—peaceful, historic, intellectual. Not tragic or regrettable. Lena tried to keep hers that way too, and she succeeded to some extent. Why not celebrate what you had had rather than spend your time mourning its passing? There could be joy in things that ended.

Still, it surprised her how much she was thinking of him here, how often she thought she saw him. Around the corner, looking out a window, sitting at a table in a café. Not a ghost or a memory of Kostos, but Kostos as he was now.

"It's weird. Now I keep thinking I see him," she confided to Bee later that day when they were canvassing people around the Paradise and Pori beaches.

"What do you think when you do?" Bee asked.

Lena considered this question as she showered before dinner.

After the scene in the motel in Providence, Lena knew she had changed. She knew she had destroyed whatever remained of her and Kostos. God, what must he think of her now?

She wasn't who he thought she was. She wasn't who *she* thought she was. She had displayed an ugliness he hadn't imagined was there. But it was a relief, in a way. If that was part of who she was, he should know it. He shouldn't be tricked. And there was a perverse, childlike part of her that wanted to get to be ugly sometimes.

She wondered about him. Had he ever really been able to love her? Did she really love him? There was undoubtedly something beautiful in longing and wishing. Their love story stayed perfect because they couldn't have it.

But could he love her imperfection? Would he accept the fact that she wasn't always beautiful? Could he allow imperfection in himself? Would he give up being lovable for her sake?

They had their imagined love. It had been wrenching and beautiful. But she wondered now whether either of them had ever had the stomach for the real thing.

The following day they tried the port of Athinios, where the ferries came in. They posted signs and they went shop to shop and restaurant to restaurant. Valia had by now trained them how to ask "Have you seen these Pants?" in Greek. They even learned to say it in French and German.

There was one moment of excitement when an ice cream scooper said, "Oh, I saw those." But after all four of them closed in on him, they realized he meant he'd seen the signs.

"We aren't getting hopeless, are we?" Tibby asked. She couldn't hide her worry.

"No," Bee reassured her.

"We'll find them. They want us to find them," Carmen said.

Tibby sensed that none of them was willing to think about it any other way. Or at least, they weren't yet willing to say so.

When they got home from Athinios, Lena's grandmother was waiting inside her door. She practically tackled Lena as soon as she saw her.

"Kostos is here!" she said. Her fingers were pressing a little too hard into Lena's shoulders.

"What?"

"He's here. He's looking for you."

Her friends clustered around her.

"He's looking for me?" she echoed.

"Oh, boy," Tibby said.

"See, he *is* here," Bee said.

"He said he's leaving the island and he vanted to find you before he left."

Lena's heart started to rampage in its old familiar way. "Where did he go?"

"He said he vould look for you at the grove." She shrugged. "I don't know vhat, but he valked up." She pointed.

Lena knew what. "Thanks, Grandma." She paused, trying to gather her feelings around her.

"Are you going?" Valia looked like she was going to go for her if Lena didn't hurry up.

"Yes, I'm going."

With words of caution and encouragement from her

friends, Lena walked slowly up the hill. It was strange. She thought she'd found some place of calm regarding Kostos. Why was her heart racing?

Why did he want to see her? What more was there to say? She couldn't have been clearer than she had been. She was frankly surprised to think she hadn't scared him off for a lifetime.

Of the things she'd said, would she take any of it back? Did she want to? Was that why her heart was racing?

She walked up and up until the cliff leveled into a sort of plateau. She was happy to see how green it was again. The rain had been good this year.

Yes, some of the things she'd said that night had been lies. Maybe she'd correct a few of those if she could, but they represented some kind of truth, and she had needed to get it out. She was glad she had, if only so she could move on with her life.

Her heart rose at the sight of his back as he stood in their grove. Some feelings you just couldn't kill, no matter how much they deserved it. He turned and saw her as she came close.

Why did he look happy to see her? Why was she so happy to see him?

"We always come back to here, don't we?" she said.

He nodded. He looked better. Not in handsomeness, exactly. He looked straighter, fuller, stronger. He'd worn a hangdog, hopeful look last time, in Providence, but he didn't look that way now.

366

He rolled up his pants and they sat side by side at the edge of the pond. The water was so cold Lena yelped, and he laughed.

He doused his feet and then he reached in and washed his hands. She kept her hands in her lap. She looked at the foot of scrubby grass separating them.

"I've been unhappy," he told her. She believed him, though he didn't look very unhappy now.

"I was awful to you," she said.

He plunged his hands into the water again and shook them out. "I have a story to tell you," he said, looking at her directly.

"Okay," she said uncertainly. She had a feeling she was going to play a role in this story.

"Remember how you asked if I thought you would rush into my arms when you saw me?"

She winced. She'd said it cruelly then. She'd wanted to hurt him.

"Well, that is what I thought," he declared unflinchingly. "When I flew to see you, I packed clothes to last me for two months. I imagined I would call my grandmother and she would send the rest of my stuff in boxes. Because I did think you would rush into my arms and we would be together forever."

As painful as this was to hear, she admired his honesty.

"I called the Greek consulate. I started working on a student visa. I got transfer applications to three universities near you."

As much as she admired his honesty, she wished he would stop now.

"I brought a ring."

Lena chewed her cheek so hard she tasted blood. How could he tell her these things? They were clearly as painful for him to say as they were for her to hear. She couldn't think of any way to respond.

"I didn't think we would get married. Not in the first few years. But I wanted to give you something to show you that I would never leave you again."

She felt the boot in the head. The unexpected tears. She felt herself softening for him; she could feel her body changing.

He was tough. He was gritting his way through this confession. She could tell he wasn't going to stop until it was done.

"I worked two different jobs, almost a hundred hours a week for the last two years, and I spent almost everything I made on the ring. It was good to be distracted and also to think I could make it up to you."

Lena's friends teased her for the humming sound she made when she felt their unhappiness. She heard herself make that sound now.

"Do you know what I did with it?"

He was staring at her so fixedly she realized he expected her to answer. She shook her head.

"I threw it into the Caldera."

Her eyes were wide.

"You know what I did after that?" The recklessness with which he told his story seemed to capture the recklessness of what he had done.

She shook her head again.

"I broke into the house of my former wife and I stole the ring I had given her and I also threw that into the sea."

Lena just stared at him.

"It didn't mean anything compared to your ring, but it gave me a feeling of ending."

She nodded.

"But then Mariana called the police, and so I confessed to the crime and spent a night in jail in Fira." He told it very matter-of-factly.

"No," said Lena.

He nodded. He actually looked pleased with himself.

"I have a mug shot," he said, almost cheerfully.

She thought of it. Lovable Kostos in a mug shot. It was insane. It was funny. But she couldn't help being impressed by him. She'd credited herself with the capacity for destruction. She had underestimated his.

"My grandfather picked me up. Thankfully, I was released without fines."

"What did he say?" It was hard to picture.

"Well." Kostos's face returned to solemnity. "He pretended it hadn't happened. We never talked about it."

Lena made the humming sound again. She realized this confession was part of Kostos's penance. It was her penance too.

369

The sun was beginning to set. The pink light on the silvery olive leaves was as lovely as anything she could remember. She knew Valia would be putting dinner out soon.

"You are leaving for somewhere," she said.

"I take the first morning ferry. I'm flying to London tomorrow."

"To London?"

"Back to the School of Economics. They held a place."

"Oh. Of course." That was the difference about him now, she realized. He was undaunted. He was sturdier than he had been before. His anger at her had burned away the guilt. He had forced himself to get over her.

How powerful it was to give up your desires. It was like bargaining for a rug. Your only leverage was being able to walk away.

"I can start where I left off. I even got a room in my old flat."

Her throat ached. "God. It's like the clock turned back. It's just like we're back to the summer we met. It's late August and you're going off to London and I'm going back home for school."

He nodded.

"You can almost imagine away all the things that happened in between," she said.

He was thoughtful as he looked at her. "But you can't, can you?"

"No, you can't." She saw the fair orange circle of sun in the still water. She put her hands in to fur the edges. She brought cold, watery hands to her warm cheeks.

He stood up and so did she. He put out his hand to shake. Hers was still wet. "I guess we should say good-bye," he said.

It was easier to be together, to talk, now that they had both given up.

"Yes. I guess it is."

"Good luck with everything, Lena. I hope you will be happy."

"Thanks. I hope you'll be happy too."

"Well, then."

"Good-bye."

He cleared his throat a little bit as she walked away. She turned around.

"There's a full moon tonight," he said before he walked a separate way.

As soon as he was out of sight, Lena felt that old feeling of missing him. It didn't cut like a raw wound. It was the ache of a flu coming on.

Had they really gotten over each other? she wondered. It seemed more like they had gotten over themselves.

Lena was quiet through dinner, watching the tanned, beloved faces of her friends, enjoying their banter. She loved how Valia laughed when Carmen teased her.

As soon as she'd gotten home they'd wanted to know everything that had happened with Kostos, and she'd told them. But she hadn't yet figured out how to tell them how she felt about what had happened.

She crawled into bed early. She half listened to the

laughter downstairs coming from Bee and Carmen and Valia. She heard Tibby talking to a series of international operators, trying to reach Brian on her cell phone.

Lena's head was so full she expected she would toss and turn for hours, but instead, she fell asleep almost immediately. And then she woke up with a jolt. She felt there had been a dream, but it receded too quickly for her to grab even a string of it.

She heard Carmen's slow breathing beside her. The particular look of Carmen's sleeping face reminded her of a hundred other nights, a hundred sleepovers through the years. Here, in Greece, it made her feel happy. So often the world was made of jumps and starts, but tonight it was round and continuous.

She looked out the window and saw the proud full moon hanging over the Caldera, seeming to enjoy its own perfect reflection below. She knew what Kostos had meant.

She spent another minute looking at the moon, and suddenly she really knew what Kostos had meant.

She crept out of bed gingerly so as not to wake Carmen. She pulled on a pair of jeans and a faded green T-shirt. She brushed her hair and padded on soft toes out of the house.

Who knew what time it was? Who knew if he'd be there or when he'd be there? But her big feet had faith as they pulled her up the hill.

He was there. Maybe he'd been there for hours; she couldn't know. He stood up to greet her, happy, not surprised.

He needed to look at her face for only a second to know it was okay to hold her.

She cried in his arms. They weren't sad tears at all, just ones that needed to get out. She cried in his shirt. She cried for her Pants. He held her as tight as he could without crushing her.

She had willed her heart to stay small and contained, but it wouldn't be. Oh, well.

The neat leaves wrinkled under the moon. The pond made slapping, watery noises. It felt so good to be right here. These were arms that felt unlike other arms.

"Do you think you can ever forgive me?" he asked her. There was no demand in his voice. She felt like she could answer yes or no and he wouldn't hug her less.

"Maybe," she said faintly. "I think maybe so."

"Do you love someone else?" he asked. It was important to him, clearly, but he let it float.

"I tried," she said. "I don't know if I can." She talked to his chest.

She could feel him nod on her head. She could feel his relief in the way his body found more surfaces to connect to hers.

"I know I can't," he said.

She nodded at his chest. They stayed like that for a while. She realized the sun was already pushing up light at the farthest edge of the sea. It was later than she thought. Or earlier.

He unbound himself from her slowly, regretfully.

She felt cold air replace all the parts he'd been touching.

Before he broke away he put his hands on either side of her face and kissed her, strong and sturdy and full of lust. It was a new kind of kiss. It was grown up and decisive. She knew without thinking how to kiss him back the same way.

The last thing he said to her was something in Greek. He said it with emphasis, as though she would know what he meant, but of course she didn't.

And all the way down the hill as the sun rose, carelessly extending itself into the privacy of her night, she tried to remember the word.

Was it one word? Two words? A phrase? It was five syllables, she thought. It was, wasn't it? She tried to remember each of them, chanting them over and over as a mantra all the way down the hill.

First thing inside the house she wrote it down with a pencil on a piece of lined paper in her grandmother's kitchen.

She wrote it out phonetically. What else could she do? She didn't know the Greek alphabet well enough to try the right way. She was unsure of how to represent the vowel sounds.

Why did he say it like that? Like he knew exactly what he was talking about and like she would understand?

Arg. He always left her with a problem.

"Do you know what this means?" she asked her grandmother when she came down the stairs, sticking the piece of paper two inches from Valia's nose. Lena wasn't quite as private as she used to be.

Valia scrunched up her already wrinkly eyes. "Vhat is this supposed to be?" she asked.

"I don't know. I'm hoping you can tell me. It's Greek."

Grandma was nonplussed. "You call this Greek?"

Lena breathed impatiently. "Grandma, can you try?"

Valia made a martyrish fuss over finding her glasses. She squinted at the paper some more. "Lena, love, how do I know vhat this means?" she said finally.

While her friends got out of bed and dressed and took over the kitchen, making omelets out of everything edible in the room, Lena sat at the table in the middle of the action with her nose in the Greek-English dictionary.

"What are you doing?" Tibby finally asked.

"I'll tell you when I know," she said.

They put on bikinis and sundresses and packed straw bags and Lena followed them down to the beach with her face still in the dictionary. She tripped over a cobblestone and skinned her knee like a baby. Like a baby, she felt she might cry.

"What is with you?" Carmen asked.

"She'll tell us when she knows," Tibby said with a note of protection in her voice.

Lena was so preoccupied she got a sunburn on her back. She kept diligently at her dictionary when her friends went to get ice cream. She tried every spelling. Every grouping of letters until at last, with the sun at the top of the sky, she figured it out. Or at least, she believed she did.

"κάποια μέρα" was what Kostos had said. It meant "Someday."

And so she did understand.

Off we go, into the wild

blue yonder.

—U.S. Air Force anthem

On the sixth day in Santorini, Lena tracked Effie down by phone at their aunt and uncle's house in Athens.

"Effie, it's me," she said. She made her voice gentle. She knew Effie was afraid to talk to her.

"Did you find them?" Effie practically exploded.

"No."

"You didn't?"

"No."

"Oh, no." She heard Effie turn instantly snuffling and teary. As mad as she'd been, Lena realized she didn't want Effie to feel this way. "Oh, no," Effie said again.

"I know."

"Since you called, I thought maybe you found them," Effie said, sniffling. She probably believed Lena would be too angry to call otherwise.

"I called because I wanted to tell you . . . it's okay." Lena wasn't sure what she was going to say until it was out.

Effie blew her nose loudly.

"It's going to be okay," Lena said again. "Okay? I know you didn't mean for it to happen. I know you tried your hardest to find them."

Effie shuddered a sob.

"It's okay, Ef. I love you."

For the longest time Effie was crying too hard to say anything back, so Lena waited patiently until she was done.

On the seventh day in Santorini, they swam for hours in the Caldera, floating with their bellies pointing to the sky. It seemed to Carmen they were putting off having to touch their feet to the earth again. The earth turned and time passed and then they would have to think about what it meant. But the hour did come, as all hours do.

"I don't think we can stay here much longer," Lena said, sitting on the sand and watching the sun go. She was the one who had to say it.

Carmen looked at her shriveled fingertips. She pressed them to her mouth.

They had been so busy with their Pants-finding attempts the first few days, but after that, bit by bit, they'd talked about the Pants less, expected less, done a little less. They'd relaxed into their long aimless stretches of talking and eating and thinking and walking and wondering about things together.

Although the overarching fact of the matter was sad, there had not been a moment since Carmen had arrived here that she'd suffered. It felt too good to be together.

There was too much joy in it, so long needed and so long overdue.

Rather, Carmen had felt an ever-growing awe at the wisdom of the Pants for knowing how to bring them together. For knowing that absence is sometimes more powerful than presence.

"I wish we could stay here forever," Carmen said.

"I do too," Bee said.

They didn't want to leave without the Pants, Carmen knew. The Pants were here, in a way. Even if they were lost, they were all around them.

"I think we might have lost the Pants a while ago," Tibby said, pressing her hands into the sand, her face abstracted. "I mean, I think we lost the idea of them. They came to us to keep us together, and I think we were using them to help us stay apart."

Carmen thought about this. "Right. It was like we had the Pants, so it was okay if we didn't see each other."

"I think that's true," Lena said. "I hadn't thought of that."

"We counted on them too much," Bee said. "Or maybe we counted on them in the wrong way."

Without thinking, they moved around to form a loose circle, like they did at Gilda's. Today there were no Pants, just them.

"They taught us how to be separate people, but we learned a little too well," Carmen said.

"We should have put them away during the school year," Tibby suggested.

"But our lives are different now," Lena said. "It used to

379

be we were apart for summers. Now we're apart all the time. Regular life used to be together. Now regular life is apart. It's impossible to know how to use them."

Carmen felt like she might cry. "Maybe it's too big a job to keep us together anymore."

Bee grabbed Carmen's raisiny fingers for a second before letting them go. "It can't be," she said. "But we can't expect the Pants do all the work, either."

"We're all in different places now," Carmen said, voicing her deepest fears. "Maybe our time is over."

"No," Lena said. "I don't believe that. You don't believe that, Carma, do you?"

Carmen was sitting there not wanting to believe it. And then, out of the blue, she had an idea that released her.

"I think I know what it is," she said. "We aren't in Bethesda anymore and we aren't in high school. We aren't really in our families and we aren't in our houses. Those are the places we grew up and the times we spent together, but they aren't us. If we think they are, then we're lost, because times end and places are lost. We aren't any place or any time."

She thought of their Pants. She pictured them blowing off the laundry line and into the air, floating and soaring until they silently merged into sky and sea.

"That's the thing. We are everywhere."

You are welcome here.

—B. C. L. and T

EPILOGUE

On our last day in Greece we took a long walk and ended up on a stony precipice overlooking the water. We sat with our legs dangling into space, part of the air. The sky was cloudless and the sea was perfectly calm.

I looked at my friends, brown, barefoot, freckled, rumpled, mismatched, happy, all of us in each other's clothes. Tibby had Lena's white pants rolled up to her ankles, Carmen had Tibby's paisley T-shirt, Lena wore my straw cowboy hat, and I tied up my hair in Carmen's pink scarf.

The sky and the sea were so still and so constant that although we squinted and stared to find the line between them, the place that separated sea and sky, time and space, liquid and air, we could not see it.

I thought of what Carmen had said about us. We aren't in any one place or any one time. We are everywhere, here and there, past and future, together and apart.

And so for a long time we sat and watched in silence because the seam was invisible and the color was eternity.

And I thought about the color and I realized what blue it was. It was the soft and changeable, essential blue of a well-worn pair of pants.

Pants = Love

Forever in Blue

The Fourth Summer of the Sisterhood

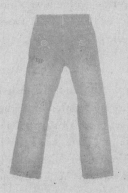

Ann Brashares

A READERS GUIDE

QUESTIONS FOR DISCUSSION

1. In the past, the Sisterhood has not shared the Pants during the school year, but only in the summer. In *Forever in Blue*, we discover that the Pants circulated among the girls while they were at college. If you were a member of the Sisterhood, would you follow suit? Or do you think the Pants should only be used during the summer? Does using the Pants year-round help or hurt the girls' relationships? Why or why not?

2. Which girl has come the farthest, or learned the most, since the first book, *The Sisterhood of the Traveling Pants*? Why do you think so?

3. Carmen and Lena reflect on the idea of home throughout *Forever in Blue*. How would you define *home*? Does a person's definition of home change as she grows up? Might your definition differ from that of a friend?

4. On page 102, Lena thinks about Kostos and whether she's over him. "She wasn't sure she wanted to be the forgetting type, even if she could be. If she forgot Kostos, she feared she'd forget most of herself along with him. Who was she without him?" Given Lena's feelings for Kostos, do you think she's ready to move into a new relationship with Leo? Will someone like Lena ever get over her first love?

5. On page 167, Bridget is talking with Peter. "*I don't have a family to talk about,* she was going to say, but she realized that it wasn't true. She did have a family. They were all under twenty and none of them related to her by blood, but they made her who she was. They represented the best of her." Do you think of your friends as your family, as Bridget does? How would having such strong friendships influence your relationship with your family? How would it affect your relationships with friends you'd make in the future?

QUESTIONS FOR DISCUSSION

6. Tibby finds herself in a very adult situation when she's afraid she may be pregnant. How well does she handle her relationship with Brian during this time? If you were in her shoes, would you have pushed your boyfriend away, or would you have wanted his support?

7. Were you surprised by Carmen's friendship with Julia? Why do you think Carmen forgets how to be herself and lets Julia take control of their relationship? What would you do if you found yourself in Carmen's place?

8. What do you think of Effie's dating Brian so soon after he and Tibby break up? What would you have done if you were Lena and had to comfort your friend (Tibby) while still supporting your sister (Effie)?

9. Pants = Love. Can you draw more equations for this book? What does Carmen equal? Bridget?

10. Where do you think the Pants are? Do you think the girls will find them one day?

11. If you were a member of the Sisterhood, what would you have done at the end of this book? Was flying to Greece as a group more about looking for the Pants, or more about finally spending time together as friends?

12. After reading all four Sisterhood books, if you could tell each of the girls one thing about what they have learned, have experienced, or know, what would it be? What would you want to know about each girl in the future?

In Her Own Words

A CONVERSATION WITH

Ann Brashares

A CONVERSATION WITH ANN BRASHARES

Q: How did it feel to write the last book about the Sisterhood? Did you feel pressure to wrap up the girls' stories?

A: I didn't feel a sense of pressure, but more a sense of inevitability. I didn't want to force change upon the girls so much as recognize that it had already taken place. I wanted to mark the end of a great time in their lives and complete the story. But that doesn't mean I won't revisit them in another part of their lives. I have a feeling these characters will live to tell another story.

Q: You went on a lengthy tour for this book. What's the best part of meeting your many fans?

A: The best part for me, I guess, is a feeling of connection with readers. We (me and my readers) spend hours in the same world, thinking about the same people, so there's kind of a built-in closeness even if we've never met before. Many girls and women come to my readings with their friends. They often tell me or show me the rituals and symbols of their friendship, and I am inspired by them, not only in my writing but also in my life.

As for the travel part, it's hard for me to leave my family, but I confess it's fun to take a bubble bath in a nice hotel and eat all the M&M's from the minibar.

Q: Did you struggle over the issue of giving Lena another chance with Kostos—and giving Bridget a chance to mess things up with Eric yet again?

A: There are often important people in your life who define you and hold you, even when you don't want them to. For Lena, many roads lead to Kostos. But this time, at least, she trips over a good deal of self-knowledge along the way.

For Bee, the unexamined life wreaks havoc. She has a natural weakness for doing a lot and thinking a little. But you can't have a real relationship unless you are willing to tame your impulses, and Eric is the person she's found who is worth that sacrifice.

6

With these characters, as with real people, the same weaknesses afflict us again and again, though often in different ways. The same people have the power to hurt us and also to move us.

Q: Despite the trip's origins, the girls spend a wonderful week bonding in Santorini. If you could get away for a girls-only weekend, where would you go?

A: I think Santorini sounds pretty good, actually. As a less glamorous alternative, I like the idea of gathering at a beach house in the off-season. I like taking runs or walks with friends along the ocean when it's chilly and kind of desolate. I like communal cooking and eating and staying up all night talking when you've got nowhere to be the next day.

Q: Have you ever had a toxic friendship like Carmen and Julia's? Do you have any advice for someone in a similar situation?

A: I have had a few friends (if you can call them that) who've made me feel bad about myself. They've tended to be competitive people who, on some level, seemed eager for my missteps and my disappointments. These were short-lived friendships, thankfully.

There's a famous quote that represents that particular toxicity: "It is not enough for you to succeed; your friends must also fail." If you have a friend who seems to espouse that philosophy, it's important to recognize that she is not actually your friend and move on.

Q: How many pairs of jeans are in your closet? What's your favorite pair, and why?

A: I have about three pairs that I regularly wear, two pairs I keep folded away for nostalgic reasons (one pair from tenth grade, another pair from college), and about seven pairs, stored in the closet of my study, which readers and booksellers have made for me over the years. I have a nostalgic attachment to those too. I guess I'm pretty sentimental about clothes. Can you tell?

Q: **This novel, along with portions of *The Second Summer of the Sisterhood* and *Girls in Pants*, will be a major motion picture later this summer. Is there anything you're hoping to see on the big screen?**

A: I loved the last movie [*The Sisterhood of the Traveling Pants*], so I guess I'm spoiled. I'm thrilled that the four actresses are back to reprise their roles. I'm hopeful that it will be as emotionally satisfying as the first. I'm very excited to see it.

RELATED TITLES

The Sisterhood of the Traveling Pants
Ann Brashares
978-0-385-73058-7
Once there was a pair of pants. Just an ordinary pair
of jeans. But these pants, the Traveling Pants, went on
to do great things. This is the story of the four friends—
Lena, Tibby, Bridget, and Carmen—
who made it possible.

The Second Summer of the Sisterhood
Ann Brashares
978-0-385-73105-8
With a bit of last summer's sand in the pockets, the
Traveling Pants and the Sisterhood who wears them—
Lena, Tibby, Bridget, and Carmen—embark on
their second summer together.

Girls in Pants: The Third Summer of the Sisterhood
Ann Brashares
978-0-553-37593-0
It's the summer before the Sisterhood departs for
college . . . their last real summer together before they
head off to start their grown-up lives. It's the time when
they need their Pants the most.

A Great and Terrible Beauty
Libba Bray
978-0-385-73231-4
Sixteen-year-old Gemma Doyle is sent to the Spence
Academy in London after tragedy strikes her family in
India. Lonely, guilt-ridden, and prone to visions of the future
that have an uncomfortable habit of coming true, Gemma
finds her reception a chilly one. But at Spence, Gemma's
power to attract the supernatural unfolds; she becomes
entangled with the school's most powerful girls and
discovers her mother's connection to a shadowy group called
the Order. A curl-up-under-the-covers Victorian gothic.

Counting Stars • David Almond • 978-0-440-41826-9
With stories that shimmer and vibrate in the bright heat of memory, David Almond creates a glowing mosaic of his life growing up in a large, loving Catholic family in northeastern England.

Before We Were Free • Julia Alvarez • 978-0-440-23784-6
Under a dictatorship in the Dominican Republic in 1960, young Anita lives through a fight for freedom that changes her world forever.

Rebel Angels • Libba Bray • 978-0-385-73341-0
Gemma Doyle is looking forward to a holiday from Spence Academy — spending time with her friends in the city, attending balls in fancy gowns with plunging necklines, and dallying with the handsome Simon Middleton. Yet amid these distractions, her visions intensify — visions of three girls in white, to whom something horrific has happened that only the realms can explain.

Walking Naked • Alyssa Brugman • 978-0-440-23832-4
Megan doesn't know a thing about Perdita, since she would never dream of talking to her. Only when the two girls are thrown together in detention does Megan begin to see Perdita as more than the school outcast. Slowly, Megan finds herself drawn into a challenging almost-friendship.

Colibrí • Ann Cameron • 978-0-440-42052-1
At age four, Colibrí was kidnapped from her parents in Guatemala City, and ever since then she's traveled with Uncle, who believes Colibrí will lead him to treasure. Danger mounts as Uncle grows desperate for his fortune — and as Colibrí grows daring in seeking her freedom.

Code Orange • Caroline B. Cooney • 978-0-385-73260-4
Mitty Blake loves New York City, and even after 9/11, he's always felt safe. Mitty doesn't worry about terrorists or blackouts or grades or anything, which is why he's late getting started on his Advanced Bio report. He considers it good luck when he finds some old medical books

in his family's weekend house. But when he discovers an envelope with two scabs in one of the books, his report is no longer about the grade — it's about life and death.

The Chocolate War • Robert Cormier • 978-0-375-82987-1
Jerry Renault dares to disturb the universe in this groundbreaking and now classic novel, an unflinching portrait of corruption and cruelty in a boys' prep school.

Bud, Not Buddy • Christopher Paul Curtis • 978-0-553-49410-5
Ten-year-old Bud's momma never told him who his father was, but she left a clue: flyers advertising Herman E. Calloway and his famous band. Bud's got an idea that those flyers will lead him to his father. Once he decides to hit the road and find this mystery man, nothing can stop him.

The Watsons Go to Birmingham — 1963 • Christopher Paul Curtis • 978-0-440-41412-4
Nine-year-old Kenny tells hilarious stories about his family, the Weird Watsons of Flint, Michigan. When Kenny's thirteen-year-old brother, Byron, gets to be too much trouble, they head south to Birmingham to visit Grandma, the one person who can shape him up. And they happen to be in Birmingham when Grandma's church is blown up.

When Zachary Beaver Came to Town • Kimberly Willis Holt • 978-0-440-23841-6
Toby's small, sleepy Texas town is about to get a jolt with the arrival of Zachary Beaver, billed as the fattest boy in the world. Toby is in for a summer unlike any other — a summer sure to change his life.

I Am the Wallpaper • Mark Peter Hughes • 978-0-440-42046-0
Thirteen-year-old Floey Packer feels as if she's always blended into the background. After all, she's the frumpy younger sister of the Fabulous Lillian. But when Lillian suddenly gets married and heads off on a monthlong honeymoon, Floey decides it's her time to shine.

Hattie Big Sky • Kirby Larson • 978-0-440-23941-3
For years, sixteen-year-old Hattie has been shuttled between relatives. Tired of being Hattie Here-and-There, she courageously leaves Iowa all by herself to prove up on her late uncle's homestead claim near Vida, Montana. With a

stubborn stick-to-itiveness, she faces frost, drought, and blizzards—and despite many hardships, Hattie forges ahead.

The Lightkeeper's Daughter • Iain Lawrence • 978-0-385-73127-0
Imagine growing up on a tiny island with no one but your family. For Squid McCrae, returning to the island after three years away unleashes a storm of bittersweet memories, revelations, and accusations surrounding her brother's death.

Girl, 15, Charming but Insane • Sue Limb • 978-0-385-73215-4
With her hilariously active imagination, Jess Jordan has a tendency to complicate her life, but now, as she's finally getting closer to her crush, she's determined to keep things under control. Readers will fall in love with Sue Limb's insanely optimistic heroine.

Girl, 16, Absolute Torture • Sue Limb • 978-0-385-73217-8
Jess has the perfect summer planned: She and Fred, lounging in the park, gazing into each other's eyes and engaging in witty repartee. And then her maddening mum announces a two-week "road trip" to Cornwall to visit Jess's dad. Something Jess might have enjoyed, were it not for the monstrously bad timing. As if all this weren't enough, Jess's mum seems to expect her to weep at the grave of every departed literary hero in Britain's long history. *It's absolute torture.*

Girl, Going on 17: Pants on Fire • Sue Limb • 978-0-385-73219-2
It's never fun when a great summer comes to an end. Particularly when one argues with one's adorable, but grossly insensitive, boyfriend the night before school starts. It's such a terrible fight, Jess doesn't know—are they broken up? When she ends up pantless in her own backyard, Jess is left to ask herself: Where did she go wrong?

The Boyfriend List • E. Lockhart • 978-0-385-73207-9
Ruby Oliver is fifteen and has a shrink. She knows it's unusual, but she's had a rough ten days. She's lost her boyfriend, her best friend, and all her other friends; had a panic attack; failed a math test; done something suspicious with a boy; had an argument with a boy; and had graffiti written about her in the girls' bathroom. But Ruby lives to tell the tale (and make more lists).

The Giver • Lois Lowry • 978-0-385-73255-0
Jonas's world is perfect. Everything is under control. There is no war or
fear or pain. There are no choices, until Jonas is given an opportunity that
will change his world forever.

Crushed • Laura and Tom McNeal • 978-0-375-83121-8
Audrey Reed and her two best friends are a nerdy little trio, so everyone
is shocked when the handsome, mysterious Wickham Hill asks her out.
Soon Audrey is so smitten that she hardly pays attention to the vicious
underground school newspaper, which threatens to crush teachers and
students—and expose some dangerous secrets.

A Brief Chapter in My Impossible Life • Dana Reinhardt • 978-0-375-84691-5
Simone's starting her junior year in high school. She's got a terrific family
and amazing friends. And she's got a secret crush on a really smart and
funny guy. Then her birth mother contacts her. Simone's always known she
was adopted, but she never wanted to know anything about it. Who is this
woman? Why has she contacted Simone now? The answers lead Simone to
question everything she once took for granted.

Holes • Louis Sachar • 978-0-440-22859-2
Stanley has been unjustly sent to a boys' detention center, Camp Green
Lake. But there's more than character improvement going on at the
camp—the warden is looking for something.

The Book Thief • Markus Zusak • 978-0-375-84220-7
Trying to make sense of the horrors of World War II, Death tells the story
of Liesel Meminger—a German girl whose book-stealing and storytelling
talents sustain her foster family and the Jewish man they are hiding in their
basement, along with their neighbors. This is an unforgettable story about
the power of words and the ability of books to feed the soul.

CONTEST

ELIGIBILITY: No purchase necessary. Must be at least 13 years old as of 4/22/2008 and a legal resident of the U.S.A. Contest starts 4/22/2008 12:00 AM EST and ends 6/20/2008 11:59 PM EST. All entries must be received by 6/20/2008.

HOW TO ENTER: Visit **www.flip.com/sisterhood** to create and submit an original Sisterhood-themed Flipbook.

This contest is presented by CondéNet, 1166 Broadway, New York, NY 10036. Prizes will be fulfilled by Random House Children's Books, 1745 Broadway, 10th Floor, New York, NY 10019.

PRIZES: One (1) Grand prize winner and twenty (20) runners-up will be selected based on the criteria of the contest. Total grand prize approximate retail value is $3000.00 U.S.; actual retail value may vary depending on the winner's city of departure and availability of tickets and accommodation. Each of twenty (20) runner-up prizes approximate retail value is $12.00 U.S.

For a complete list of winners, visit **www.flip.com/sisterhood** on or after 6/27/2008.

Visit **www.flip.com/sisterhood** to enter and for full rules of eligibility.

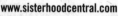